Midnight in Malamulele

Darla Bartos

Midnight in Malamulele

Book design by e-book-design.com.

ISBN 978-1502945044

Printed in the United States

Thank You

A note of deep appreciation to those in South Africa ...

To Sister Hilda Mahiteh Tucker, principal of the Holy Rosary School in Malamulele from 2000-2009, and the religious nuns who gave me friendship, love, prayers and support.

To Jacinta Baloyi, Rose Mangani, Margaret Asithi, Aminata Sannoh, Hawa Sannoh, Alfred Lavalie, Lansana Mara, Johanna Thabathi and Rendani Mabusa for their friendships.

To Detective Donald Hlongwane and the amazing commanders and detectives at the Malamulele Police Department.

To Mike Perry, owner of African Reptiles and Venom in Johannesburg who kept me honest about snakes.

To Ouma Lucy Poppie Matibula of Giyani for her love, support and visitors' quarters.

To Salva Matusi, a Mozambican refugee, who selflessly raised three orphans in Malamulele.

... Australia and U.S.

To the Rocky Mountain Mystery Writers of America critique group, including Mike Befeler, Becky Martinez, Jedeane Macdonald, Barbara Graham, Bonnie Biafore, Lori Lacefield and Rick Gustafson.

To Rex Burns and Joan Johnston for their encouragement.

To Linda Kent and the Volunteers-in-Policing program at the Denver Police Department.

To members of the West Highlands Book Club for invaluable feedback.

To Cheerleaders Phil Bartos, Stacy Ann Baugh, Chris Bartos, Anne-Marie Braga, Benjie Bartos, Benjie Blasé and Tom Sheely.

To Donna Bowman and David McHam for constant support.

To editor Victoria Hanley and text designer Gail Nelson.

To Narra3D for the excellent book cover.

One

Murder in the Convent

A scream pierced the night. At first I thought the noise was only the psycho rooster, but then I remembered that the blasted bird had already struck. It crowed at 2:17 every morning. Never early, never late. This had to be something else. My reporter's instinct kicked in, and I fumbled for the side table and switched on the gooseneck lamp. The clock said 3:40. There it was again—a human scream and no mistake. Throwing off the heavy covers from my narrow convent bed, I scrambled up and threw on my thick robe. The concrete floor was ice cold and jarring, reminding me to slip on my wool socks.

Sister Bridget, wrapped in a baby-blue blanket, stumbled in from her adjoining bedroom, her dark eyes filled with questions. The nervous twitch in her cheek was tap dancing. "What was that?"

"I don't know." Grabbing the torch, I managed to twist the key in the lock to the outside door. I held my breath when I stepped into the night with Bridget close behind. Maybe someone had only stepped on a snake. Like last year. Maybe. But my gut told me it was something much worse.

A little more than ten feet ahead on the walkway stood Sister Mary, consoling a distraught Sister Benignus, the oldest of the nun bunch. Others were running out of their rooms in nightclothes, pulling themselves together, shivering in the freezing night air. As I watched the frenzy, I wondered again why a Denver crime reporter—that's me—felt the urgency to volunteer here in the African bush. I'd never been nun material, and yet here I was staying in a convent. My friends thought I was crazy. Maybe I was.

I glanced around and counted. "Where's Sister Valaria?"

Benignus grabbed her forehead and let out an agonizing cry reminiscent of the screams heard moments before. Someone shoved a plastic green lawn chair beneath her. I walked over and crouched beside her as she concentrated on deep breathing under the direction of Sister Mary, the psychiatrist in residence.

"Take your time." I patted Benignus' weathered hands. "What did you see?"

Benignus pulled from her left sleeve a small kerchief with a tiny embroidered shamrock and wiped her nose, then took small nervous breaths. Her arm shook as her crooked finger pointed in the direction of Sister Valaria's room.

"Blood, blood everywhere. She's dead, she is."

I glanced up at the fragile faces filled with absolute terror.

The women stood under the tin roof that covered the sidewalk leading like a square yellow brick road to their rooms at the Mother of Angels convent. Reminded me of a scaled down Holiday Inn back home.

"Blood, blood, blood," Benignus chanted.

Sister Mary's eyes moved quickly from nun to nun. "Come." She stepped aside as she pointed her flock toward the kitchen. From the back, they reminded me of refugees carrying nothing but uncertainty and desperation. Someone would automatically put the black kettle on the stove for hot tea, and one by one they'd move to the adjoining dining room.

Sister Mary turned to me, and as our eyes met we both headed for Valaria's door. Surprisingly, my heart was pumping like I'd been in a train wreck. I grabbed Sister Mary's thin arm as she touched the door handle. "Prepare yourself."

Although I didn't know how bad it was, I knew how bad it could be. As a reporter in America, I'd been present at more than a few crime scenes. It was a sure bet I'd be able to handle whatever we found better than Sister Mary. Although she was a psychiatrist who had dealt with horrendous calamities in Zambia and Rwanda, her gentle nature always found violence hard to accept. She inhaled, then slowly opened Sister Valaria's door. My breath caught in my throat. The small light on the bedside table was dim, but not dim enough. I could see Valaria sprawled across the once-pristine white bed linens that were now mostly a brilliant red. Blood spatter decorated the walls, the floor, and even the ceiling. "Annabelle, be careful," Sister Mary said, as I stepped in front of her and bent to inspect Valaria's head, which tilted sideways. It was severed from her neck except for a thin thread attaching it to what looked to be the spinal cord. It looked like the killer had attempted decapitation.

"Dear God." I said it automatically. When you run with nuns, you pick up the lingo.

Sister Mary peered over my shoulder, then bolted for the small porcelain basin in the corner of the bedroom. After losing her supper, she rinsed her mouth, patted water on her forehead, and wiped her face on her sleeve. "Jesus, Mary, and Joseph." She made a wilted sign of the cross.

I tried desperately to control dry heaves as I concentrated on what we both needed to hear. "She was asleep. She never felt a thing."

Sister Mary stared at me. "But, who could have done this to us?" She began to pant uncontrollably.

I gently led her out of the room and closed the door. I pulled my cell out of my pocket. "I'll notify the police."

She looked alarmed. "First, we must clean...."

"No, no, Sister Mary! This is a crime scene. We cannot. touch. a single. thing." I said the words with such authority it shocked me. I eased Sister Mary down the walkway to join the others and then stepped out of earshot to make the emergency call. When the police answered, I announced, "There's been a ... a ... murder at the convent." Even as I said the words, it seemed impossible. Was I in a dream, a nightmare? How could this be happening? Especially to these women?

I rubbed my forehead as I struggled with what lay ahead. Investigation. Suspicions. All this in Malamulele—one of hundreds of villages not even on a South African map. Everyone in the surrounding area knew these nuns, who had spent ten years building the Mother of Angels Elementary School, not to mention the refugee work they'd conducted in villages all over Limpopo Province. But I knew how quickly reputations would be damaged if this murder wasn't handled perfectly.

I dashed to my room and pulled my mid-sized suitcase from the closet. I unzipped it and grabbed my camera case with my digital single lens reflex, then headed to Sister Valaria's room. Before I opened the door, I pretended it was just another crime scene. I concentrated on taking small breaths, ignoring the smell of fresh blood and body fluids that always wreaked havoc on newbies. After I snapped pictures in all directions, I concentrated on detailed close ups. Might come in handy. Who knew what the village police would be like?

As I closed Sister Valaria's door and stepped out onto the walkway, the chill of early morning flooded over me. No one but the nuns were here, the dearest people you'd ever want to meet. Then a dark shadow flashed before me. Someone else had indeed been here. No need to take chances. I walked into my room and placed my camera at the back of the very highest shelf in my closet.

I hadn't touched a thing in Valaria's room, but still I felt a need to wash my hands. I stopped at the basin in the corner of my room. Scooping water from the small tap, I caught a glimpse of myself in the mirror. My eyes, now a dull sea green, stared back at me. What was I thinking coming here all the time? Why was I involved? Was it because I had no personal life? I clumsily wrapped my shining glory into a twist and clipped it up. Mom must be turning in her grave. What kind of woman thinks about her hair at a time like this? A nun had just been killed a few doors down from me. Tears welled in my eyes. Yes, I had appeared brave and in charge. The truth was, ever since the death of my aunt, Sister Cecilia, worry and self-doubt had followed me. But now I heard Aunt Cecilia's voice: *"Straighten up, Annabelle."*

It had been seventeen minutes since I'd called the cops. I needed air. I walked outside. Staring up at the night sky from the open courtyard reminded me I was indeed in Africa. No ambient light, no streetlights, no neon billboards. Not even a moon tonight. Was there any place on earth darker than here? I glanced at the Southern Hemisphere constellations. Brilliant, perfect stars should be beckoning romance, not murder. My first trip here had been to see my aunt. I'd stayed in the convent as a chance to reconnect and find serenity. Was I cursed, that crime would find me even here?

As I passed through the kitchen, I grabbed a piece of toast hoping it would settle my stomach. I forced my demeanor into that of a professional as I paused at the doorway to the dining room, then took a chair near the end of the table. I glanced at wet and distraught faces. It was obvious Sister Mary had filled everyone in on most of the details. No one sitting here could possibly be a cold-blooded murderer. Nevertheless, it would be easy to keep an eye on them, being that there were only six nuns currently living in the convent. *Make that five.*

From my life as a crime reporter, I knew the authorities would automatically zero in on one of us. Why wouldn't they? The convent had been locked down. We'd all had opportunity. And when the police sifted through facts, my dear friend Sister Bridget, the principal of Mother of Angels Elementary, would probably become the key suspect. She was the one with motive, though she wouldn't hurt a fly.

So then, how had the killer gained access?

Certainly not through our windows. Each bedroom had one large picture window fitted with metal latticework designed to keep intruders away. Small, elongated windows framing the larger one could be opened if you slipped a hand through the latticework and lifted a latch. But no one, not even Houdini, could come through one of those small windows. Or get out.

Sister Ann, the Mother of Angels' young novitiate, freshened each nun's cup with steaming black tea. Then Sister Mary, with her mug in hand, stood and motioned for all of us to follow.

She headed toward the lounge where we gathered at night eating our prepared meals on metal trays. Now a darkness settled over the room as if there had been a power outage—but this time electricity had absolutely nothing to do with it.

Sister Mary sat upright, head bent, rubbing her forehead with all ten fingers. "Could anyone shed any light on who might have done this to Sister Valaria?"

The nuns eyed each other, then shook their heads back and forth. I looked quickly at Bridget, then picked at the one loose thread on my robe. I remembered my aunt suggesting I befriend Bridget. She needn't have asked. The minute I laid eyes on that zany nun, Bridget and I could not stop talking. Believe me, nothing was happening to her on my watch.

No one uttered a word, so Sister Mary continued. "Sister Benignus, please tell us once more how you happened to find her."

Sister Benignus sniffed and twisted her shamrock kerchief. "I was up early, I was." Her gray hair, usually in a bun, fell loosely over her shoulders. The same arthritic fingers she used to plant flowers in the garden now rubbed a brown sunspot on her cheek. "I couldn't sleep. I went to the kitchen to fetch tea and heard a noise. Sister Valaria's light was on, so I lightly tapped on her door. There was no answer. I figured she'd gone back to sleep, maybe had a bad dream. I walked toward the kitchen, but then I heard a door close. So, I returned to check on her."

Sister Benignus leaned forward, then quickly straightened up, sitting tall as if she had suddenly remembered her instruction in the Irish Catholic girls school seventy years ago. She wiped her bulging eyes. Sister Ann moved closer on the cushioned rattan couch and eased her arm around Benignus, whispering too softly for me to hear.

I had studied these dear, sweet nuns for years. They sacrificed each day, working long, difficult hours – always for others. Still, I'd always believed under the right circumstances anyone could be pushed over the edge. But a beheading? No. Absolutely not. Too gruesome. And certainly Valaria's murder had to be premeditated because a simple knife would not have been able to do the damage I'd observed. A machete would surely have been required for such a devastating blow.

Was someone trying to send the nuns a message?

A loud pounding on the front door propelled me into action. I jumped up and threw my hands in the air. "I'll take care of the police." Running down the walkway to the entry foyer, I grabbed a large skeleton key from the old school desk in the corner, slipped it into the lock and twisted. I automatically stepped back as an African man ducked his head and walked inside.

"Detective N.F. Baloyi," he said. "You have a murder?"

He surprised me. The detective wore dark blue jeans and a trendy black leather jacket. I took a deep breath and held out my hand. "I'm Annabelle. Annabelle Chase. And you are?"

"Detective. Detective Baloyi. I believe I just said that."

"Sorry." I must be even more upset than I'd realized, but I was determined to treat him as one professional to another. But hadn't he also said N.F.? Those were unusual initials, weren't they?

I led him three doors past the chapel to the northwest corner of the convent. Taking a deep breath, I opened Sister Valaria's door, stepping aside and allowing him to walk in first.

Despite the murder, I couldn't help but notice that Baloyi

was absolutely nothing like anyone I'd encountered since I'd been here. Certainly he was different from the paunchy officer at the speed trap, when I had been going 40 in a 25. He had grabbed the 40 rands I offered him and looked the other way. I wasn't proud of bribing a policeman, but going to court was too complicated for a foreigner out here in the bush.

This detective was different, though. Somehow I doubted that Baloyi would have accepted any bribe, no matter how high. Now he pulled latex gloves from his hip pocket. Smooth. I liked that. Always prepared. His dark eyes surveyed the room with no reaction whatsoever. It was obvious he'd seen death before but probably not much worse.

"That's all. Thank you." He turned his back to me.

All the words I could find were, "I'm sorry?"

As if he didn't think I understood, he turned back and faced me. "You may join the others." He nodded toward the door.

"You're dismissing me?" I felt my head jerk back when I said it.

He controlled a smile twitching in the corner of his lips. "If that's the way you want it. Look, it's a crime scene. Let us do our job. I've got it."

"Who is us?" He ignored what I said, so I continued. "I have crime scene experience."

He folded his arms in a way that could easily be intimidating. The man was tall and—I couldn't help noticing—extremely well built. "And just where did you have experience with crime scenes?"

"I am, that is, I was a crime reporter." He made me feel like a child, my professionalism stripped bare.

He looked at me squarely. "Bet you were good, too, but that

crime reporter thing—it don't count for much out here."

I walked out the door, but leaned against the wall outside and listened. No clicks. He wasn't even taking pictures. What kind of cop was he? Then magically, I heard snapping. Camera hidden in his jean pocket. Must be a point and shoot. Certainly not an SLR.

Twenty-one minutes and six seconds later the door opened. His eyes grew wide then settled down when he saw I'd been vigilant. "What's an American nun doing here in Africa?"

Instantly, my composure fell. If the situation hadn't been so serious. I would have laughed out loud at the absurdity. "I'm no nun. I told you I was a crime reporter."

He rubbed the back of his neck and looked down at me with his head cocked to the side. "So, if you're not a nun, why are you here?" For a split second, his eyes caught mine. Dark eyes like hot cocoa. Eyes I could get lost in.

"My aunt was a nun here." I lowered my eyes, unwilling to tell this stranger about the ache in my heart, about how I missed Aunt Cecelia and mourned her every day. I cleared my throat. "I teach crime reporting in Denver nine months out of the year, but I spend my summer vacations here."

"Whoa! Gotta be better places. For vacations, I mean. Not many Americans out here."

I nodded.

"Just flew in from Austin myself." He pulled his cell from his jacket pocket.

"I'm sorry?"

As he repeated it, his voice grew hoarse. "Flew in from Austin." He hit speed dial.

"Austin? As in Austin, Texas?" But his accent had no trace

of the American South—it was pure vintage South African.

"Is there another?" This time he shot me a smile that made me glad I could see him in the light remaining on the walkway. He turned his back to me as he spoke into his iPhone. "Body at the convent." He hesitated. "Convent. Yeah, that's what I said. Didn't believe it either." He put his cell into his jacket pocket and faced me. "Where were we?"

"Your first name again? Did you say N.F.?"

"N.F., yes." His tone told me not to ask what the initials stood for. "Everyone calls me Baloyi."

So he was sensitive about his name. "And my American friends often call me Belle," I said. "What were you doing in Austin, Baloyi?"

"Picked up my criminal justice degree." He paused. "To fill in from time to time for the Malamulele commander, who you'll find out is my grandfather." We moved away from Valaria's room as he pulled off his latex gloves, wadded them up and looked around probably for a dustbin, then stuck them in his right jean pocket.

When we reached the front door, I pointed to the small metal trashcan in the foyer. He pulled the latex gloves from his pocket and dropped them in.

"So what's it like being a detective in this village?" I asked.

"Samo, samo. Little funding. Bribes. We do what we can. Oddly enough, there's plenty of crime."

"Don't you have a partner?"

He shook his head and exhaled. "It's not like in America. We walk into the office, take whoever's there. Partners change every shift." He stared out into the night, then turned to me. "And seriously, don't mention I came alone. I have enough going on."

"Grandfather?" It seemed like a good guess.

"Yeah, that and the number one rule is you never, ever leave the precinct without a partner. But honestly, when I heard murder at the convent, I thought it was a prank. What are the odds?"

"Indeed. And now I have something on you." I smiled.

Baloyi studied his jeans as if he thought he'd brushed up against something.

"No, no. I was kidding." I hesitated and stared at my sneakers, then looked up. "Where's the closest place for autopsy?"

"Thohoyandou."

"Closer than Johannesburg." Then surprisingly, exhaustion hit me like a two by four.

"Yeah, I get it. Tiredness all round. Been back five days. Still got the jet lag."

Baloyi's cell chirped. He looked at his text. "Driver's here." He leaned toward me in a conspiratorial manner. "Don't be impressed. He was three blocks away."

I watched him walk out to the ambulance, exchange a few words with the driver, then slip on new latex gloves. He waited as the driver rolled the gurney out of the ambulance. I nodded when they passed me headed toward Sister Valaria's room. Minutes later on the return trip, Sister Valaria rode on the gurney, zipped up in a shiny black bag.

Keeping my distance, I watched as the driver slid her into the ambulance. When I turned back to the convent, the nuns had gathered beneath the dim light on the front stoop. I walked over and spoke quietly with the middle-aged driver. Luckily, he understood a bit of English, and I was able to tell him what I knew Sister Mary would want me to say. "The victim is a nun and must be treated with respect." He nodded sleepily, then entered his ambulance and slowly pulled away. The nuns turned to go back inside.

I shivered and pulled my robe closer, then followed the detective to his beat up bakkie. He opened the passenger side door, pulled out a roll of crime scene tape from the disheveled glove compartment, and closed the door.

"Seriously, about the partner thing."

"Seriously, don't report me." Half smiling, he held up his hands in midair like he'd been caught.

We walked to Sister Valaria's room. He stretched the white tape with blue lettering depicting crime scene across the door, then locked it and took the key with him. "Are there other keys for this room?"

"Probably."

"Don't let anyone in until Forensic Services leaves."

"Okay, but keep me in the loop."

"Can't." He looked down at me. "Well, not officially."

His smile was endearing, but I struggled to ignore it. "Could you at least wait until morning to interview the nuns? They're exhausted and they'll be on their knees praying in the chapel."

"I shouldn't, but there's a bunch of 'em." Baloyi yawned. "Okay, I'll be back in the morning with two more detectives and techs."

I checked my watch. 5:15. "It's already morning."

"See you in a few." He nodded and ducked his head, leaving the same way he'd come.

Detective Baloyi drove away and I closed the front door listening to the soft steady hum of community prayers drifting from the chapel windows into the courtyard. Officially, I was patrolling the inside perimeter. Unofficially, I needed fresh

air. My mind was twisted in so many directions sleep was not
even an option. There was a murder to solve. I stared at the
brilliant stars in the constellations above me. I couldn't figure
out how someone had slipped into the convent to kill poor
Sister Valaria. And why Sister Valaria specifically? Although
she did nothing but stir up trouble, why would someone want
to actually kill her?

And then there was that other thing.

Baloyi.

Two

Interrogation

Sister Bridget hovered over my bed like a dorm mother, balancing an aging metal tray with a stack of toast, hot coffee, milk and sugar on the side. "The police want to talk to the outsider."

I sat up in bed. "Now? Are you talking about right now?"

"Yes, now."

"What time is it?" I waited for her response rather than check for myself.

"Half past three."

The afternoon sun streamed through the windows. I groaned, realizing how much of the day I had missed. I quickly downed the coffee.

Sister Bridget turned to leave then shot me a glance. "Eat the toast."

"I will."

"Oh, and sorry, no hot water." She left.

I was used to cold water, but that didn't mean I liked it. My routine for no hot water began. I bathed key areas with ice cold water, dried off with a new yellow towel the nuns had given me when I arrived, then hopped into my jeans, T-shirt and red sweater. No time for glamour, which admittedly, I seldom went for while living in the bush. I dabbed on a bit of lip gloss and was out the door.

Bridget spotted me and waved me in from across the courtyard like I was a 747 on approach to landing. Amazing how calm she looked, as if she had absolutely nothing to worry about when in truth she had the most to lose. The police eventually would hear about Bridget and Valaria's confrontation, although it wouldn't be from me.

Bridget pointed me toward the dining room. I hesitated outside the door, took a breath and stood as erect as possible.

The dining room had been transformed into a police interrogation room, despite the faded lace curtains and teacups strung out along the low credenza. A uniformed officer, who had a distinctly unfriendly face, motioned for me to sit in the chair across from her and her co-worker. "You are from A-mer-i-ca?" The uniformed interrogator wore square black glasses on her ample nose. The other official with short thick-cropped hair glowered as she wrote in a five by seven black notebook.

"Yes, Denver, Colorado."

"Why are you here?"

"I love it. I've volunteered here in Malamulele for ten summers," I said with pride.

The assistant's pen scribbled away.

"But it's winter. Why do you come here now?"

"No, no, I volunteer here during *my* summer in America. Opposite seasons." I watched to see if she understood. I didn't want her to think I was insulting her intelligence. "Sorry, I know you know that. I come here to help at the school." Should I offer more conversation about myself?

I decided to take the plunge. "My aunt was a nun. Ten years ago, she invited me here for a visit. And, I've been coming back ever since." I hesitated, wondering if I should tell her more. Perhaps about the fact I'd had a failed marriage at 24. Before I had time to think any further, I blurted out, "Even after my aunt was killed in a car accident eight months ago." I blinked and nearly missed a flicker of sympathy.

Her scowl began to soften. "You have a job in America?"

"Yes, I teach at Denver University."

"Did you know Sister Valaria?" Her tone bordered on accusatory.

"I met her last year." I thought of the last time I'd seen Valaria, all huffed up and angry, totally ignoring Sister Bridget, who was angrier than I'd ever seen her.

"It's odd to see you here." She cocked her head to the side.

"What do you mean exactly?" *Did she mean white or educated or blonde.* She was pissing me off. I realized part of my irritation was my exhaustion. Knowing I was becoming defensive, I changed the direction of the conversation. "Where is Baloyi?"

The interrogator cocked her head, raised her eyebrows and shot me an odd look. Without saying a word, she shuffled her papers, slid them into her portfolio, stood and then strode out of the room with her assistant close behind. As if she'd had second thoughts, the interrogator poked her head back in. "*Detective* Baloyi was called to Johannesburg."

I slumped down in the dining room chair to think. I had to be objective about this murder. Could I be missing anything? Experience had taught me that people like Valaria could push someone over the edge. It happened all the time. Anyone could become a killer in a split second—not necessarily intentionally. Not many people decide to become killers. But murder was serious business. I didn't want to do the wrong thing by keeping Bridget off my imaginary suspect list because of our close friendship.

I stumbled into the kitchen as Sister Bridget dumped rice into the boiling water and lowered the temperature for a slow cook. I studied her movements. She handed me a bright red metal tray. I placed my tea and toast on it, while she found another tray for her own tea and her rice. We walked into the lounge to sit together.

I should just ask her the question on my mind. We'd been friends for so long, there weren't any barriers between us. Bridget and I had clicked from the moment we met. Not only that, but she'd also been a dear friend to Aunt Cecelia. And how could I ever move forward until I knew for sure that Bridget was innocent? "Bridget," I said, after swallowing my bite of toast.

She looked up at me with her usual open smile. "What is it?"

"Did you kill Sister Valaria?" I felt like a criminal as soon as the words left my lips.

She stared at me with incredulous eyes. "What?"

"I'm sorry. I don't really think you could have killed her. I'm just torn up about this investigation and I need to hear it from you. Tell me you didn't kill her."

Bridget set down her teacup. "Annabelle," she said gently. "You know me. You know I'm called to God."

I gulped. "Yes."

"Thou shalt not kill. Murder is a mortal sin, and I would never betray God in such a way. You can't believe I could do that." Her face was serious and sad. "No, Annabelle, I did not kill Sister Valaria."

I pressed both hands against my eyes. "Of course. And I'm so sorry for asking." When I lowered my hands, I saw the hurt on her face and knew I would feel the same pain if my dear friend had questioned me the way I'd just questioned her. But I doubted the question had even crossed Bridget's mind—even though I was the outsider and I was young and strong enough to swing a machete, her faith in me was complete.

What had I done? To satisfy the objective side of my mind and eliminate her as a suspect, I had asked this woman of God an absurd question. I felt like Judas. "I see how wrong I was," I said. "Can you forgive me?"

Bridget gave me a sunny smile. No clouds. "I forgive you." She picked up her teacup again and shook her head ruefully. "I will admit I harbored anger in my heart towards Sister Valaria. She was mean and I hated her for making my life miserable. But I never thought to kill her." Her voice dropped to a whisper. "Though I'm glad she is not here."

My toast forgotten, I sat lost in thought, considering the other nuns. Sister Margaret was 75 years old, tall and a string bean. She handled accounting and engaged in little physical activity. I doubted she could even lift a machete, let alone swing it. It takes a lot of strength to decapitate a person. Sister Benignus, 85, no way she could have done it. Sister Ann was a light-weight. Nix to her. And Sister Mary was strong at heart but frail enough that she could not have done the deed. I could understand why the police would suspect Sister Bridget.

Bridget was strong as an ox, and the only one from the convent besides me, who could have physically murdered Valaria. The Ethiopian sister had harassed her at every opportunity. That's the way the cops would see it.

I lifted my head. "Bridget, please be careful. The police could try to pin this on you. Because of your history with Valaria, they'll think you had motive and opportunity."

Bridget shrugged. "God knows I'm innocent. He will take care of me."

Just then the door opened to Sister Mary.

"Are you okay, Annabelle? How did it go with the police?"

"She didn't ask me anything, really." I considered my interview, how my words could have been misinterpreted, and wondered what impression I had made on the officers. The female cop evidently didn't realize that I'd been up all night with Baloyi. Unless, of course, maybe she did.

"Praise be to God." Sister Mary looked relieved as she pointed behind her at the hallway. I was about to ask what she was praising God for but I stepped out of the lounge and spied the reason why. A group of crime scene techs in navy blue jump suits were hauling equipment out of Sister Valaria's room.

We walked them to the front door as if they'd been guests in our home.

As the last tech exited, he practiced his English. "Okay to clean."

We were cordial and thanked him. The miserable and thankless job of cleaning would go to dear Flora, our housekeeper, who had ample reserves in case she was ever locked in a closet far away from the fridge. It was Flora who cooked and cleaned the convent and took the odd job with locals some evenings.

***

Shortly after twelve that night my tossing and turning had worn on me. I turned on my bedside lamp, and from the drawer I pulled a yellow-paged novel that surely had entertained a wide number of insomniacs over the years. But no amount of reading seemed to lull me to sleep.

I jumped when there was a knock on my bathroom door.

Sister Bridget walked in and plopped down on the end of my bed. "Saw your light." Since the guestroom at the convent was connected to Sister Bridget's bedroom by a joint bathroom, she and I had assumed a college roommate relationship. "Can't sleep." Bridget pressed her fingers on her forehead and inhaled. "I know she hated me and made my life ..." She hesitated.

"A living hell? I'll say it."

"Yeah, for sure. But no one should die ... not like that." Bridget froze. Our eyes locked when we heard a noise outside my bedroom door.

I seized the key and my torch from the nightstand, then clicked off the small lamp. I felt my way to the door with Bridget close behind. She held onto my shoulder as I moved to unlock the L-shaped door handle. I don't think you could have slipped a piece of spaghetti between us. Carefully, I opened the door. It was pitch black outside, except for a small light mounted on the stucco wall at the far side of the convent. A comforting candle shined through the stained glass chapel window and reflected out onto the courtyard.

I could hear my own heartbeat as I crept down the walkway with a faint stream of light bouncing ahead of me. Then suddenly, nothing. I shook my torch and wrote batteries on my imaginary shopping list. I vividly remembered Sister Valaria and how her head cocked to the side, her body lying in her blood-soaked bed. *Snap out of it, Annabelle!* I stepped quietly, so quietly I had no trouble hearing Sister Bridget's gasp as the only light in the courtyard went dark.

Three

Accomplice

Sister Bridget held onto my shoulder as I blindly navigated. We had been near Sister Mary's bedroom when the light disappeared, and I knew the laundry room would be the next doorway. Feeling brick by brick, I led us to the southwest corner of the convent. The cold night, or maybe sheer fright, caused my stubborn feet to move slowly.

Reaching the corner we turned, knowing the kitchen door was to our immediate right. As I opened the door, I tripped and landed flat on my knees.

Bridget grabbed for me and helped me to my feet. I groped to the wall where the refrigerator should be, then touched the large switch plate. I flipped everything. Nothing happened. "Electricity's out."

"Oh, thank God, that's what's wrong." Bridget released my pinched shoulder.

Rural electricity was temperamental, especially when it rained. I relaxed despite the darkness. "Just the rain," I said.

"Annabelle?"

"What?"

"No rain." Bridget said it with a strange voice like she was either scared or thought I must be out of it completely.

I stepped back out onto the walkway. Sister Bridget stayed right behind me. I led us toward the lounge where there was another light panel – the one that controlled the exterior walkway lights; maybe it was on a different circuit.

"Call police, please," Bridget whispered frantically.

"Shhhh." With my ear against the lounge door, I slowly opened it. Movement, something, brushing up against my legs. I let out a yell. "Son of a ...."

"What in the name of heaven is going on?" Sister Mary bounded out onto the walkway from her room, pointing a powerful bouncing beam in our direction.

I looked down at our intruder. Plato. Sister Margaret's homeless cat.

Bridget and I broke into hysterical laughter. We held onto each other, screaming with delight when suddenly a large dark figure barreled past us into Sister Mary, sending her and her flashlight rolling onto the small patch of grass in the courtyard.

Bridget rushed to check on Sister Mary, while I flew down the walkway unable to see anything ahead of me. I stopped short, my bravery collapsing as I realized I had no defense against a stranger with possibly a machete in his hand. The sound of unknown footsteps grew fainter all the way to the side door.

I returned to the two sisters. "He got away."

"Oh, Jesus, Mary and Joseph, not again. Get everyone to the chapel." Sister Mary shouted.

We rounded up everyone and prayers began in the chapel. Though bleary-eyed, everyone was accounted for. Until daylight, the nuns would pray and stay put.

I took a working torch and inspected the side entrance of the convent. The area appeared untouched except for the top drawer of the flat-topped desk, which was open, showing a bunch of labeled keys. My stomach churned as if I'd drunk milk 10 days past the expiration date. I knew with only a glance which key had been taken—the key to the side door. It was distinctive, easily recognizable and at this moment missing. I wanted to be wrong. I spied the halfway open door. My torch caught the lock. Dangling in it was the keychain with a picture of the Virgin Mary inside a clear plastic square.

Assuming that Valaria's killer had scaled the wall, he would have had to drop down into the garden. Then with unlocked bedroom doors, he would be home free. That was the only way for someone to gain entrance to the locked down convent. Plus, it would have taken someone extremely fit to have scaled a wall, not to mention dropping quietly down into the garden. Then he would have had to reverse the process to leave. Or maybe he simply walked out the side door. And maybe he had help with that? Or, speaking of help, someone might have let the killer into the convent, which would implicate one of the nuns.

I contemplated the possibilities. If the intruder was being chased, he would have only seconds to select the correct key to the side door and escape. That meant he was familiar with the convent and that key in particular, or else there was an accomplice saying prayers in the chapel.

Four

The Letter

A ten-year celebration of the Mother of Angels Elementary School was roaring to life with hundreds of school children anxiously awaiting their very first competitive soccer match. I stood shading my eyes from the glorious sun and scanning the horizon searching for Sister Bridget. I knew she wore the colors of her country, a black, red and gold dress representing Ghana's national flag. As I studied the crowd, I saw many teachers sporting long elaborate dresses representing their own African homelands. A hive of teachers busied themselves arranging snacks and drinks on a long table under the feathery silver-leafed branches of the Weeping Wattle tree.

I didn't count them, but I guessed that almost all 752 children, stair-stepped according to grades, were standing on the soccer field in their new uniforms rehearsing songs and cheers while four honor students struggled with flagpoles three times their size.

A sleek silver bus decorated with screaming children hanging out the windows jolted to a stop. Students on the field broke ranks and rushed forward to greet the new arrivals.

I reached Bridget. "Who would ever believe this?" she asked gleefully.

I patted her back. "It was *your* dream. You believed in this." My mind returned to ten years ago when the school consisted of two rooms in a rundown building across the dirt road with unsupervised children running up and down the streets for entertainment. No playgrounds. No toys. Now, there were sixteen brick buildings comprising a small campus set amid lavish landscaping done by a Mozambican refugee.

One of Sister Bridget's dreams had been to prove that an African woman could indeed build a school. She'd overcome the prejudice of the African parents who believed their children's school would be better, perhaps elevated somehow, if white Irish nuns were in charge. Sister Bridget, determined to gain their confidence, found grants and donations with the help of her religious sisters. And she dreamed big. I could hardly contain my excitement a few minutes later as Bridget stood at the rented podium introducing her staff to the local chiefs and other dignitaries. But even as I enjoyed the beauty of the moment, my inner voice told me something dreadful was coming.

Festivities of the soccer match stretched into a celebratory supper for the five residents at the convent. As the nuns awaited dinner, Sister Mary quietly motioned for me. The last time I'd followed her, there'd been that murder to deal with. Now she led me to the small chapel filled with two kneelers and straight back chairs against one wall.

While I warmed my cold metal chair beneath the street side window, she pulled a letter out of a stiff vanilla envelope stamped with the seal of the Johannesburg diocese.

Sister Mary handed it to me. "I'm the only one who's read this."

I scanned it.

Headquarters of the Mother of Angels Congregation
256 Canto Degli Italian
Rome, Italy

Dear Sisters,

Wishing you a Happy Feast day of the Archangels. I trust that you all had a beautiful celebration in your Community. After a lot of reflections, prayers and discernment the headquarters of the Congregation has decided to close your community and hand it over to the Congregation of the Sisters of Maria from Rio de Janeiro with effect of the 2nd February 2015. This day will be a symbolic gesture as it is the feast of the Light of Christ which is the feast for all Religious. Let us celebrate as Missionaries to go out through the nation and bring Christ's light to all through our various ministries.

As Sisters of The Congregation of Mother of Angels, we are called to be missionaries and have a pioneering spirit and above all to serve with obedience to our Constitution. In obedience to your Superior General, I call on all the Sisters in your Community to hand over the convent to the new Congregation and move to the Provincial House in Johannesburg where each of you will be given a new mission.

It is a big moment of grace for the whole Congregation and especially for you. We are all united in prayers at this time as you move out. We trust that the new Congregation will settle down soon to continue God's work in the vineyard.

*I send you greetings and grace of our Lord and Savior
Jesus Christ.*

Wishing you all God's Divine Grace and Blessing.

Yours Sincerely,
Rev Sister Mary Michael of all Angels
Reverend Mother Superior General

I reread it twice. "Does this say what I think it does?" I could
feel Sister Mary's eyes. I looked up. "They can't do this!"

Her face was a pasty white and she stared straight ahead. "It
appears they already have."

"Did you know about it?" I could not hide the accusatory
ring in my voice.

Sister Mary sat up straight. "Of course not. There's been no
rumor this time, nothing." Then, hearing footsteps outside the
chapel door, Sister Mary went silent.

I leaned over and whispered. "Do you think it's because of
the murder?"

"I don't know, but I don't see how word of the murder could
have reached them in time for them to deliberate and then inform
the sisters from Brazil, write the letter, mail it... In any case,
this news will keep until tomorrow. Sister Bridget deserves her
special night after that beautiful celebration today."

I shook my head in disgust. "We'll just ruin her world
tomorrow." I could be sarcastic when I felt the need. I took a
breath. "You must find out why they're doing this!"

"I have a thought."

"Who and why?"

"Let me ... investigate. I'll let you know. And meanwhile,
not a word of this to anyone." Sister Mary, as pale as the white

sweater she wore, moved quickly from a sitting position to kneeling and making the sign of the cross.

"I promise." I treasured Sister Mary's trust, but it would be hard to keep this from Bridget.

As I moseyed down the walkway, outbursts of laughter filled the air. I closed my eyes, wiping tears away as I breathed in the chilly night air. In effect, Bridget had been fired and would have to leave her school, the school she built, the school she loved. It would be like pulling a mother away from her screaming baby. Couldn't a person do a better job if her whole heart was in it? And Bridget's heart was buried deep in Malamulele. Surely, they wouldn't force her and these other sisters to leave? These nuns had sacrificed themselves for years working eighteen-hour days living in dire conditions. Now that they loved it here, now that they were beloved by the community, why send them away?

I joined the others at the long mahogany table in the dining room, remembering that the last time we'd congregated there was the night Sister Valaria had been murdered. Flora was setting a feast on the table for the 10-year celebration. Boiled potatoes, salad and roast for the sisters. Fried chicken for me, plus an assortment of sweets for all of us to enjoy later.

Knowing about the letter, I had difficulty with conversation. Still, I was determined to toast the nuns. Not only did they fulfill tough assignments, but also no one received individual credit. Usually.

But, come to think of it, Bridget had been involved in an international story a few months ago. A British Broadcasting Corporation crew had interviewed her for an African education piece. Could it be that uprooting her was a form of reprimand for standing out? Could jealousy have played a part in this stupid and heartless decision to pull her out of Malamulele? In my travels, I'd seen politics play a role in every walk of life. Why not here?

I raised my water glass, my eyes on Sister Bridget. "Never have I been more proud of you." It was understood that all the sisters got credit for the team effort. But privately, the nuns gave individual credit to Sister Bridget for her splendid work at the school.

Later when Sister Bridget and I were alone, I raved. "You pulled off quite an event. Absolutely amazing. Honestly. I'm so proud of you."

Bridget's face glowed. Her head bobbed up and down. "Remember your first visit? You asked why kids played in the streets?"

The vision of children in threadbare clothing racing down muddy streets came back immediately. "I do."

"I told you we didn't have tuition for them, remember?"

"Yep."

"And you told me to find the money, remember?" Bridget paused, waiting for me to pick up the story.

"Then on my next visit the streets were empty." I shook my head. "Absolutely amazing." Being privy to the letter announcing that the nuns would be forced to leave Malamulele weighed on me. I could hardly breathe.

Bridget picked up on it immediately. "What's wrong? You sick?"

"I have headache." I lied. I was sworn to secrecy. The news could wait until tomorrow.

Then the shit would hit the fan.

The next morning I groaned at the incessant knocking on my door. Bridget had left early for school. Who could be waking me up this early? Who would even be in the convent at this hour? Besides Flora. And why hadn't I heard from Baloyi? And where did that come from? I stumbled to the door and eased it open. Sister Mary walked in dabbing her red eyes with a tissue.

"Why aren't you at the hospital?" I didn't mean to be so blunt, but usually she left before sunrise and saw patients 'til supper.

"It's my day off." Her worried eyes grew darker. "I'm so sorry to intrude."

I pulled out a chair from under the desk. "Please ... sit."

"The news keeps getting worse and worse." She looked around my room searching for nothing in particular. "Are we alone?"

"Bridget's gone, if that's what you mean."

She shivered and pulled her worn sweater closer.

"How can the news get worse?" I regretted saying it the moment the words rolled off my tongue.

Sister Mary dropped her shoulders. "Annabelle, you are our trusted friend."

"Of course."

"I know I can talk to you in confidence."

"Of course you can."

"Sister Ann ... she hasn't looked well. I'd prayed my suspicions were wrong."

"But...?"

"She tested positive." Sister Mary pulled a new tissue from her pocket.

I could feel pain emanating from the back of my eyes. "She's pregnant." I shook my head.

Sister Mary looked at me incredulously. "Of course not!"

"Then what?"

"She's HIV positive."

"HIV, but how..." I stopped in mid-sentence.

"She didn't say, but a nun getting HIV reflects poorly on the whole congregation no matter how she contracted it. People's minds jump to promiscuity automatically. And since she hasn't had sex, it must have been a blood transfusion or something from years ago."

I didn't ask how she knew Sister Ann hadn't had sex, but I took her word on that. I reached for my bottle of Panadol pain reliever on the nightstand, shook two tablets into my hand, rethought that and grabbed another one, downing all three with a half glass of water.

"I'm very troubled to be burdening you, Annabelle, but you're the only one who's not one of us. Plus, you were an AIDS activist in America, isn't that so?"

Yes, I knew something about AIDS. And I had a mantra. "The absolute worse thing you can do is NOT talk about it." My heart was sick for the nuns. I knew what they would be going through. Plus sweet Sister Ann must be terrified of not only the disease itself, but also the process of hiding her diagnosis.

Sister Mary rolled her eyes and look heavenward, or maybe it was just the ceiling where a rather large black red-belly spider was lowering itself down ever so slowly. "You must not divulge this, Annabelle. No one must know."

"Who else does know?"

"Well, the mother general in Ireland would know ... she receives a health report automatically. We try to keep it quiet, because ...when someone hears, it goes like a bush fire." Suddenly Sister Mary looked ten years older.

"What meds is she on?"

"She didn't say." Sister Mary stood to leave. She took a deep breath and held it for a moment, then exhaled. "So tonight when are we telling the group about..."

"Leaving?" I hate it when I complete the sentences of others, but sometimes people talk too damn slow.

"Right. I think you should be there, Annabelle. It'll make it easier. That way no one has to give you an update later."

"Wow, what a week." I pressed my hand to my forehead.

Sister Mary stood up and pulled her sweater tight. "It's only Monday, Annabelle."

Before I could respond, she left the room and closed the door behind her.

Murder, my nun friends being uprooted from a life they dearly loved, now HIV. Could it get any worse?

Five

Mamgoboza

The day's weather was next to perfect in every detail. Blue skies. Not a cloud as far as the eye could see. I stepped out of my rental car, grabbed my bag, and stood still for a moment. I breathed in Africa. Where had my passion for this continent come from? I loved the people and the very soil that lay beneath my feet. Had Aunt Cecelia known this would happen when she invited me here for that first visit?

I hesitated at the door of the school Admin building. I'd left Sister Mary behind for her day of rest and decided to join Bridget at the Mother of Angels this afternoon. My mind reeled with so much trouble on its way. I wanted to give Bridget a heads up about the impending move to Johannesburg, but I had to respect Sister Mary's confidence. Besides, was it any of my business? When I returned to Colorado, the nuns would live and work things out without me. Yet, I felt so very involved.

A perky young woman in a short black skirt and a ruffled purple jacket greeted me from behind a vintage wooden desk. *Check in here* was written all over her face. "May I help you?"

Before I could respond, a staffer I'd known for years rushed over with a huge apologetic smile on her face. "No, no, this is Sister Bridget's excellent friend from America." Then she turned to me beaming. "Good morning, Ms. Chase. So excellent to see you." This was Junie, a mid-thirties Tsonga woman with knotted hair and purple glasses. She smiled and gave me a welcoming hug.

"You're stepping up in the world." I glanced around at the new digs.

"Isn't it lovely?" She talked on and on, but all I could think about was that this building would be the last one Sister Bridget would ever build. At least in Malamulele. I walked on to the principal's office where I found Bridget shuffling papers at a desk the size of a Ping-Pong table. "Come with me." Bridget grabbed her wool throw with a flourish and slung it over her shoulders.

"What's up?" At first, I thought she'd found out about Johannesburg.

"We have work to do."

"But It's three-thirty. I'm here to take you home."

"Come, come, I'll explain."

We piled into my white rental and due to the dropping temperatures, I started the engine immediately, flipping on the heater. "Tell me what you need to do." I hated afternoon surprises.

"Listen here, you remember the teacher from the other village?" Her voice grew soft. "His wife arrived today."

"That's great."

"No, not great."

"He's not glad to see his wife?"

"Not with his girlfriend living there."

"Ooooooh."

"He has a Zimbabwe woman who knows nothing about his wife. Today his wife walked in and both women were shocked

... how do you say?"

Shit hitting the fan was a definite no. "The fur flew?"

She shook her head impatiently. "I have to talk to them." She flapped her hands in a forward motion, which meant I should accelerate. "Go, go."

"Whoa! Bridget." I faced her. "You shouldn't get involved."

Puzzled, she looked at me as if I had landed from another planet. I didn't waver. "Honestly, it isn't any of your business."

"Yes. It's my business. I know them."

"The Zulus have a word for that." I hesitated. "They call that being a Mamgoboza" I was glad I'd learned their word for a busybody.

Her eyes flew wide open in surprise.

"Seriously, let it alone." I said it with authority. After all, I'd been married. This was one time I was way ahead of Bridget.

"Mamgoboza." Her head bobbed back and forth and she let out a giggle. "You call me a Mamgoboza?" She lifted her eyebrows at me significantly.

Okay, so she had a point. Reporters are famously nosy. But in this case, I was right and I stood my ground. "Look, I have experience in these issues," I said. "Take it from me. Leave it alone."

"I know such things."

"And how do you know such things?" I squelched a smile out of respect.

"I had a sexuality class."

"Oh really, and what did that teach you?"

"It was about ... relationships. Married relationships."

"Did it include catching someone in the act?" I asked.

"What?" She stared at me with child-like eyes.

"Someone in the act. Making love with someone else's spouse or someone not your partner?" Ouch! Had I stepped over the line?

"No, but I can handle it."

"You're not equipped to handle it. Trust me." I took a breath. "Tempers can flare in these situations and the anger can land on innocent bystanders. What if someone hurts you?"

"Annabelle, I'm only obeying my vows. Please, just drive."

I rubbed my hands together and held one in front of the heating vent. Then, knowing I could not win this argument, I slipped on my gloves, backed the car out and headed for the front gate at the entrance of the school. We waved to a group of children playing outside waiting for afternoon pick up. Two teachers waved back.

Bridget directed me down the dirt road, then toward the other side of the village. Chilling air and a haze of smoke from coal fires settled over Malamulele. People bundled up in blankets waited on street corners for buses to other villages. Students scattered to their homes, while a few cool high school students in shirtsleeves hung on corners laughing, smoking and texting.

We rolled up for the surprise visit. Sister Bridget told me she'd only be a minute as she went inside the small mint green house enclosed by a cinder block fence. She had absolutely no idea what she was walking into, but I decided that despite the temperature drop, I would sit in the car and wait for her. I turned up the heater.

Twenty-five minutes later the front door opened. Three people walked out. Sister Bridget was one, and she turned and hugged the other two. I recognized the tall, handsome teacher from my last visit. The other person was a petite African woman whom I suspected was his wife. I wondered where the other woman had taken refuge.

As Bridget approached my car, she turned and waved again. Apparently she was under the impression that everything had gone well. But from my vantage point—and the couple's body language—those two were definitely estranged. Bridget should have taken my advice.

"So how did it go?" I asked.

"They both listened to me. I told you so. It went very well." She was beaming.

"But what did they say?"

"Oh, the Mambogoza wants to know?" She cocked her head.

I couldn't help laughing. "Come on. What did they tell you?"

"They listened."

Just like I thought. What I'd observed from watching them from afar told me everything. They were irritated. I had observed the couple's, distant, long faces and their body language. They were headed for divorce court.

"Bridget, you need to be more careful. I worry about you. No matter what you think, people resent being told what to do—."

My iPhone's ringtone interrupted me, blaring *I love the rains down in Africa* .... I didn't recognize the number, so I pulled off the road to answer the call. Low clouds threatened a torrential downpour as lighting scattered across the night sky.

"Ms. Chase?"

I would have recognized his voice anywhere. The detective with the dark chocolate eyes had finally called.

"So you need me after all?" I laughed, silently reprimanding myself for my suggestive remark. Only maybe it didn't sound that way to him. "How can I help?"

"Nine tomorrow at Wimpy's. Tzaneen mall. Can you make it?"

"Absolutely." I wanted to say with bells on, but I didn't think he'd know what that meant. I tossed my cell into the outside pocket of my purse lying between Bridget and I.

"Was that the policeman?" Nothing slipped past Sister Bridget.

"Yeah. The detective wants me."

"Why?"

"No idea." I forced a straight face as I considered the endless possibilities.

At first chance, I pulled into the afternoon traffic. Funny to think there was traffic here at all. Not quite like the I-25 at home, thank goodness, but traffic nevertheless. Then I remembered what we were headed toward. Suppertime and Big D Day. As in Big Downer Day.

Sister Bridget received a call on her cell and began talking animatedly in French—one of the six languages she spoke. I drove, listening fondly to the rich cadences of her voice and wishing I had the power to remand the new orders from the Superior General.

I pulled up onto the gravel driveway at the convent. Sister Bridget jumped out and locked the wire gate as I parked the car under the carport. Her phone never left her ear. As we hurried inside, our Sister Margaret flashed into my mind. She'd returned earlier today from her trip to Ireland. I only could imagine how she would take the impending news. Welcome home, then wham!

Hurriedly, we threw our things into our rooms, freshened up and joined Sisters Ann, Benignus and Mary with apologies for being a few minutes late. Sister Mary said Margaret had arrived mid afternoon, offered a brief hello and retired to her room immediately due to severe jet lag.

The rest of us piled extra food onto our plates, slipped them atop individual trays and were eating Sister Margaret's share, as well as our own. But my stomach played havoc with the food. I should have known better than to eat right before watching the rug jerked out from under all these wonderful women.

When dinner was over, one by one we carried our trays into the kitchen and washed up. The teakettle whistled and each of us poured our own cup of tea and headed back to the lounge to watch the International News. The nuns wouldn't be expecting the local news that Sister Mary was about to deliver.

Minutes later, Sister Margaret walked into the lounge balancing a hot cup of tea.

"Here, let me take that," I offered, as I put the steaming cup on a table near her favorite chair. She relished our welcome back hugs, took her regular seat, and smiled in surprise as the homeless cat jumped into her lap.

Sister Margaret stroked Plato as it lazily stretched out in her lap. "She remembers me."

"Sister Bridget, please, would you turn off the television?" Sister Mary looked around the lounge. "Where is Sister Ann?"

"Sister Ann has a migraine." Bridget offered to fetch her.

"No, it's quite all right. I'll speak to her in the morning." Sister Mary's tired eyes surveyed the room. "As you know, we have been here for ten years." She hesitated. "I remember my arrival in Malamulele wondering if I would ever learn to like it here. I didn't think it was possible to love anywhere more than Zambia, where I'd been for twenty years. I had friends there, my work was important. It had quite honestly become my home. Plus, the hospital needed me ... and the people needed me." A wistful look passed over Sister Mary's face like a cloud on a sunny day. Then she pasted an unsettling smile on her face and continued.

"Now, even though I've been here for ten years, it seems like yesterday when I arrived. And I do most certainly love it here." Her eyes glazed over for a second, then she blinked and sipped her tea. Her mouth twisted as she searched for words. "I have news that will affect us all ... as a community." She took a deep breath and forged ahead. "The Sisters of Maria from Rio de Janeiro are sending a group of nuns to relieve us of our obligations here so that we can move on to other projects in Johannesburg." She stared at her lap.

All I heard were gasps. Everyone was speechless as if they were being controlled by an invisible entity.

First to speak was Sister Margaret, who stood up and seemed to have grown a foot. "What on earth will we do there?"

"What about a fair?" Sister Benignus was a bit deaf, and now she looked from face to face for an explanation.

Sister Margaret repeated the news louder in Sister Benignus' direction.

I finally found the nerve to look at Sister Bridget just as she spoke. "And how does that affect the school?"

In truth, Sister Mary said the only thing she could have. "Well, the school isn't ours, never was."

"But, the school ... " Sister Bridget sat back deep into her chair and shut her eyes. A moment later she stood and quietly walked out of the room. Clearly, she was stunned.

Halfway to her room I caught up with her. "Look, we'll find another project. Something even better."

Bridget turned and stared straight through me. We entered my room as usual, then silently she walked through our bathroom and into her own room, closing her door.

I waited five minutes and gently tapped on the door. When she didn't answer, I quietly turned the handle, then pushed it open to take a peek. Sister Bridget snored under a pile of covers with a tiny space heater going full blast three feet from her bed. I tiptoed out. Sleep was the best medicine.

I couldn't help pondering where I would fit into this transition. Malamulele had been a second home to me. When the nuns left, I might not ever return.

Six

Boomslang

I drove like a crazy woman toward Tzaneen—a small town in Mopani District Municipality, population about thirty thousand if you included the surrounding villages, on my way to my nine o'clock Wimpy breakfast with Baloyi. No matter the gloom that should have hung over me because of the nuns' circumstances, I could not deny my smile at the thought of seeing the detective.

Parking underground, I took the aging escalator and arrived at Wimpy's, the mighty fine coffee and hamburger establishment on the second floor of the Tzaneen Mall. I checked my watch. Early. I adhered to my mom's theory: "When you're on time, you're late."

Wimpy's lipstick-red and ebony décor was reminiscent of the 1950's era—a surprise to me the first time I visited. At the back of the restaurant, the theme morphed into futuristic, reminding me of the *Jetsons* cartoon. I was lucky enough to grab the last black faux leather booth. I ordered coffee and pulled out my Sudoku puzzle.

When the coffee arrived, I stared at the white ceramic cup, steam rising, the thick foam tempting me. I added a touch of sugar, then savored the first taste like it was pure heaven. I checked my watch. Eight-fifty. The longer I sat in the booth, the less I seemed to be able to concentrate. I felt uneasy. I had so much to tell Baloyi, but why hadn't I asked exactly why he wanted to meet? Had he discovered a lead in Sister Valaria's murder? Maybe the autopsy report had come back. Of course, we didn't need an autopsy to tell us that she had died from a swift blow from a blade.

At 9:45, my phone showed no calls. Why would Baloyi be late, especially since he'd called the meeting?

At last, my phone rang. "Bridget?" I was surprised to hear from her.

"There's been an accident. The detective's in Malamulele Hospital."

"What kind of accident?"

"I'll explain when you get here." She hung up.

I slipped my arms in my coat, threw my crossover bag over my head and dropped rands on the table. Racing to the parking lot, I imagined various scenarios. Must have been a traffic accident. What other kind of accident could it be? Fell and broke his ankle or worse?

Twenty minutes later I drove through the black wrought iron gate at the entrance to the Malamulele Hospital. I stopped for security, then followed their directions to Emergency, parked in the first available space and rushed inside. I asked the first person I saw where Detective Baloyi was. A tall nurse with wild braids looked at me with a flash of surprise and a gorgeous smile. She pointed me to the corridor on the right. "Room six."

Although small, the hospital was surprisingly busy. Nurses carried out their morning rituals, ignoring me as I rushed by searching for the correct room. When I found it, I walked in and saw a narrow bed with Baloyi sound asleep. No cast in sight. In fact, he looked much better than I'd imagined. The only movement in the room was the steady dripping of a clear liquid into his veins from an IV hanging off a metal frame. That and the heart rate blip on another monitor.

I bent low and spoke softly. "You stood me up. What happened?"

His eyes strained to open. He raised his hand and crooked a finger. "Snake." His eyelids closed, then lazily opened again, his full lips smiling. "Boomslang ... in my bed."

"In your bed?" That was even more ghastly than anything I could have imagined. But even with this deadly serious attack, all I could think of was ... who else was in your bed? Annabelle, what is wrong with you?

"Not much venom ... rear fanged." He took a breath and smiled up at me.

"Right, rear fanged. But, a Boomslang is a tree snake. You're sayin' a tree snake ... was in your bed?" How on earth had a tree snake slithered under his covers?

His eyes struggled to focus, but it was clear the meds were transporting Baloyi into another reality. "You know Boom ... slaaaang?" He gave me a medicated smile. Good to know he was alive in there. "You know snnnaaakkkes?"

"Research." My mind was flooded with the facts. The timid Boomslang loves trees ... extraordinarily dangerous ...human fatalities rare ... venom "affects the body's natural blood clotting mechanism, causing bleeding of internal organs"... fangs at the back of its head.

I bent closer to Baloyi. "Hey, what did you want to tell me? Do you have a suspect?"

His eyes rolled around, then closed. I thought I'd lost him, but he took a slow breath and forced himself awake. "Sis-ter Bridg-et."

"Sister Bridget didn't do it," I snapped.

"Would you like a glass of water?" A nurse had slipped into the room behind me. Baloyi shook his head. She closed the door behind her.

"Are you with me?" I gently moved my hand to Baloyi's arm and shook it slightly.

"I hear ..." His eyes flicked open, then settled into a semi-open position. "... she threatened Sister Valaria."

"On for heaven's sake," I cried. "That again?"

His eyes were more alert now. "Explain."

I threw up my hands. "It's my fault."

The detective blinked. "*Your* fault."

"I don't mean ... just listen! Sister Bridget has spent too much time with me. The thing is, Valaria could be ... exasperating, and one day, Sister Bridget's American slang kicked in. She said, 'Sister Valaria, I could just kill you.'" I rolled my eyes. "You know what I mean—you've been to America. Well, Valaria took it literally. For months, Valaria told absolutely everyone that Sister Bridget was trying to kill her. She was sullen and moody. I don't know if she really believed it or she was just trying to make trouble, but Sister Valaria even wrote to the Bishop, to the Irish order, to everyone she thought would listen to her! But everyone discounted it, for they could clearly see that the problem was cultural. Everyone except Sister Valaria. Of course, Sister Bridget didn't mean she wanted to actually kill her. But no matter how much we explained it, Sister Valaria refused to hear us."

Baloyi's eyes drooped again, then closed.

"It's just an expression. *I'm going to kill you.* We said it all the time when I was growing up in Texas. No one ever took it seriously. Except Sister Valaria." I knew I was ranting a bit, but somehow saying it all out loud gave me comfort. "You have to believe me, Baloyi!"

But he seemed to be dead to the world now. I felt like swearing in frustration but instead I told him goodbye. "You get some sleep, we'll talk later." I almost leaned down to kiss him but caught myself. What was I thinking? Where did that impulse come from? I walked out of the hospital room and hurried down the hall. I had nothing but questions racing through my head. How did a damn Boomslang get into Baloyi's bed? Was he seriously considering arresting Sister Bridget? And for heaven's sake, why did I almost kiss a man I just met?

When the nuns heard about Baloyi and his snake, they had a lot to say.

"What kind of blarney is this? How ever did a snake get into Detective Baloyi's bed?"

Sister Mary, who'd spent years in Zambia and Uganda, shook her head and crossed her arms. "I don't believe it. The Boomslang wraps around branches. It's a tree snake. That's what Boomslang means!"

"Only one way it could have happened. Someone with a grudge *put* it there." Sister Margaret spit it out as if she were shocked that no one else had thought of it.

I wanted to tell Bridget she was under suspicion but I just couldn't bring myself to deliver even more bad news. And besides, Baloyi had been drugged when he said that. Maybe he'd just been rambling and delusional.

For two days, nothing at all happened regarding Valaria's murder. Life had gone back to normal, for what else could we do? But then during dinner the aging front door bell rang alerting us to unexpected company. Sister Mary, as if she half expected trouble, stood up and left in a huff. When she returned, she wore a sober face and looked directly at my suitemate.

"Sister Bridget, Detective Baloyi would like a word."

I ran to the door ahead of Bridget and saw Baloyi standing in the foyer with that awful female interrogator who'd interviewed me the afternoon after the murder. She was the same—in uniform sporting the mean stare.

"Hey, Baloyi, how are you feeling?" I was determined to act nonchalant until I knew what he was here for.

"Better." His eyes looked beyond me as Sister Bridget walked up.

"Sister Bridget, you're under arrest for the murder of Sister Valaria." He cuffed her so quickly she didn't have time to react.

Words flew out of my mouth. "What are you doing? That's absolutely ridiculous. What did that snake venom do to your brain?"

Sister Mary pulled me near her and jostled me softly, trying to keep me quiet. It had the opposite effect. I yelled, "Baloyi, she didn't do it! She's a nun for God's sake!"

Baloyi reached for my arm and pulled me out onto the walkway.

"Annabelle, I have to arrest her. I don't see her for it, but the Chief wants an arrest. Don't worry. The investigation is not over."

"You're makin' a mistake. Take me!"

He stared at me like he was thinking about it. Instead, we returned to the foyer. The female cop had Bridget by the arm and was walking her down the steps.

"It's okay." Sister Bridget glanced back. She had the look Joan of Arc must have worn as they lit the fire.

"I'm right behind you. I'll take care of this." The nuns pulled me back, as the female detective turned around and glowered.

The police car drove away, and I ran to my room for my jacket and car keys. "Don't worry, I'll take care of this," I shouted to no one in particular. Sister Mary shook her head as I raced past her. The nuns were all retiring to the chapel. I couldn't understand why they weren't more upset. I was livid and backed out of the driveway like the proverbial bat out of hell. My heart raced and I pounded my palms against the steering wheel. "Shit, shit, shit!"

Little more than five minutes later I walked into a crowded police station. Sister Bridget sat in handcuffs on a bench next to an African man holding a bloody T-shirt on his head. The concrete floor looked like someone had done a half-assed job of cleaning it up by smearing the blood around. The man removed his T-shirt from his head to show his friend a gaping wound and mentioned a word that sounded like machete. What the hell? Two other guys sat in handcuffs waiting to be transferred somewhere. At least that's what I picked up from listening to the conversation that transpired in English.

A skinny wide-eyed woman with wild disheveled hair and a wrinkled forehead weaved back and forth as she was led down a disappearing hallway. Then there sat Bridget, the nun from Ghana, who had given her life to serve God, chatting to prisoners, switching languages like she was changing her order at a deli. I sat down quietly next to her and stood out like a vanilla wafer in a package of chocolate cookies.

Baloyi walked over and motioned for me to come with him. He lifted the counter drawbridge and I walked beneath it straight toward the hallway leading to holding cells and what I suspected were interrogation rooms. He motioned me through a doorway. We sat in the only two chairs. He hovered over me.

"First, I want to know what you know, Ms. Chase."

It was time. I could feel it. I figured I might as well tell him again, this time while he was awake. He'd find out anyway. "Okay, okay. From the moment Sister Valaria arrived at the convent she saw how well respected Sister Bridget was. Valaria became enamored with Bridget's popularity. She wanted to work at the school like Bridget. Soon it appeared she longed to be Sister Bridget. Sister Bridget gave her assignments at the school. With each task, it was apparent that Sister Valaria couldn't cut it." I winced at my choice of words.

"Thanks."

"For what?"

"For confirming what I've heard from others."

"But Bridget's heart is two feet out in front of her. Can't you see that? She would never hurt anyone, least of all try to cut off someone's head!"

Just then, Bridget walked into the room, followed by an officer. He uncuffed her.

"I don't have space for her tonight." Baloyi's eyes were downcast. "How about house arrest? I turn her over to you and the sisters, Annabelle. She stays inside the convent until something changes." He pointed a finger at me. "But you have to vouch for her."

Relief swept over me. "Of course, yes, of course I'll vouch for her." I exhaled. I saw the corners of Baloyi's lips turn up for a split second, but he corrected it so fast that I couldn't be sure I wasn't imagining it.

Ten minutes later Bridget and I surprised everyone when we walked back into the convent. The nuns huddled around while I explained the rules of house arrest. Then Sister Bridget and I said our goodnights to relieved faces and took tea to our rooms. Basically, Bridget was like in jail, but here instead. And just maybe the food was better.

A short time later, Bridget knocked at the bathroom entrance to my room.

"Come in." I watched Bridget plop down on the end of my bed. "Well, that was some experience, Bridge."

"Yeah." She grinned. I saw no worry on her face whatsoever.

"You were lucky, you know. Someone was watching out for you."

"I told you, God will take care of me." Bridget answered her cell and began conversing in yet another language I couldn't identify, one that made her sound like she was singing into the phone.

Her arrest had taken a toll on me. I was too tired to change so I slipped into my bed fully clothed and watched as Bridget paced up and down in my small room talking on the phone, occasionally laughing delightedly. I pulled heavy covers over my head.

Finally, she hung up. "What, you've gone to bed?"

I managed to open my eyes. "I'm exhausted."

"This would never have happened if I had just stayed in the other room." She walked into the bathroom closing my door.

I lay there trying to sleep, but her words kept bouncing around in my head. *"If I had just stayed in the other room."* What did that mean? Finally I got up and walked through the bathroom and knocked, then pushed open the door to Bridget's room. She lay there in her bed looking up at me.

"What did you mean when you said 'if you had stayed in the other room'? What other room? Is this not your regular room?"

" No. This is the guest room. When you have a guest, you stay here."

The hairs on my neck stood at attention. "Which one is your regular room?"

Bridget sat up. "If you must know, I'm usually in Sister Valaria's room."

I couldn't breathe. "Dear God." I held onto the door jam. I stared at her. "If your room was Valaria's, someone may have been trying to kill you, not Valaria."

Bridget nodded. Apparently, she was way ahead of me.

Seven

Arrest

Baloyi's call awoke me early the next morning. He'd barely said hello when he blurted out what I'd been waiting to hear. "Got the tox screen results."

My eyes struggled to focus. It'd been a late night after Bridget and I considered the fact that she might well have been the target, that Sister Valaria's killer had made a mistake. But I'd save that bit of info for later. "And?"

"Sister Valaria was taking an anti-paranoia prescription drug that I can't even pronounce."

"I need to talk to you and I'll buy coffee. Half an hour?"

"Sure, Grocery Mart?" He agreed to coffee so quickly, I knew he must be a caffeine addict like me.

"Perfect." I said goodbye and threw on jeans, a long sleeve black sweater, blush and added just a touch of lip gloss. My curls I threw up in a clip. Bridget had closed her door. Complete silence. Since she couldn't leave the convent, I decided to let her sleep. I'd check in later.

I backed out of the driveway, drove two blocks and to my astonishment recognized a familiar figure walking in my direction. I drove up beside Bridget and rolled down the passenger side window. "Excuse me, what part of house arrest do you not understand?"

"I'm just trying to make it easy." Her braids were in disarray, moving in all directions.

"What? What are you talking about?"

"I want to make it easy for whoever wants me dead." Her face was somber.

"What kind of talk is that?" I ratcheted up the volume of my voice and ordered her to get in the car. "Do you have any idea how dangerous it is for you out alone?"

"I'm never alone, Annabelle. God is always with me," she said, but she got in beside me.

I blew out a big intake of air and held my temper as her history flitted through my head. The favorite daughter, parents killed in a coup, then an orphan. The nuns in Ghana had bundled up Bridget and her siblings and sent them to the orphanage. When she hit eighteen, she joined the nuns. It was all she'd ever known, this nun's life. I pulled into the driveway of the convent.

"Look Bridget, you have to obey the rules. You must stay inside the house or you will look guilty of this murder."

"I didn't murder anyone. This way, I can draw out the killer, and no one else will die."

"Alone? Bridget, I know you're brave, but you're only one person." I immediately saw by her expression that I'd get nowhere with that argument. "Please," I said. "Cooperate with the police. They've been extremely lenient under the circumstances. You are damn lucky to have only house arrest."

"But people can be under damn house arrest for years!"

I stared at her. I did not want to go down for teaching a nun to curse, so all I said was, "I've given my word you won't break the rules. You fall, I fall."

Bridget gave her irresistible smile. "Okay, okay, I'll stay. For you, I'll stay."

"Thank you." I tried to match her smile but knew I'd failed.

After she walked into the convent, I eased the car out of the driveway and headed for Main Street. A few locals were opening their small wooden stands to sell fresh vegetables and fruits, woven fabrics and trinkets. I searched for a parking place. Not one available. If I'd been at Aspen Grove back home, I wouldn't have been surprised. But here?

In front of the appliance store, I spotted a car reversing to leave. After I parked, as if by magic Baloyi opened my car door and handed me a cup of steaming hot coffee in a Styrofoam cup. Smiling at catching me off guard, he closed my door and walked around to the passenger side. He extended the seat back, then maneuvered his long legs and sat down in my car. I could see his breath as he tugged the door closed. I looked at him and wondered if he knew how happy I was to see him. I hoped not.

"You're spoiling me."

"I hope it's to your liking."

"Oh, the coffee? Something dark and tasty." My heart picked up a few beats realizing my comment said more than intended.

"What's on your mind?" he asked.

I coughed, took a sip and began. "You aren't going to believe this." My thoughts tumbled out before I had a chance to think. "Until the day before I arrived, Sister Bridget occupied Sister Valaria's room." I waited for his applause and was disappointed he didn't react.

He pulled his coffee cup from his lips, looked over at me with squinted eyes. "And?"

"Just think. Bridget lived in Sister Valaria's room for a very long time .... " I stopped in mid sentence and quickly cut to the chase. "I think Valaria's killer believed he was killing Sister Bridget."

His head jolted back and you could see his wheels turning.

I sipped my coffee, proud of my plausible theory, as he wrapped his head around the new information.

"I get it. So the killer would have thought it was Sister Bridget in that room."

"The killer had the information, but it changed when I arrived. Apparently, the murderer did not get the memo that Sister Bridget switched to the guest's adjoining room. I mean, who would have known that except the nuns?"

"Hmmmmm," he said and then took another swig. "If that's true, and I say if, then Sister Bridget may not be the killer."

"For sure." I didn't say I told you so.

Baloyi laid his lips on the rim of the cup and let his mind wander. His eyes traveled over to mine. "What you say makes sense. I'll run it by the Chief. Maybe he'll rethink house arrest, at least until we have conclusive proof of Bridget's involvement." His coffee cup slipped, splashing his jeans.

I handed him my napkin and spoke softly. "Maybe the Chief will at least realize a nun would not be capable of such a crime."

Baloyi downed the rest of what was left in his cup. His eyes studied his jeans. "I understand your loyalty. And I admire it, I do, I really do."

"But?"

"But, it's not inconceivable that a person of the cloth, nun or priest, could kill. Or perhaps hire someone, leaving themselves feeling uninvolved."

"Nuns and priests just don't think like that."

"Excuse me, Annabelle." His words suddenly had an edge to them. "You're not African and you're not a cop. You do not see what I see every day." He collapsed his empty cup. "I'm not indicting nuns or priests—it's just that through personal experience I know that under the right circumstances anyone can be provoked to kill. Either for themselves or to protect someone."

That was my own philosophy, but hearing Baloyi mouth it irritated me. Silence fell over us. "So you're not helping her?"

"Ms. Chase, my job is not to help you, but to find the killer. Or did you forget that?"

"Detective, the difference is I know the truth. Sister Bridget wouldn't hurt anyone. That's what I know and what you can't seem to accept." I pulled my purse onto my shoulder. "So you'll call the minute you speak to the Chief so I can at least get Bridget out of the house?"

He cocked his head, resolve written all over his face. "She was out this morning."

A flush fell over my face. "You saw?"

"Oh, yeah. Another woman who doesn't take orders."

I hesitated. "Not so much."

"I can relate." Then he climbed out of the car and waved his hand without looking back.

Eight

Witch Doctor

Returning to the convent I found Sister Mary in the kitchen staring intently at the electric teakettle.

"I could use a cup." What I really wanted was a triple brandy. Baloyi's words sat on my shoulder like fresh thorns ripped off a bush. The nerve of him. Women following orders. I was so furious I could hardly speak. He had seemed so progressive.

"Annabelle, is something wrong?"

I blew out air and put my hair behind my ears. "No, Sister Mary, just police stuff."

"What happened?"

I rotated my head in a circle carefully and then looked at her. "Just that infuriating detective."

"Oh, never you mind." She looked up at me with a faint smile as I selected the white mug with the South African flag emblazoned on it.

"That was your aunt's favorite cup."

"Yeah, it makes me feel close to her." I studied Sister Mary's shoulders holding up the weight of the world. "Did you sleep well?"

She poured boiling water into our cups. I plunged mine twice with a rooibos tea bag, then pulled it out and set it on a saucer. She dunked her tea bag in her cup and left it. "Let's take our tea to the lounge."

During the day, the lounge was a casual meeting place for the nuns or for guests who popped in unannounced bringing their own set of problems with them. When we stepped inside the room, Sister Mary pushed back the heavy drapes and opened the blinds allowing sunshine to cast shadows of trees on the lounge walls. Although wintertime produced brutally cold mornings, as the day progressed, one usually could expect a beautiful sunny afternoon. Sister Mary settled atop a worn beige cushion in her rattan chair. Pulling her navy blue sweater close, without much ado she chose a topic of conversation I didn't expect.

"I don't mind moving on, you understand. I took the vow of obedience in Ireland over fifty years ago. Sometimes I wanted to move, you know, to relocate, sometimes I didn't. I never wavered. But, this time ... it's complicated." She put her teacup to her lips and quietly took a sip.

I listened, enjoying the warmth of the hot cup of tea.

"When I go, I will have to leave patients at the hospital who depend upon me. Patients whom I have worked with for ten years, like Grace."

"Grace?"

"A desperately ill woman." Her eyes blinked away tears. "She could barely walk when I first met her. Her family had accepted that she was dying. Nothing worked. After weeks of medical tests and research, I discovered that she was on the wrong medication and had been for over sixteen years. Everyone believed she had an unknown illness. Instead, it was a simple misdiagnosis. Can you believe it? After I eased her off the strong medication, she recovered in a few months and was right as rain. Her family was overjoyed, as you might expect. It felt like a miracle, even to me."

"Wow." I stared admiringly at her. This woman sitting in front of me was changing the world—or certainly someone else's world. And I was furious that she was being made to return to the city when she was so desperately needed here in Malamulele.

"I worry about all those people falling through the cracks." She steadied her cup with dry wrinkled hands. "I know God can take care of them but ... God has so much on his plate." She studied her cup with painful eyes as if she were reading tealeaves.

I had to ask the question. "But you believe that this is God's will, right?"

Sister Mary adjusted her glasses as she focused her eyes and looked up. "After fifty years, I've learned a thing or two about God's will. I think sometimes He has to work around man's plans to get His will done, if you know what I mean."

She surprised me by her remark. "Uh-huh, actually, I do know what you mean." I repositioned myself on the lumpy couch. "So if you don't think it's a good idea to leave, why don't you do something? Maybe God's plan is for you to speak up. To speak out." After spouting my radical idea, I sat back and wondered how all those words had come out of my mouth. Me, practically an unbeliever at this point.

Sister Mary looked me squarely in the face. "Maybe. But, I've always followed the rules of our order, the rules of obedience. I took that vow. And it's too late to go back now."

"Maybe." I took a quick breath. "But maybe not. Too late, I mean."

There was a faint knock on the door, then Sister Ann walked in pale as a corpse. She sneezed into her Kleenex. "Sorry, I didn't realize anyone was in here."

"It's okay, come in." Sister Mary stood and gave her a hug. "My dear, you don't look well."

"I've surely been in my room a year." She feigned a laugh. "I needed a change, but I don't want to make you ill."

Sister Mary walked Sister Ann and her touch of flu out into the courtyard where the dazzling sunlight shone down upon them reminding me of a picture I'd seen in a book of saints. I closed the door and thought about God's will and how these women had given up absolutely everything for their beliefs. Just like my aunt. I watched Sister Mary put her arm around Sister Ann's shoulder and walk her back to her room past the bright red poinsettias climbing up to the roof.

Bridget in the far corner on the left walked out of her room. She saw me standing in the doorway of the lounge, then turned and retreated to her room. House arrest really sucked.

When I went back to my room moments later there was no noise coming from Bridget's room. She must have gone back to bed, and who could blame her? Moments later I stepped out of the shower and dried off, threw on my robe and checked messages. A text message from Baloyi. He'd convinced the Chief to release Sister Bridget from house arrest until they had additional evidence to support the theory that she'd killed Sister Valaria. "Yes!" I couldn't help but shout. I knocked on Bridget's door, but there was no answer. Under the circumstances, I opened the door. Bed made. No Bridget. It appeared, once again, she'd gone rogue. This surprised me, because Bridget wasn't in the habit of breaking her word.

Could she have gone to the school as if this were a normal day? I needed to find her. Twenty minutes later when I walked into the school admin building, staff members and teachers were flying through the halls shouting in African languages. I couldn't make out what had happened so I raced to Bridget's office. She was there, all right, dressed in a bright green African dress. And on the desk in front of her lay a crude brown rubber snake.

"Some kid messin' with you?" My grin disappeared when Bridget's eyes narrowed into a serious stare.

"It's a warning."

An unexpected thud on Bridget's office window surprised me. I looked up to see a dark red liquid sliding down the glass from the place of impact.

"What on earth? That looks like blood!" I went to the next window and watched as a young African woman with wild cornrow braids threw more blood. I shrank back as she held up a bloody chicken claw and flicked it toward me. I flinched, then screamed. "What is she doing?" She seemed delighted with my reaction.

"She thinks she's protecting me," Bridget answered softly.

"From what?"

"From snakes."

"Bridget, it's rubber. It's a rubber snake!"

"No, the snake was alive."

Bridget was a smart educated woman. I stared at her with disbelieving eyes.

"The healer thinks she's releasing the curse."

"What curse?" I toned down my voice and did my best to

remain calm. "Bridget, you're a brilliant educator. How could you believe in such nonsense? And you're a nun!"

She shook her head. "Of course I don't believe it. Nuns are not superstitious, you know that."

"So she thinks someone put a curse on you?" My voice grew high pitched.

"You Americans don't understand. It's their culture. I am a guest in their country." She studied the floor and then continued. "I was working at my desk and this snake crawled across the floor. I screamed and ran to get Hero. When we came back, this snake was on my desk."

"And it's rubber." I tried to be rational and at the same time respect where I was, where unexplained things happened from time to time. But still, a live snake could not turn into rubber. And yet, here was a witch doctor splashing blood all over the windows.

I tossed out an idea. "Okay, but maybe someone switched the snakes."

"Switched the snakes?" She stood and paced around the room. "That's it exactly. You are brilliant Annabelle!"

"Yeah, someone messing with you. It would have scared anyone."

Bridget looked up as the witch doctor unexpectedly walked into the room, saw me and did an about face.

Had she heard our conversation? "Does she speak English?"

"Yes. She studies at Witwatersrand University in Joburg. She was visiting her grandmother who sent her to release the spell. Being a Witch Doctor or a healer is how she pays her tuition."

"What's her name?"

"Shari."

Through the open door I saw Bridget's administrative assistant pay the witch doctor as she passed her desk. Still, I took out a notebook and wrote down the name Shari, as a person of interest. I would give it to Baloyi.

As if by magic, Baloyi appeared in the doorway. He passed me and spoke directly to Sister Bridget. "I went by the house, as in house arrest, but you weren't there."

The look on Bridget's face must have been the same one she had as a child when she was naughty. It was priceless. For a split second, she displayed an impish grin.

Baloyi was using his official voice. "I'm here to inform you that thanks to your friend Annabelle, I spoke to the Chief and you are allowed to go wherever you want. Just don't leave the area. Understand?"

Suddenly she was Sister Bridget, Principal, once again. "Thank you, for all you've done." She stood as tall as she could. "I *am* innocent."

"We'll see about that." But as he turned his back to her and walked to the door, I saw a quick smile he didn't bother to hide. With a twinkle in his eyes, he said, "Annabelle, you have a nice day."

I stood directly in front of Bridget's desk, and it seemed to divert her attention. "I hope you know how lucky you are. You could be in jail right now."

Bridget grinned. "God takes care of me."

Thinking about Baloyi's smile, I added a thought. "And me."

Nine

Target

In the seat beside me, Bridget was already snuggled against the window. That woman could sleep anywhere. I envied her. As we drove down Main Street and cut over to the highway, it hit me. Baloyi had said not to leave the area, but I rationalized he hadn't been clear what that meant exactly. What area? We were on our way to Tzaneen, which was a mere 45 minutes away. That could be part of the area. If I believed that, why was I so paranoid he'd find out?

I spied a cop car hiding behind a grouping of young fever trees on the side of the two-lane highway. I glanced at my speedometer and then into my rear view mirror. Thank God I wasn't speeding.

Bridget exhaled loudly.

"Not to worry. Baloyi won't find out. And if he does, it's on me." I looked in the rearview mirror. Nothing. "I just wanted a relaxing meal where we could sit across from one another and talk. Is that a crime?" Apparently it could be in our situation. Bridget nodded and laid her head against the window again, closing her eyes.

A chill ran through me, but it wasn't the temperature. "Bridge, have you told anyone about how the nuns will be leaving Malamulele?"

She straightened up, twisted toward me and answered defiantly. "I'm not leaving."

"What?" My eyes bounced from Bridget to the road and back to Bridget.

"I'm staying. People depend on me."

All I could say, albeit to myself, was woe betide those who stand in the way of a determined nun. It was an interesting dichotomy: Sister Mary, nearly twice as old as Bridget, would obey because of an oath she took fifty years ago, while Sister Bridget, young, sharp, and confident, had taken the same oath but now had a new attitude.

I decided to challenge her. "So what will you do if they insist you leave?"

"Listen here, it's time the Mother of Angels order caught up with the times. You can't order people around anymore. You have to dialogue, talk to the people and see what they want, what they think God wants them to do. Do they think God only talks to the white hierarchy, the white Irish nuns? What about what God says to us Africans?" Bridget's rich lilting voice added beauty to her words. She inhaled deeply and grew quiet for half a minute. "They want me to go to Johannesburg just out of the clouds. Did they ask what I thought? Did they ask any of us?" She answered her own question. "I'll tell you. No, no they didn't. Well, I won't do it. I need to stay here. This project isn't over." With furrowed brows, she crossed her arms and blew out a breath of air. Just for the sake of argument, I dove in. "But didn't you agree to the obedience clause?"

"Yes, but I've changed. I'm different. I've had training, I've learned a lot. I want dialogue. I want to be a nun, but I don't want to be bossed around like I don't have a brain in my head."

"So it's just the obedience angle that's bugging you?"

"That and other stuff."

"Like what?"

"Like I don't want to talk about it anymore." She stared out the window in the direction of an avocado farm we were whizzing by.

"No problem." I kept quiet until I couldn't stand it anymore. "I don't remember you ever shutting down before."

"What do you mean 'shutting down'?"

"You know, quit talking."

"You shut down when you need to think."

Bridget was absolutely right. When I needed to think, I did shut down.

Silence took over as we whizzed past cars, bakkies and vacation trailers, orange groves, and fledging entrepreneurs hawking marble sculptures, carved wooden baskets and trinkets. Finally, we reached Tzaneen. Today congestion was at an all time high. Tzaneen was a hub where everyone congregated to shop for groceries, clothing, vehicles and other essentials. I drove through the entrance to underground parking. We locked up the car and waved to a young man whose livelihood depended upon watching cars. He sported a broad smile knowing he'd get a tip when we returned.

Entering the mall through a heavy glass door, we found our way to the battered escalator that took us to the first level. We passed Milady's, Bridget's favorite shop that sold accessories and clothes in flamboyant African colors, then arrived on the second level near Woolworths. Before we indulged in shopping, we zeroed in on Wimpy's.

A young eager waiter greeted us immediately, leading us past booths of shoppers with early purchases and school age children stuffed in beside them. En route to the empty booth, I glanced around and there was Baloyi staring right at us. We were so busted. Taking the high road, I headed straight for his booth with Bridget reluctantly in tow.

"Hey there, we thought we'd catch up with you today and buy you a late breakfast." I sure hoped he bought it. And I wasn't talking about the food.

He blinked a couple of times, as if considering what to do with us.

"Are you alone?" I asked.

He nodded.

Bridget whispered into my ear that she needed Panadol, then headed for the chemist, leaving me to deal with Baloyi. I thanked the waiter, who had followed us to Baloyi's table, as I took a seat across from the detective and nonchalantly picked up a menu.

Baloyi looked up from beneath a burnt orange baseball cap that read "Longhorns." "What's up?" I was desperate to act natural. Then words I had no time to prepare tumbled out of my mouth. "Okay, I'm sorry. I wasn't thinking about the 'stay in the area' thing when I decided to come to Wimpy's. Don't blame Sister Bridget. She was just a passenger. It's my fault completely. I'm so, so sorry. It won't happen again."

And just at that moment, a shrill scream in the mall caused Baloyi to bolt from our booth with me right behind him. Baloyi rushed toward a knot of people bending over someone. Being with a cop threw me right into the center of the action. As I pushed my way closer, there was Bridget with a bloody forehead lying on the ground.

"Oh, my God, Bridget!" Bending down, I jerked off my scarf and wrapped it around her head. "Are you okay? What happened?"

I stared up at a young woman in jeans hovering over us. "A man pushed her down. I saw it."

"I need a description, don't run off." Then Baloyi turned to Bridget. "What did he look like?"

She was struggling to get up. Baloyi took one arm and I took the other. We lifted her.

"Describe him," Baloyi demanded.

"Large man, tall, thick."

Baloyi probably figured that was all he would get from her. He hurried toward the young woman who'd come forward. I knew the protocol. Baloyi was searching for witnesses who could give a better description of the attacker. "Large and thick" wasn't going to cut it.

Bridget leaned against me as we hobbled over to a seating area where a woman with children quickly dispersed. We thanked her and settled ourselves on the bench. In the distance I watched Baloyi giving info to mall security and local police.

"Bridget, tell me exactly what happened." I emphasized *exactly*.

"I went for Panadol. A big man grabbed me. I pushed him. Then, he pushed me hard and I tripped and fell."

"Did he know you were a nun?"

Bridget looked at me like I was from outer space. "How could he tell?"

I checked out her navy blue tracksuit. Nuns now wore street clothes, so how could he have known? Unless someone told him or gave him a picture. Who wanted my friend dead? And why, dammit?

Baloyi hurried over to us, bent down on one knee in front of our bench as if he were going to propose, and began questioning Bridget. "Could you think very hard, Sister Bridget? What did the man look like? Was he dark skinned or light? Young or old?"

Bridget, exhausted I was sure, avoided his eyes and reiterated the same facts she'd told him the first time.

Baloyi escorted us to the chemist two doors down and requested the nurse on duty to examine Bridget. Then after instructing us to return to Malamulele, he left to assist with the search.

The nurse taped a white gauze bandage around Bridget's forehead. "It looks as if you'll be good as new in a day or two, but head wounds are tricky," she said. "If you feel extra tired or you get dizzy, be sure to see a doctor."

When we got in the car, I made sure the car doors were locked and drove slowly toward home while Bridget rested her bandaged head against the passenger side window on the left. I watched through my rearview mirror to make sure no one followed us. The only traffic behind us was a dilapidated white van that sported a faded "electrical" sign on its side.

The moment we drove through the convent gate the piano riff on my iPhone played. I was surprised to hear Baloyi's voice.

"How's Sister Bridget?"

"As good as she can be."

"We need her at Malamulele Headquarters in an hour. Tzaneen Police are bringing two suspects to see if she recognizes them."

The Malamulele Precinct was housed in a small nonde-script brick building. Sister Bridget and I took a seat on the long wooden bench to our left. With no fanfare, two handcuffed men were hustled in through the front door by Tzaneen officers. Baloyi came from behind the counter. The officer led the men down a hallway and into an interrogation room. Then Baloyi turned to Bridget.

"Did you recognize either of the men?"

"No."

"Are you absolutely sure, Sister?" Baloyi looked very skeptical.

"Yes."

Baloyi towered over us with a no nonsense face. "Because a very reliable witness identified one of them."

"No, not him." Bridget stared out the window.

I stood up, signaling we were leaving. "Thank you, Detective Baloyi. Sister Bridget needs rest." I held my hand out to shake his. As our hands touched, our eyes met and held for a moment, and in that instant something stirred deep inside me. I nodded and followed Bridget who was already walking out the door.

Bridget was silent as we walked out of the building. I had a nighttime tiredness nagging at me, and it was only 3:45. But I didn't have time to be tired. As we drove up the street, I saw a chemist and pulled into the parking lot. "Bridge, ever get your Panadol?"

She shook her head.

"Okay, then. Keep the doors locked. I'll only be a minute."

Due to the long queue at the drugstore, my errand took longer than I had expected. Relieved when the clerk handed me my change, I hurried to the car.

It was empty.

"Don't panic." I raised my phone to speed dial Baloyi just as I caught sight of Sister Bridget at the side of the building. Cancelling the call, I eased closer. I could hear her talking to a tall, heavy-set man. When he spotted me, he turned and ran. I recognized him as one of the men the Tzaneen police had escorted to Malamulele headquarters, someone Bridget said she'd never seen before.

"Bridget, what is going on?" Could this be the man who had attacked her?

She was dead calm. "He is a man I met at the Indian shop."

I didn't even ask what Indian shop. "Was he the one who knocked you down today? Do you know him? Why on earth did you not identify him?" I spit out questions and couldn't seem to quit.

"He's a friend to my cousin." She studied the dirt-filled area between the buildings.

I threw my hands in the air. "You lied to us – to me, your friend, and to Baloyi, a police official! What's wrong with you?"

Bridget stared at me with big wide eyes. "He is Bennie, a friend to my cousin from Johannesburg. He gave me warning."

"Warning? Warning about what?"

Bridget studied the rock as her shoe moved it back and forth. "He said," and she hesitated, "someone offered his cousin R100,000 to ... to kill me."

For a minute I wondered how long I could go without taking a breath.

"Pushing me down was an accident," Bridget continued.

"He said to me, 'Damn, lady what did you do to piss somebody off? Ain't you a nun?'"

I barely controlled my wavering voice. "But then why didn't you tell Baloyi all this? It absolves you—shows they were after you all the time, not Valaria."

Bridget sighed." I couldn't betray my cousin's friend. He only meant to help me."

Ten

Footsteps

"Where are we going?" I asked Bridget that evening. Wearing my heavy coat, I traipsed right behind her as she opened the side door of the convent. Now that I knew for sure that someone wanted to kill her, I didn't want to let Bridget out of my sight. I agonized about whether to tell Baloyi and try to get Bridget some police protection. But I'd already talked myself blue in the face arguing with Bridget, who scoffed at the idea, stubbornly clinging to her faith that God would look after her, and absolutely unwilling to cause trouble for the man who'd given her the warning. "Fine, then," I'd told her. "But that means you're stuck with me."

Now I wrapped a knotted scarf around my neck, bracing for the cold. While Denver had hit one hundred and two that afternoon, Malamulele was a wintry thirty-five Fahrenheit, about four Celsius according to the thermometer on the wall.

"We're going to the Indian shop," Bridget answered.

The cold wind took my breath away. And if that hadn't done it, surely the brilliant constellations above us would have. Only those stars and a sliver of moon lit the darkness as we carefully navigated the gravel road leading to Malamulele's Main Street.

The thick air smelled of coal fires. A white haze hovered

over the rooftops of the village dwellings. The lucky ones lived in homes built of brick or cinder blocks. Mud homes with open fires inside the huts were scattered on the outskirts of the village. Hundreds of less fortunates lived in cardboard dwellings. By now, stragglers had returned from work and were in their homes, if they had one, or staying with family or friends if they didn't. Homeless people were invisible here. Someone always took them in at night.

We hit the main road. On the corner stood a small shop with an aging white bakkie parked out front. We walked through the door of the Indian shop and Sister Bridget greeted a small man with round wire glasses and a quiet persona. She spoke in Tsonga but then motioned to me and switched to English. "This is Annabelle, my good friend from America." She smiled broadly. "Annabelle, this is Punjab."

"Velcome." The confidence he exuded while wearing a warm and engaging smile, hinted that he was the owner. He introduced me to the two men playing chess on low stools near the potbelly stove. "They also from Punjab."

The men looked up, nodded and continued their game.

Immediately Bridget and Punjab switched to Tsonga again, so I strolled around the small store. From the ceiling to the floor were shelves displaying electrical devices, odd farm equipment, and rocks with mineral deposits. At the back of the store against the wall were out-of-date kitchen appliances under heavy duty plastic wrap. I saw nothing to clue me in on why Bridget was here.

A young boy, eleven or twelve, popped his head out from a doorframe, then vanished. "Raj," the owner called out. A string of impatient words flew out of his mouth in yet another language. I suspected it was Hindi, India's national language, although it easily could have been any of the three thousand languages spoken there.

The boy reluctantly walked in.

"Are you in school?" Bridget asked in English.

His father spoke. "No. I want him to go, but he gives me trouble."

"Can he read?"

His father answered for him. "Not much."

"Send him to my school. He must learn." Bridget spoke in her principal's voice, as if giving an edict, not a suggestion.

The owner put his hand on his son's shoulder and spoke quietly. Raj shook his head. His father didn't need to translate, but he did. "He won't go."

An unsettling sensation washed over me as the boy ran to the back and disappeared through a door. I wondered if Punjab actually had asked Raj about school. How could we know? None of us spoke their language.

Bridget slipped Rands to Punjab and in return he gave her a small card, which she stuck into her pocket. She thanked him and we left.

"What did you buy?" I knew it couldn't be drugs, but I was curious.

"Time."

"Time?" My mind tripped to a parallel universe. How wonderful if we could buy more time. Sister Bridget looked at me and smiled, taking pleasure in the fact that I seemed baffled.

"Air time for my phone." She gathered her scarf around her neck. "I buy new time every night." I suspected she was smiling, but without ambient light, I couldn't be sure. I knew Sister Bridget had family and friends all over the world. Cousins in Texas and Alabama, an aunt in London, sisters in Ghana and religious friends in Zambia and Nigeria and probably many more I hadn't even heard about. Talking with these friends by phone was her entertainment and her company.

"You walk here by yourself every night?"

"Yes."

I supposed buying time every night was one way to budget her tiny stipend. Because of all the calls she got, it made a certain sense. But I couldn't allow this to continue—not now, with a killer on the loose. "Bridget, until we catch that murderer, you can't be going out alone every night in a predictable pattern." I could see her getting ready to protest and I pushed my face right up to hers. "Do you want me to die of anxiety?"

Just then I heard a noise behind us. I grabbed Bridget's arm. Footsteps ... growing louder. I looked back but saw nothing in the dark. Being that we were a half block from the convent, Bridget and I sprinted. Only after we locked the side door did my pounding heart begin to ratchet down. "Now do you believe me?" I squeaked.

In between deep panting she managed to say "I will not ... let anyone ... control me."

I wanted to yell and scream and shake her. For God's sake, she could lose her life with that attitude. Besides, wasn't she a nun who'd been controlled by her superiors for years? She should be used to being controlled by now. But then I remembered what she'd had to say about the orders coming from Reverend Sister Mary Michael. Not only that, but at that moment a snippet of my failed marriage appeared and gave me insight.

I realized exactly how Sister Bridget felt.

Eleven

Cobra

As I entered the lounge with my coffee cup, I realized that if I closed my eyes, I couldn't tell if I was inside or outside. I turned the space heater up to high and pretended it was my fireplace, curling up in the rattan chair next to it. My eyes roamed over the room. I'd better appreciate it while I could. I spotted the marble sculpture of an African head sitting on top of the television. Without touching, I knew he was cold as ice.

A light, steady rain tapped a gentle melody against the windows. Compelling myself to relax and consider how to move forward in this murder investigation, I was convinced Bridget was the target. The question was: why would someone want to kill her?

A clap of thunder startled me, causing coffee to splash over the rim of my cup and down the front of my robe. I wiped it with a Kleenex from my pocket and jumped when the door opened. "Oh my gosh...Sister Ann, you half scared me to death."

"Sorry, It's only 4:30. Couldn't you sleep?" She placed her tray on the coffee table.

"Just restless, I guess. How are you feeling?"

Sister Ann was way ahead of me. Face scrubbed. Breakfast

on a tray. "I'm feeling much better." She spoke with a delightful lyrical tone.

"Migraine's gone?"

"Yes." She sat with her tray in her lap and took a small bite of toast. "I've missed a ton of emails and I'm quite behind in my research. I have to get with it, as you Americans say. Thought I'd work until time for Mass."

"What are you working on?"

"The AIDS clinic north of Tzaneen is my primary responsibility." Sister Ann paused. "Didn't I hear that you were an AIDS activist?"

"I was. A friend of mine struggled ...very traumatic." I wished I could have bitten off my tongue. Sister Ann was HIV positive, but I wasn't supposed to be privy to the information. Well, maybe it was good I said what I did. At least she wouldn't think I knew.

"Right." Sister Ann warmed her hands with her teacup. "It is tough work, but drugs are more powerful now and I feel hopeful ... for the people."

"Of course, the drugs are miles ahead of what they used to have."

Before I knew it, this petite woman with short, walnut brown hair, had finished her breakfast. "Time to go." She whisked her tray to the door. "See you for dinner."

As she left, I remembered something Sister Mary had said. The local people buried family members every week dying from pneumonia, lung disease and heart attacks, which actually were caused by the HIV virus turning into full-blown AIDS. Here in Africa, it tended to be a silent death sentence no one would speak about.

My coffee was cold, despite the warmer room, and I was frozen to the bone. At that moment, if I'd had a magic button that would transport me back to the Denver summer, I would have pushed it.

Boisterous children raced toward my vehicle as I drove through the double gate of the Mother of Angels Elementary School Monday morning. I pulled under the open carport on the far side of the school property. As I stepped out of the car to the screaming crowd of children in blue gingham uniforms, I knew how it felt to be a rock star. Beautiful shiny faces radiating jubilant smiles stared back at me. A teacher walked over and instantly children stood erect and greeted me properly in the way they'd obviously been taught.

"Good Morn-ing Sis-ter Ann-a-belle." These children persisted in calling me Sister even when I told them I wasn't a nun. It was easy to understand their mistake, for they always saw me in company with Sister Bridget.

Heating "Sister Annabelle" reminded me that my aunt had encouraged me to be a nun. But with my faith next to nothing, there was no way for me to live the life of a nun. It required sacrifice. I'd sacrificed enough already.

"Good Morn-ing Child-ren." Today, I didn't bother to correct them.

After quick hugs, the group scurried away toward the swings in the distance. The teacher smiled at me with a twinkle in her eye as she followed.

I walked into the admin building searching for Bridget. I found her leading morning prayers in the staff meeting.

When she concluded and walked in to her office, I questioned her. "Could there be anyone, a parent or co-worker here at the school, who might wish you harm?"

"Good morning to you, Annabelle," she said, reminding me of my total disregard for manners. I ignored her. I had important things on my mind, not social graces.

Her grin subsided, causing me to notice her tired eyes. "You think someone *here* would want to kill me? Someone I know? Are you kidding me?"

"Maybe that teacher whose mistress had to leave?" She shook her head. "How about a disgruntled parent? Anyone who might have been irritated by one of your policies?"

"No."

"You have to at least consider the possibilities."

"No, I have to buy bricks for the auditorium we're building. Come."

Bridget threw a red wool throw around her shoulders and grabbed her bulky purse. As we passed Junie, she kept typing at a feverish pitch and barely waved.

At Bridget's direction, I drove down Malamulele's Main Street passing the shops, the Police Station on the left. When the road ended, I turned right, passed the petrol station on the corner and headed southwest. "Seriously, where are we going?"

"To buy bricks. I told you." Two hours later we turned off the main highway and drove through an open gate connecting a cyclone fence. Batches of freshly made bricks rested on crisscrossed two-by-fours in front of a small flat brick building. Bridget opened her door and walked up to the office to talk with a burly Afrikaner I could see from the distance. In less than five minutes she returned, slid in and slammed the door. "Let's go."

"You didn't like the bricks?"

"Yes, I did."

"So when will he deliver?"

"When I pay him." She shook her head and her braids flew from side to side.

"And why didn't you pay him?" Confused, I turned the key and started the car.

"He won't accept a check."

"What?" I could feel my eyes pop.

"I am an African woman. I must bring cash tomorrow, then he'll deliver in three days."

"So he doesn't trust you ... but you have to trust him."

"That's how it is here."

I thumped the steering wheel with my fingers thinking about that. "But Bridget, does he know you're the principal of the school?"

Bridget rolled her eyes, stared out the window and shook her head.

I drove down the highway, but found that I could not let it go. "Are you telling me that we have to drive four more hours tomorrow to pay him and then we still won't have the bricks?"

Sister Bridget exhaled. "It's okay. Junie can drive."

She'd missed the point. Or maybe she hadn't.

A half-hour into our trip back to Malamulele, the two-lane road was swollen with traffic. Rain pelted the windows, reminding me of my aunt's accident. The driver of a bakkie passing a car at the top of a hill had run head-on into my aunt's vehicle. Because of the weather, emergency vehicles were not able to reach her for over an hour. When the ambulance arrived, the paramedics discovered that Aunt Cecelia had suffered a collapsed lung, broken pelvis, dislocated shoulder and fractured hip. Of all the things I feared in South Africa, a car accident ranked number one.

Lightning flashed brilliantly decorating the sky as the rain turned into a ferocious downpour slamming against the windshield. Within minutes water filled the gully beside the two-lane road. Traffic was bumper to bumper, reminding me of Denver's I-70 during rush hour. Who would have thought?

Sister Bridget pulled out her African music. When she slid in the CD, the song "Mamgoboza" filled the air.

Bridget and I both laughed and started singing along, our voices harmonizing. But as we sang, the traffic came to a standstill. Looking ahead at the line of cars, I turned off the motor. I glanced at the rearview mirror, and when I did, my heart began to pound like a thousand drums. What I thought I saw in the rearview reflection was impossible. Surely I was delusional. A poisonous black spitting cobra was swaying less than a foot behind me.

I whispered to Bridget. "Don't move."

She turned enough to see I was terrified.

My mind struggled to recall my research on the Rinkhals. These snakes would spit venom in a victim's eyes right before striking. Ultimately the venom would kill or blind you unless you received immediate medical attention.

No ambulance could get here in this traffic. But I'd be damned if I would let myself and Bridget die today on the same road as Aunt Cecelia.

From my peripheral vision, I could see Bridget's bulging eyes staring forward. I whispered. "On three, run."

"One, two, three." I hit the door locks and we bailed out of the car. I didn't look back until I hit an ankle deep puddle on the far side of the road. Bridget ended up three feet from the car in a wet ditch.

A driver in a black SUV behind us honked his horn and stuck his head out. "Blazes, what ye doin' mate?"

"Snake, snake!" I screamed.

The large man in a hunting jacket leaped out of his SUV toting a shotgun and rushed to our car while we stood on the sidelines and watched. He opened the driver's side door, looked inside, then leaned the shotgun against our vehicle. "It's dead!" He bent back roaring with laughter, as he reached into the car.

It was like seeing an accident in slow motion. I could not scream fast enough. "Nooooooo...it's....."

Sporting a huge grin, he scooped up the limp snake and turned to show us just as the cobra came to life and struck the Good Samaritan's face full force.

I ran over and grabbed the man's shotgun that had shimmied to the ground, aimed and pulled the trigger, catching the tail end of the cobra as it slithered into the underbrush. The threatened Rinkhals had rolled over and played dead with his forked black tongue hanging out of his mouth—its protection mechanism. The stranger, apparently ignorant about South African vipers, had assumed the snake was dead. Now, this bulky guy dropped to his knees, then collapsed on the ground writhing in pain.

I dialed emergency services repeatedly. Sister Bridget opened the trunk of our car and pulled out a piece of poster board to use as an umbrella for our hero lying flat on the ground. The man's face was swollen within minutes.

I ran back to his vehicle, discovered a brown weathered satchel in the front seat of his Explorer identifying him as Joe

Bagot, an Australian business owner. Several strangers climbed out of their vehicles and came over offering their help.

One man and woman bounced from car to car asking if anyone had anti-venom serum for a Rinkhals. Of course it was a long shot, but South Africans living in isolated areas frequently stored anti-venom in their fridges. It would have been a miracle if someone had been returning from shopping with the exact anti-venom vial we needed.

Even as the rain poured down, word traveled car to car. A heavily bearded man hurried over to offer anti-venom for the Puff Adder or the Boomslang but unfortunately nothing for a Rinkhals. And unfortunately as well, the wrong venom would cause Mr. Bagot even more problems than he had now. I did remember that from my brief Internet research months ago for a story in Denver.

Lightning filled the sky and the thunder was relentless. Bridget and I knelt, comforting the Australian. She said a rosary while I continued contacting emergency services. My call to Baloyi went to voicemail. There was nothing more to do than sit back and embrace the hero desperately clinging to life on this narrow African highway far, far away from home.

Twelve

Deliver Us From Murder

While Sister Bridget remained by Mr. Bagot's side, I searched for a long stick, walked over and peered into my car. I eased the door open, then with the far end of my stick, touched every possible crevice inside the car to make sure there were no backup snakes. I also prodded underneath the car and even under the hood until I was satisfied nothing was lurking there.

I locked the car doors, then joined Bridget and Mr. Bagot, who now was unconscious. Bridget wiped her red eyes and continued praying while I paced around the two of them, stunned by the course of events. Was that snake meant for Bridget, or for me? Plenty of people knew I was the one driving Sister Bridget more often than anyone else, but the Rinkhals could just as easily have struck me as my passenger.

Forty-three minutes later, the traffic finally cleared enough for an ambulance to arrive. Medics loaded poor Mr. Bagot and sped away to the Tzaneen Hospital.

Bridget and I settled back into the rental. "I've thought about this Bridget," I said, "and here's my conclusion. Someone is after you, and whoever it is doesn't seem to care if others are killed so long as there's a chance of murdering you. Now do you see why I worry about you?"

She looked absolutely stricken. "I can't stand the thought you could have been killed!" she cried. "But who would want me dead? I don't understand."

"I agree, it's completely incomprehensible." Who could she have angered so much? Bridget's life was full of good works and kind deeds. "But Bridget, we have to tell Baloyi about this. There's no one you need to protect this time."

She nodded, her hands clasped. "Yes, yes, tell the detective. But Annabelle, you have to promise me you won't say anything about the man who warned me—or what he said."

I wanted to argue with her, but she looked so sad and tired, I just sighed and agreed.

We made our way to the hospital, feeling terrible that the stranger who had been so brave might end up giving his life to help us. Bridget prayed nonstop for Mr. Bagot, but the best I could do was keep myself from nonstop cursing.

When we arrived at the Tzaneen Hospital, doctors confirmed Mr. Bagot had slipped into a coma. From his appointment diary, we learned he had simply been in the wrong place at the wrong time. Plus, it was evident that he had no knowledge of African snakes. The officials were notifying his relatives in Australia that he might not make it through the night.

Bridget and I headed back to the convent. My poor friend was completely exhausted, and within minutes of driving down the highway, Sister Bridget began to snore with her head resting against the window. It gave me a small bit of solace that one of us was resting, but as for me, I could not quell the jumble of noises in my head.

I was now 100 percent convinced that Valaria had not been the target on the night she was murdered. And that whoever was after Bridget was relentless. During my career as a crime reporter, I had learned that nothing was more dangerous than a *frustrated* killer. But frustrated killers usually made mistakes. Now that I thought about it, hadn't this killer made several already? He had entered Valaria's bedroom and assumed that Bridget was under the covers. Although they were the same height, approximate weight, both African and lying under piles of blankets, only someone who didn't know them would have simply assumed it was Bridget.

As I crested the top of a hill, I slammed on my brakes skidding off the road barely avoiding the herd of cows ambling across the road. My heart felt like it might stop! To calm down, I counted the 31 cows. Sister Bridget merely looked up, gave me a half smile, then resumed her sleep. A young boy carrying a six-foot stick shouted at the herd, flailing his arms to move them. I didn't understand a word, but his apologetic eyes said enough. I waved as he passed.

Waiting for the cows to finish crossing the road, I made a mental list of car alterations for the Bevis Car Rental company. In addition to the fender repair for the shotgun blast that had pop-corned the side of the car when I took out the cobra, they might need to check the tires ... and maybe the brakes.

Sister Mary let out a shriek when we walked into the convent. Truly we looked like we'd been plucked from the war-torn pages of "National Geographic." Sister Bridget's navy blue pantsuit was mud-stained from kneeling in the rain to pray for Mr. Bagot, and her cornrow braids were decorated with twigs. I hadn't seen a mirror, but I could only imagine how I looked. Sister Mary grabbed Bridget's arm and escorted both of us to the warm lounge where she'd been watching the news.

Minutes later Sister Ann brought in a pot of steaming black tea and two cups on a tray. Sister Margaret glanced at us and ran for warm wet towels. Benignus sat tentatively on her chair asking if she could help. Basically, though, the nuns couldn't fool me. They had gathered for the story.

Questions, as if we were the central figures of a CNN investigation, bounced back and forth. I began the story with Bridget interjecting comments. Tonight, I refused to pretend that I didn't know that Bridget was the target of a brutal and relentless killer. As I laid it all out for the nuns, four sets of eyes grew wider and wider. And Bridget had to go along with it, because I wasn't going to allow her to dismiss this latest threat to her life.

By the time I finished, everyone was shaken.

"But why?" They all had the same question, now that the cat was out of the bag about someone being after Bridget.

"No one seems to know," I said, relieved to have confidants and allies at last. No nun would have put a cobra in my car, I was quite sure. "If any of you can think of anything, please please tell me, and I'll pass it on to Detective Baloyi."

The nuns nodded soberly. After we snacked on the plates of food that had miraculously appeared, we all said good night. Then Sister Margaret and Sister Mary insisted on walking us to our rooms. I didn't know what help these two older women could be in a fight, but somehow their presence helped me feel at least a little better—as if their faith formed a powerful shield that would protect Sister Bridget and me.

Once inside our little "suite," Bridget and I began scanning the floor. Sister Bridget stood by with an aging broom handle as I slowly opened the closet door. We closed windows that opened no more than six inches and locked our outside doors. I stuffed washcloths and socks down the drains of the sinks and the bathtub in case someone could have gained access to our rooms and delivered us another snake delight. Then we thoroughly checked Bridget's room. I was paranoid and with good reason. Luckily, we found nothing.

As soon as the sun arose, I called Baloyi. I needed to tell him about the recent snake episode. Just thinking about it sent shivers up my spine. He didn't answer. I'd talk to him later.

Next I called the Tzaneen Clinic and inquired about Mr. Bagot.

The nurse who answered must have left the phone on the desk because instead of hold music, I could hear noises of a small hospital. I was so glad to be in Africa at that moment. They'd never heard of HIPPA. The nurse returned to the phone and spoke to me in perfect English. "The doctor would like to speak with you."

A deep voice with a thick African accent said, "I am Dr. Chake. You inquired about Mr. Bagot."

"Yes. How is he?" I held my breath.

"A Rinkhals bite to the face dispersed venom swiftly to major organs. We did everything we could. He died at 3:17 this morning. The police will notify his family in Australia."

"Thank you." I closed my eyes and choked back tears. I would forever remember that snapshot in my mind of Joe Bagot laughing at the snake that killed him—the snake intended for my dear friend, Sister Bridget.

Baloyi finally answered.

"Where have you been?" I asked.

"Just where do you want me to be?"

His voice was seductive, raspy as if he were just out of bed. I could have answered that question in oh so many ways. Instead, I willed my mind to stay on course. "I need to talk to you." I hesitated. "It's important." Even I noticed that my voice sounded unsteady.

"Are you okay, Annabelle?"

I detected a hint of alarm in his voice.

"Now I am. But I almost wasn't. How 'bout you buy fat cakes and I'll tell you the story."

Within 20 minutes I was sitting in Baloyi's cop car in front of the SPAR grocery store. I'd pimped myself out for fat cakes by promising him details. And I knew that the Rinkhals tale would not disappoint.

Within minutes I'd shared the adventure, complete with vivid imagery of the storm and traffic down to our checking our rooms for snakes when we returned to the convent.

His hand caught mine as his eyes studied me. "You've got to be careful, Annabelle. That was a definite attempt on either your or Sister Bridget's life."

"Not me. Surely you must see that it's Bridget someone's after."

"What did the police say?"

I must have looked at him so strangely because he stared until I came up with an answer.

"I was so busy surviving, making sure Bridget was okay and trying to save Mr. Bagot that I never even thought about calling the police." My head felt as if someone was squeezing it with giant hands.

"You're scarin' me. You look awful."

"Well, thanks for that." I shook my head and faked a smile.

"No, Belle, you know what I mean. I'm worried about you." His voice calling me Belle for the first time felt extremely intimate somehow. He quickly pulled me into his arms and held me for only a moment, just long enough for me to melt.

"Snakes, snakes, snakes. Someone loves'em. Your dancing cobra, and didn't Sister Bridget find a snake on her desk at school?"

"Yes, and what about the Boomslang in your bed?" I said, feeling baffled and frustrated that I couldn't connect what seemed to be an obvious series of dots. "Was that because you're on this case?"

He went silent for a moment, and when he spoke he didn't answer my question. "I'm going to put an undercover police officer in Bridget's office. It'll go through normal channels and even Bridget won't know who she is. Sound good?"

"Sounds great to me. It would relieve some of the stress for sure." Without this measure in place, I was sure I'd go absolutely bonkers with worry.

"I'll use Detective Aimee Malanga from Joburg. She'll fit right in and no one will recognize her here."

I felt weak with relief knowing that Bridget would be protected. Suddenly, my exhaustion pushed forward. "I need to go back to the convent, Baloyi. Thanks for the coffee ... and the protection."

During late afternoon prayers I walked into the small chapel no bigger than a bedroom where behind the altar a pewter savior stared out at three nuns sitting in padded chairs against the wall.

Sister Benignus, the oldest nun, knelt on an individual kneeler affixed to the back of a chair in the center of the room. Bridget was on the floor, her back against a pillow, her legs stretched out in front of her crossed at the ankles. As Sister Mary read from The Divine Office, or Breviary, I considered their devotion.

Exhausted, they prayed twice a day, at five in the morning and five in the afternoon. During the week, a local priest said Mass in the convent chapel. Sunday would find the nuns at the village church a few blocks away. There, they were always treated like dignitaries. It'd been a while since I'd attended church in America, but here in Africa, God seemed vivid, more vital. I said a few prayers as I sat in the chapel. I didn't see how the nuns could pray so much. Five minutes and I'd be half asleep. What did that say about me?

Deliver me, that is, deliver us from this crazy mess. Was that a prayer? Could that even be a prayer?

Thirteen

Muti Killers

Next morning after seeing Bridget safely to school, I dialed Baloyi. I wanted to be kept in the loop and in case Baloyi needed encouragement, I'd bring out the big guns and promise him hot coffee and more fat cakes.

"Minjhani."

I paused, wondering if our connection was amiss. "Who is this?"

"Who do you want?" His voice was gravelly.

"Detective Baloyi," I said.

"Oh, it's you. I must sound awful." Then there was a loud cough.

"Are you even up?" I waited for his reply and checked my watch.

"I'm up just now."

I loved that South African expression "just now." It meant within minutes he *would be* up, as in he *wasn't* up just yet. "Detective Baloyi, I never asked you if you've recovered from your Boomslang?" I said, half laughing.

"Oh yeah. Plus, got new info." He cleared his throat.

"Me too. When and where?"

I heard stirring and new energy in his voice.

"OK Furniture. Half hour, African time?"

"Let me put it this way, Detective Baloyi. In thirty minutes I'll have fat cakes and steaming hot coffee. After that, it'll be cold."

I dressed in a flash. Pulling back the aging sheer curtains, I checked the sky for the instant weather report. A soft blue. But, by the chill in the room, it was cold. I'd need layers until midday.

Locking my bedroom door behind me, I traveled down the walkway to the carport, exiting and closing the door. I locked it with the key dangling from the Mother Mary key chain, then placed the key in my coat pocket. I jumped into a mighty cold car, but it started without a hitch. Poor baby. So many pockmarks it looked like it'd been in a war zone. Luckily, the windshield wipers worked and swished away most of the frost.

In six minutes I arrived at the grocery store where I purchased fat cakes and two tall hot- as-fire coffees. No sleeves. I placed the bag of fat cakes under my arm, picked up the coffees after wrapping two serviettes around each and headed for the car.

It wasn't hard for Baloyi to find me as he drove up in his bakkie. Pale faced woman in a white rental car. He stepped out and as he headed over, he stopped and ran his hand across the popcorn surface of my car. He opened the passenger side door, moved the car seat back as far as it would go and slid his tall frame inside.

"What's up with your car?"

"Do you want coffee or not?" I held one cup in each hand and playfully pretended I wasn't going to give it away just yet.

He yawned, then grinned. "What do I have to do to you to get coffee?"

I handed him a large Styrofoam cup filled to the brim. As he took it, his dark fingers touched mine in the exchange. I shivered.

"Freezing," I said, as I shook my shoulders. In case he'd noticed.

I waited until he'd had a sip to ask the crucial question. "Do you miss Starbucks?"

"Whoa, would love one of those babies." His eyes danced as he said it. "Had a part time job at Starbucks." He laughed and rubbed his eyes, then took a sip. "This'll work too."

"Up late?"

"You might say."

He turned to face me and those eyes stared directly into mine. "What happened to your car, seriously?"

He whistled softly when I again repeated the end of the story. "You took out a snake with a shotgun?"

"Yep. Remember not to piss me off, Detective," I said, smiling. "Now what's your news?" "We got another murder."

"Another? You mean another snake murder?" My voice squeaked.

He shook his head. "No snakes. And girl, believe me, you don't want to know about this case." He took a careful sip and cuddled the hot cup in his hands, drawing out his news. Was he teasing me? But he sounded truly solemn.

"Tell me. Maybe I can help."

His dark eyes darted in the direction of the appliance store. "Okay. Professional courtesy?" He waited for my nod. "We think the ritual killer from 2012 is back."

My jaw dropped. A ritual killing? "What sort of ritual?"

"We had a series of ritual murders back then, mostly women

and children." He hesitated and looked at me. "Are you sure you can handle this?"

"Yes, of course." But of course, I wasn't.

"Body parts cut off." He shifted a bit and I could tell he was watching for my reaction. "Several kidnappers got life, but many got off for lack of evidence. In general, the killings slowed, but recently we've come to believe that they might never have stopped."

I shuddered. "Are you talking about muti killings?" I had researched a slew of stuff before coming to Africa. The gruesome I'd tried to forget. I'd read that many witch doctors continued to do good work. These were people motivated to heal. But rumors claimed that there was another class of witch doctor that practiced the dark arts—they liked to mix herbs with cooked-down body parts. The result was known as muti or muthi, a substance believed by some to bring good luck. Muti killers were said to take human eyes, genitals and other body parts from women and children, then sell them to the cruel witch doctors who'd turn them into muti and sell it—to shady businessmen, or even to some coaches before an important game.

"You know about muti?" Baloyi asked.

"Yes."

"Muti killings, yes. One this month is all." His iPhone buzzed. He pulled it from his pocket and listened. His face grew quite serious. "I'm coming." He pocketed his phone and looked over at me. "Make that two this month." He took a deep breath. "You don't want to come." He said it as a statement, but I knew it for what it was—an invitation.

"I do. Absolutely."

"It's a dead and mutilated child. A boy."

"You look as if you could use a friend."

He nodded. "But you have to do what I say, okay?"

"Course."

I climbed into his bakkie and slammed the door.

Baloyi continued talking as he drove. "Most kills happen in the bush." He gulped his coffee. "In isolated areas. But the worst part about it all is the fear." He took a turn and continued. "Parents are terrified. They try to keep their children safe, but kids have to go to school. Sometimes they walk a mile or more by themselves."

"Do you know who's buying the body parts?"

"That's anybody's guess, but body parts always sell. A head sometimes goes for R20,000." His voice turned more bitter. "Provides good luck, strength."

All I could think of was Sister Valaria's head, nearly severed. Was there a connection? But if so, why had the killer left her head behind? What if someone had been in the process of taking her head for a buyer, then been spooked by Sister Benignus' insomnia? R20,000 was a lot of money.

Baloyi flashed me a glance. "You okay?"

"I'm fine." I'd lied to him twice now. "So they kill the victim, then slice off body parts and sell them." That dovetailed with my research.

Baloyi paused. "If only."

I blinked and my eyes bore into him. "You don't mean ...?"

He didn't wait for me to finish. "The louder a person screams, the more luck ...." Baloyi left the sentence hanging.

"They cut off the parts with the person still alive?"

"Yeah, I'm afraid so."

Baloyi navigated us down a dirt road lined with scraggly

acacia and fever trees. A police car was parked on the left side of the road. He pulled up behind it and we stepped out. Through a thicket of scrub trees, we fought our way toward a clearing. A small African woman with three clinging children stood nearby. Baloyi walked over to the only policeman on scene.

A small piece of black vinyl covered something on the ground about twenty feet away. The poor woman had either found the murdered child or, God help her, the child was hers. I suspected the latter. I pulled latex gloves out of my hip pocket where I always kept a pair. Just in case.

Baloyi walked over to me. "You need to stay back."

"Of course." I walked a distance away out of respect. Plus, I didn't want this to be my only African crime scene. Denver cops had taught me well. Even as a reporter I'd had to stand behind the crime scene tape like everybody else. Still, I'd attended the Citizen's Police Academy in Denver. It was for sure that I knew more than the detective thought I did.

As the lead policeman and Baloyi spoke with the woman, I nonchalantly drifted away to search for clues. I stepped carefully so as not to disturb the area before the techs arrived. Suddenly, I saw something. I caught Baloyi's eye and waved at him. Baloyi wandered over as the policeman talked to the woman on the sidelines.

"Look." I pointed at a chicken claw stained with blood. I was astonished at how much it resembled an old woman's skinny hand with long yellow fingernails. I shivered all over realizing it may have been used in the ritual.

Baloyi pulled a plastic bag out of his hip pocket and gave me permission to drop the chicken claw inside. He stuffed the bag inside his jacket, zipped it up and walked over to the policeman.

I stared down at the plastic covering the victim, then dropped to my knees, whether to pray or beg forgiveness for humanity's crimes, I wasn't sure.

Baloyi walked over as the first officer on scene drove away with the mother and her other children. "You okay?" he asked, crouching beside me, then pulling us both back up.

"No. No, I'm not okay." I couldn't hold back the tears. Very unprofessional. Baloyi put his arms around me and held me close. Also, very unprofessional. He pulled a handkerchief out of his pocket and handed it to me. Then he asked me a question I didn't have an answer for. "Think we can get fingerprints from a chicken claw?"

I wiped my eyes and laughed at what should be humorous. Then I answered honestly. "I don't know."

After a few minutes of searching the area, we decided we had what was probably the only piece of evidence with any merit. The claw. I edged over to the child's body and gently lay my hand on the blanket, wishing I could give Last Rites. I promised myself I'd help find the killer.

Baloyi pulled the plastic sack from his jacket and shoved it under the car seat.

"Are you allowed to do that?" I asked.

"Officially? No. Don't tell me you do everything you're told, cause you'd be lyin'."

When we got back to the shopping area, Baloyi asked if I was hungry.

"No, I'm good."

"Wait here." He jumped out and headed for Shoprite.

I slipped into my rental and turned on Jacaranda 94.2 FM

thinking we'd hear about the murder on the hourly news. I rolled down the window and leaned back in my seat. The cool breeze reminded me of the Colorado Rockies.

Then I saw them. Four toughies in front of OK Furniture. One wore a short-sleeved T-shirt and probably was the leader. They gestured with their hands, laughing with one another, then glancing at me. I turned my attention elsewhere. A couple minutes later I glanced back. My breath came fast. They had advanced and were three feet from my car. My ten-point radar alert had jumped from a two to nine. I hit the door locks. The tallest of the four bent down, his leering face staring through my window just as Baloyi walked up. He spoke to the boys in Tsonga and for a few minutes bantered back and forth. Laughing at Baloyi's last remark, whatever it was, they returned to OK Furniture.

I unlocked the door. Baloyi handed me two sodas and three small sacks of food with an aroma of roast chicken and fries, but my mind was elsewhere. "Do you know them?" I tried to control my high-pitched voice.

"Seen 'em around." He glanced away. "They wanted to know why a white girl was hanging out in Malamulele. But they won't bother you."

"How can you be sure?" I turned and looked back. They were still watching us.

"I told 'em you were here on official police business, and when that didn't seem to impress 'em, I told them you were my girl. They seemed to go for that. It'll keep 'em at a distance."

I hadn't felt that protected since the eighth grade when my first boyfriend Jeremy popped a boy for trying to kiss me. Kind of fun to think Baloyi was protecting me. "Good idea."

His eyes met mine. "Did they scare you?" He opened his sandwich and discarded the pickles.

"Well, they looked like they'd been drinking. So yeah, I locked the doors."

"They won't bother you again."

"I've never had trouble in Malamulele, not in ten years." I grabbed his pickles and put them on my sandwich.

Baloyi blew out his breath through pursed lips. "Times change. Plus, they've had a few beers, maybe somethin' else. It's boredom. No jobs. They hang around shops and street corners. I feel for 'em." Baloyi handed me one of the smaller sacks with a toasted chicken and mayo sandwich. My favorite.

I took a few bites until I suddenly remembered the chicken claw in the sack below Baloyi's feet. I took a huge gulp of soda hoping it would settle my stomach.

"And dessert." He handed me a package of Smarties.

"Yummy."

He pulled out an orange for himself.

"So you give me the sugar stuff and keep the healthy stuff?"

"I'll trade," he said with dancing eyes. But I could tell he wanted the orange.

Out of the corner of my eye I noticed the guys staring at us. "They're making me nervous."

Before I could say anything else, he laid his orange on the dashboard. He turned halfway in his seat and pulled me close. He leaned over and whispered in my ear. "Go with it." He kissed me and turned me loose, his eyes searching for my reaction. I could barely breathe, but I smiled. Then he pulled me back and kissed me strong and hard. I put my arms around his neck and returned the favor. When we pulled apart, he touched his forehead to mine and lingered a moment.

"What was that?" I managed a gulp of air.

"To make sure they believe you're my girl. Now you won't have any trouble for sure. I'm a detective and you're mine." He took a deep breath. "Okay, then, I'm going."

As he stepped out of the car, I turned to check the guys on the corner. Their attention was devoted to a hot African girl sporting the world's shortest mini skirt.

It was a good thing that Baloyi didn't wait around. As I watched him drive away, I couldn't move. My axis had just been knocked into a spin.

I drove back to the convent in minutes, pulled into the driveway, then turned off the motor. I closed my eyes and sat there like I was sixteen. Baloyi and I had major chemistry. Did he feel it too? But as my fantasies took me away, a distant voice reminded me that he had kissed me to keep me safe, not because he wanted to. I, on the other hand, had kissed him back on purpose.

Fourteen

A Kiss is a Kiss

I opened the door to my room and there sat Sister Bridget on the end of my bed.

She took one look at me. "You kissed the policeman."

I could feel heat rise to my face, so I walked over to the miniature desk. I put my purse down giving me seconds to prepare. First, it wasn't any of her business. And second, how on earth did she hear about it so fast?

"What are you talking about?" Playing dumb was not something I was proud of, but it was an automatic response.

"I heard." She gave me a stern look.

"Bridget, if you must know, he kissed me to keep me safe." And my intellect told me that although it was unfortunately true, it sounded absolutely ridiculous.

"How does kissing make you safe?"

"Four big guys harassed me when Baloyi went inside Shoprite to buy sandwiches. I was rattled." I made the explanation short, sweet and totally believable. That was what had happened.

"The boys?" Bridget asked, as if she knew them.

"Well, they were big guys, Bridget, and they stared at me in a ... well, you wouldn't understand. Anyway, Baloyi told them I was his girlfriend."

"Oh?" she said.

"So they would leave me alone. That's all."

Bridget twisted her mouth to the side and furrowed her brow. I wasn't sure she'd bought my story.

"So to make them believe it, that I was his girlfriend, he kissed me. That was all. It wasn't because he wanted to."

"Uh- huh." She rolled her eyes.

Suddenly I felt like a harlot. Ridiculous! It was a simple, innocent kiss. But Bridget had never been kissed and had no knowledge of chemistry, or how overwhelming it could be. How absolutely wonderful it could be. "Why do you care about Baloyi?" I asked.

"Gossip." She waited for my reaction.

"Gossip? Since when are you concerned about gossip?" I let out a laugh. I couldn't help it.

Bridget stood and put her hands on her hips. "Everyone thinks you're a nun. They call you Sister Annabelle."

"But, Bridget, you know I'm no nun." I wanted to tell her it wasn't fair for her to think of me as one of the nuns. It screwed with my psyche. I was a healthy woman with needs that the nuns could never understand. Yet, here I was in two worlds and living in neither 100 percent. I wanted a relationship with Baloyi. Yet it would wreck my image with the nuns.

"My friend saw you."

"You have eyes everywhere." I was controlling my temper and at the same time trying not to laugh.

"I knew he liked you."

"Bridget, he was protecting me. He doesn't like me."

"He does."

I didn't want her to see my smile. Maybe he did like me, just a bit. Not only that, but he had arranged protection for Bridget, easing my mind.

─────────

For the next several days I drove Bridget to school and picked her up, carefully monitoring her movements whenever she was out of sight of her new undercover protection. I went with her to the Indian shop in broad daylight after school to be sure she didn't run out of airtime, and double-checked the locks in the convent every night.

When there weren't any more attempts on her life, I began to relax slightly about Bridget. I knew I should keep the same level of vigilance, but it wasn't in my nature. Besides, I had other things on my mind: I was waiting for the Malamulele detective to call me. The fact that he didn't was excruciating.

The morning of the third day, I called him.

He answered on the second ring, and I cut right to the chase. "What's happening?"

"Another muti killing."

My heart sank. "Sorry." A deep sadness filtered through me. How awful for Baloyi to see these victims.

"Guess you have no time for a Wimpy run?" I held my breath and chastised myself for being so crass to think of him ... or coffee. Dear God, what was I doing?

"Nine okay?"

"Sure." I changed the venue. "Post Office."

"Okay, see you."

I heard a tap at my door and when I opened it, there magically lay a stack of clean clothes in a plastic yellow grocery bag. I'd pay Flora later. I quickly brushed my teeth and when I applied Tantalizing lip-gloss, I remembered how my lips had felt on Baloyi's. He had set the bar high. I pulled my scooped neck, long sleeve T-shirt over my head, brushed my hair and let it fall to my shoulders. I threw on my black leather jacket, hoping I didn't look like I'd tried too hard.

Fifteen

Zula

I skirted by Sister Bridget and Sister Mary, waving with words that made me shiver. "Another murder." I made my way to the car close to nine. But I was on African time, which meant I had a license to be late.

I backed through the narrow wire gate feeling somewhat guilty that I never asked Bridget to join Baloyi and me. I knew without a doubt that he would never talk about the murders in front of her. Plus, I felt guilty wanting to keep Baloyi to myself, but I deserved a NNAD. *No Nuns Allowed Day.*

My heart picked up a beat as I pulled up in front of the post office. He was waiting for me, his cell at his ear. I jumped out, hit my key fob, and walked over to his bakkie.

Baloyi stretched over and opened the passenger door from the inside. I stepped up into the bakkie as he put his cell into his jacket pocket.

I began talking immediately. "Did I ever tell you I did a couple of ride-alongs with the police in Denver?"

"And?" He turned the key and began to back up.

"Most of the time, nothing happened."

"What'd you expect?" He headed south and seemed preoccupied.

"Arrest, a car chase, anything."

"I can't promise any thrills." It was hard to tell if there was a double meaning to his words. I was reminded that I'd been away from the dating game way too long. Clever conversation did not come easily. Maybe I needed to forget that kiss and admit that he had kissed me to protect me. I stared at him, handsome, smart and full of energy. My heart was working overtime, while Baloyi drove in silence.

I felt a need to talk and said the first thing that popped into my mind. "How old are you, Baloyi?"

"How old do you think?" He glanced at me with a half-smile, then his eyes locked on the road ahead.

"Do you always answer questions with questions?"

"Don't you?" He laughed with that sleepy early morning rasp.

"I'm sorry, I shouldn't have asked something that personal."

"You can get as personal as you want." Then with a twinkle in his eyes, he said, "You're my girl, remember?"

"Oh, you mean the story?"

"Yeah, what'd you think I meant?" He gave me an impish grin.

"Nothing." I chastised myself for any thoughts I might have had about romance. What had I been thinking?

"Thirty-seven."

"Excuse me?"

"I'm thirty-seven."

"You look twenty-seven."

"Yeah. I hear that a lot." He cut his eyes over at me. "What about you?"

"Thirty-four," I answered. "So have you ever been married?" Dear Lord, control my mouth. Don't let me keep asking these stupid ass questions.

"Nearly."

I laughed. "What does 'nearly' mean?"

"Like, almost."

I loved his sense of humor. "I mean, what happened?" I could not take my eyes off of him.

His sober face fixated on the road. "She died. Long story. Maybe I'll tell you one day."

"Dear God, I'm so sorry. I didn't mean ... you know, to bring up something painful." I felt terrible, like I'd stepped on a landmine and couldn't get off it for fear of blowing us both up.

"It's okay. It's been a while. That's when I decided to—what is that expression? Oh, yeah, get the hell out of Dodge. So I applied for scholarships, left for UT."

We were halfway to Tzaneen when the traffic crawled to a stop. Baloyi turned the siren on and we sped around several vehicles. When we arrived at the accident, two SAPS cops were questioning the drivers involved. Baloyi stepped out of the bakkie and walked over to them, then surprised me when he returned.

"That was fast."

"They got it under control. Driver freaked, snake in his car."

My eyes flew to his. "You're kidding."

Baloyi's eyes danced. "Yep. Just a fender hit." He laughed heartily.

I playfully hit him on the arm with my clenched fist.

It seemed in a matter of minutes we were settled into a comfortable booth at Wimpy's, ordering coffee and platters of breakfast food.

When the waitress delivered the coffee, I closed my eyes

taking in the fragrant drink and enjoying it to the fullest. When I opened my eyes, Baloyi was staring at me from across the table.

"What?"

"Never seen anyone make love to a cup of coffee." Then he hid behind his own cup, but I could see his dark flirty eyes above the white ceramic coffee mug. Did he have any idea that when he said "making love," my whole body reacted?

"I actually dream of this coffee when I'm in Denver. All I think about is coming back to Wimpy's and Africa. When I'm here, I'm home. I never want to go back, except of course for my family."

"You love it here?" His eyes locked onto mine.

"Oh, yeah." I said it softly and even I could hear the love in my voice.

"Move."

I stared at him. The pure simplicity of his thought process was absolutely refreshing. "But what would I do?" I slipped my fingers through a strand of my hair and pushed it behind my ear.

"Teach. Be a crime consultant. I won't say you're good yet, but with my tutoring, you could be."

I laughed.

Baloyi took a sip of coffee and his face grew serious. "So, like I told you we've had another murder."

Before I could respond, a tall waitress in a red Wimpy's apron pulled tight at the waist over fashionable jeans sashayed up to our table and laid down bacon and egg platters. "Anything else?"

We shook our heads.

She walked away bouncing to the rock n' roll music filtering through the restaurant.

Baloyi picked up his knife and fork and began to cut up his

eggs. "It wasn't kids this time. An old woman from Polokwane."

"So tell me."

"Let's talk about this later." Baloyi gestured at the food.

"Good idea."

I watched him scarf down his breakfast, then contemplated the question I'd been rehearsing. "Why did you kiss me the other day?"

He coughed, sipped water, hit his chest, coughing again. "Sorry."

I sat still, remembering the one tip I'd picked up from my summer sales job after my sophomore year in college. Ask the question, then be quiet.

"Sorry, got something stuck there." He shook his head, wiping his mouth with his napkin. "Now, what was the question?"

When I didn't speak, he looked like the accused in a courtroom drama, his eyes darting toward the door then back at me. "I wanted to." He tilted his head.

"And, what did you think?"

"It was okay." His shoulders tried to reach his ears so quickly I almost missed it. Then he sipped his coffee again, only I was sure it was empty by now. And the waitress was sure too because she came and completely filled it again.

"That's all you got?"

"How was it for you?"

"I asked you first."

"Yes, yes you did." He winked. "It was awesome, Ms. Chase. Absolutely awesome. Does that satisfy you?"

Baloyi had picked up the American lingo, and his dark eyes had melted into warm chocolate that I would have eagerly poured over my ice cream sundae.

"Awesome, huh?" I was energized and could not fight a big grin. There might even have been a Hallelujah chorus playing inside me somewhere.

"So how about you?" Baloyi sat back.

I hadn't thought about the repercussions of asking pointed questions. I stammered around then finally came out with it. "I ... was never more surprised."

"Uh-uh, not acceptable. How was it for you?"

"The same."

"No, you can't copy. *Your* words."

I fidgeted with the napkin. "It may be one of the best kisses ..."

"May be ... ?"

"Okay, it was the best kiss I can remember." To protect myself, I wanted to say I had a short memory, but I decided to be brave and vulnerable.

As the waitress whizzed by pouring refills of coffee again, the one who cleared plates asked if we were done. I nodded. As they vanished, Baloyi drew my fingers into his hands and moved them to his lips. It was a good thing he wasn't talkative because my lungs needed air so badly I couldn't believe it. Parts of me quivered, my heart feeling weak as if it might stop at any moment.

When we slid into the bakkie, all I could think about was how I hoped he wasn't taking me home.

After ten minutes down the highway, he peeled off onto an unfamiliar dirt road. Soon we were in a partial clearing in the middle of absolutely nowhere. A few scrub trees and the African veldt, a vast stretch of pale, waist high elephant grass, stretched on forever.

Baloyi reached into the backseat and pulled out a folded blanket. "Come, I want to show you something," he said, and walked me to the clearing. My heart was racing. Was this the crime scene? I detected the fragrant aroma of wildflowers as I followed him.

He spread the blanket on the ground, then held out his hand. "Come, we need to talk." He gently pulled me down with him.

It was then I saw his smoldering eyes and realized that talk was not what was on his mind.

"We need to take this slow," I said.

"Whatever you want, whatever you need."

Did he have any idea how seductive his words were? Holding back wasn't what I wanted. My heart begged for full speed ahead. Baloyi wrapped me so close I could feel his chest rising and falling, his heart beating wildly. His long fingers slipped through my hair. I could barely hang onto my senses as he kissed me, his lips softly melting onto mine.

Then his hand clamped down over my mouth.

"Listen."

A shrill scream, and close.

Baloyi jumped up and jerked me to my feet. Ahead of us was an open field to nowhere with patches of thigh-high elephant grass. I followed Baloyi, but the screams were growing weaker.

"Wait," I said. "What's going on? Why would someone be out here, now, screaming?"

He shrugged. "Crimes almost never explain themselves," he said, "but someone's in trouble."

I tugged on his sleeve. "What if the Muti killers know who you are and they're following you? What if those screams are a ploy to lure us both straight to them?"

Baloyi gave me an incredulous smile. "Girl, you sure you're a crime reporter? You should be writing fiction. What an imagination!" He cupped his hands around his mouth and called out in Tsonga.

Instantly, the screams were filled with renewed energy. The woman had to be somewhere directly in front of us. But where? Baloyi walked ahead of me, then stopped abruptly, throwing out his arm and saving me from a disastrous fall into a four-meter borehole. We stared down at a petite woman in the bottom of the pit wrapped in a thin blanket, which never could have kept her warm last night.

It was obvious why she had not been able to escape. The hole was deep, and the sides consisted of dry clay, hard as concrete. Baloyi ran back to the bakkie and I scanned the immediate area for anything that could help us.

I decided the best thing I could do was stay with her and reassure her. I bent down beside the borehole. "Annabelle," I said, putting my hand over my heart. "Annabelle."

The woman touched herself. "Zu-la." Then she let out a string of sentences. I didn't need to speak Tsonga to understand how frightened and frustrated she was. I continued talking with a calmness that I hoped would soothe her.

When I heard a motor, my muscles tensed. I was relieved to see Baloyi's bakkie. Definitely, I'd watched too many crime shows. If I'd been writing the scenario, the muti killers Baloyi was after would have thrown the victim into the borehole as bait, using her cries to bring them unsuspecting victims—especially Baloyi.

Now, Baloyi anchored the rope to the trailer pull on the end of the bakkie and spoke to the woman in Tsonga, apparently directing her to tie the other end of the rope around herself. Then he climbed into the bakkie and eased it forward. I stood at the edge of the borehole waiting to assist Zula. When she was at eye level, I could see her bleeding hands clinging to the rope. Once she was out, I signaled Baloyi to stop. Zula collapsed on the ground in sobs.

"Let's get her out of here," Baloyi said. He showed great compassion as he helped Zula into the bakkie and tucked a blanket around her.

As we drove away, he turned up the heat full blast. Zula spoke and Baloyi interpreted. She claimed she had been searching for food and had fallen into the hole the day before. Tears trickled down her face as she told her story. She had left her ten-year-old daughter Amica to care for her baby and three other starving siblings. No milk and no food.

Baloyi sped up as we approached Malamulele. First stop was Shoprite where we purchased bags of miele pap, an African staple, milk, bread, eggs and treats. Then we hurried to the other side of Malamulele to Zula's small refugee village.

When we arrived, I opened the door to the vehicle and Zula rushed into her mud hut calling out to her babies. I didn't need an interpreter to hear the relief in their crying voices as the children wrapped themselves around their mother. Amica handed the screaming infant to Zula, who pulled out her engorged breast and fed her hungry baby. A look of contentment settled onto the mother's face as the barefooted children huddled around her, devouring bread Baloyi had given them.

A small fire in the center of the hut was all they'd had to keep warm. The dirt floor had been swept perfectly clean. As my eyes scanned the hut, I saw a small rubber ball standing alone against the wall of the hut. I offered the children Smarties, and they looked at the box as if they'd never seen anything like it. When I approached the two-year-old, he promptly let out a horrendous scream and scurried to his mother.

The woman spat out words in Tsonga apparently admonishing him. Baloyi looked directly at me.

"What?" I asked, completely bewildered.

Baloyi translated with an amusing smile. "You're scary." Before I could speak, he explained. "He's never seen a white person."

I retreated to the side of the hut and sat down against the wall. The children satisfied themselves with more bread as Zula handed the quieted baby to Amica. Zula put miele pap into an old pot of boiling rainwater sitting on the fire. The two-year-old clung to his mom's tattered skirt, his face popping out from time to time to look at me.

"No young girl could keep a starving baby from crying all night." Baloyi's eyes grew serious.

I couldn't imagine a worse scenario than being a mother unable to reach her children. As we left, I made a mental note to ask Bridget to make this family one of her special projects.

But as Baloyi drove me back to my car, I began to ponder the unlikelihood of Zula's story.

"Baloyi, what was a borehole doing out there right next to where you planned to picnic with me?" He gave me an unconcerned smile, but I was in full reporter mode, all my suspicions aroused. "Are boreholes common? What are they for? Catching animals?"

He spread his hands. "Some Africans hunt that way."

"And this one caught a human? The whole thing seems crazy. Why was she so far from home?"

"No food around here," he answered.

"Something doesn't add up," I said.

He put a hand on my knee. "All's well that ends well."

The day ended well, at least. To keep the guys at OK Furniture happy, he kissed me goodbye. It kept me pretty happy as well, despite my anxiety about Sister Bridget and my fears that the Muti killers were hunting Baloyi.

Sixteen

Keep it Simple

The next morning when I drove Bridget to the Mother of Angels School, I belted out "I love the rains down in Africa." Life was good. No more attempts had been made on Bridget's life, and Baloyi and I were getting closer.

I wanted to confide in Bridget about Baloyi, even though I wasn't sure if she could understand how I felt. Instead, I burst into the story of how Baloyi and I had rescued Zula from the borehole. I went into detail of how we had taken her home to her children, and then I began my plea for her to help me set up a plan to help Zula's family.

"Bridget, they have nothing! Absolutely nothing." I explained how the children had no food, how the baby had screamed all night. When I finished, Bridget sat forward and crossed her arms.

"And, why were you in a field with the detective?"

I felt as if I was under a microscope in a science lab. After all I'd told her, this was what Bridget picked up on? Despite every effort, my face grew increasingly warm. "Baloyi was showing me the place where a murder had been committed. I told you that." Dear God, had I just lied to a nun with the sin of omission? It was not easy to fool Mother Nature or Sister Bridget.

"Uh-huh." She cocked her head. "You're different." "What do you mean I'm different?"

"You are.... bright." She twisted her lips and scrunched her forehead as if she were searching through a filing cabinet looking for information.

Nun or not, Bridget was my friend, so I told her about the kiss. Nothing more.

Her brows fell over her eyes. "That Baloyi's dangerous. Stay away from him."

"What? Why on earth would you say something like that?"

Bridget didn't reply. She got out of the car and waved cheerily then turned her back to go inside.

She had spoken to me as a nun and a principal, as if I were a child. Grown up Annabelle did not follow her into the school but drove away instead, forgetting until later that the real danger was to Bridget

---

I waited for Baloyi to call. He would make me feel all better. I could not wait to talk with him. I kept myself busy reading a novel, writing in my journal, and checking my phone several times. That night the nuns and I had Irish stew, salad, and beets. I went to bed dreaming of Baloyi. He'd probably been busy all day.

The next day I volunteered at the school as usual, and covertly introduced myself to Officer Aimee, Bridget's watchdog, a tall, slender undercover detective who was now acting as a secretary at the school. She greeted me with a secret smile, but it was hard to keep up my spirits knowing that 48 hours had gone by since I'd talked to Baloyi. I filed papers, while Bridget did her own thing. At noon, I left for the convent to sit in the plastic lawn chair and live in the moment. I admired the six-foot tall poinsettia plant climbing to the roof. I said prayers and played back absolutely everything Baloyi had ever said to me. I longed for him in a way I had never longed for anyone. Not just physically. I longed for his humor, his laughter and his smile. Why couldn't Sister Bridget be happy for me?

On the following day, I talked to children on the playground after Bridget shooed me out of her office. Basically, I was miserable. Baloyi must have changed his mind. Or perhaps he'd been leading me on? What did they call that in Tsonga? Maybe I was one of his many women. I checked my messages. Nothing. Well, I was fed up. My happiness did not depend upon Baloyi. What was I thinking? How had I let myself get so involved? And so quickly? I could do without him, thank you very much. I couldn't believe I had been considering moving to Africa. I would not change my life for him or for anyone.

He still didn't call.

The nuns asked what was wrong. "Nothing," was my standard answer. I faked a smile, but Sister Mary was the shrink in residence, so she could probably see right through me. However, after Sister Bridget's response to my interest in Baloyi, I was scared to confide in any of the other nuns, including Sister Mary.

And he hadn't called. Maybe there was nothing to tell after all.

A week had passed, one of my three before I had to return to the U.S. I felt panicky. Would I see Baloyi again? Then suddenly it hit me. We weren't living in the frickin' dark ages. Why had it taken me so long to come to that realization?

I dropped off Bridget in the morning, then picked up my cell.

He answered on the second ring. "Baloyi." His voice sounded so different.

"Where are you?"

"Malamulele PD."

"I'm coming over. Stay there." This was not going to end without a conversation. My heart pounded at the thought of seeing him. I wanted to be calm and simply ask why he had led me on. What was it about me that he had obviously come to dislike? Had to be the kiss. Was it that he needed more than I was giving? Most men would. Would he even tell me? Ten minutes later I walked into the precinct.

Baloyi stood behind the counter. His face was drawn and he looked like he'd been ill. He had no expression whatsoever.

"I need to talk," I said tersely.

He led me to a small office down the hall and stood to the side to let me walk in first. He left the door open and leaned against the wall. I closed the door and leaned against the opposite wall. I couldn't stand it any longer.

"What in the hell is wrong with you?" I fought back tears.

"What?"

"You haven't called. You kiss me like that, and I don't hear from you for over a week. Is that how you do it here in Africa?" The flip of my head punctuated my frustration. Okay, so I scrapped being calm.

He cocked his head and stared as if he didn't understand a word I'd said.

"And I'll know if you're lying to me, Baloyi. Remember, I was a crime reporter. I know when a police officer's lyin'." Slight exaggeration.

"Okay." He shifted his stance, glanced around, as if he

wished he could be anywhere but here.

"What? What happened to you that suddenly you don't have any feelings for me whatsoever? What a jerk to lead me on like that!" I gathered up my purse and was headed toward the door when he blurted out a string of words.

"Sister Bridget told me. I get it."

I turned back and stared at Baloyi. He had taken up a new pastime of studying the concrete floor. "Sister Bridget?" He could have been speaking Tsonga or Venda for all I understood. "What on earth are you talking about? She told you what?"

"Sister Bridget ... explained you shouldn't see me anymore." He glanced at the ceiling. "It's okay."

I let out a stream of air I didn't even know I'd been holding in. "She told you what?"

"That you didn't want to see me anymore. It's okay. I get it." His eyes looked everywhere but into mine.

"No, you idiot, you don't get it. Even I don't get it!" My anger opened a flood of emotion and I could hardly control myself. "What a freakin' Mamgoboza!" I pivoted around willing my arms to stay at my side as I paced back and forth in the small square room. I wanted to punch something. I couldn't wait to get ahold of her.

"If Bridget didn't already have someone wanting to murder her, I'd kill her myself. She told you I shouldn't see you anymore?" My head kept time with my steps, as I bounded from side to side with my hands on my hips. I turned to Baloyi. "She only said that because I told her you made me happier than I'd ever been in my life." I took a few steps toward him. I softened my voice and calmed myself. "I cannot get you out of my mind." I waited a moment for him to say something, but my impatience got the best of me. "Unless you weren't serious. Or you lied to me." I held my breath waiting for his response. "Or it was a lousy kiss after all."

I had hardly gotten the words out before Baloyi reached me and kissed me with an intensity that if I'd had socks on, would have blown them right off.

He pulled away and searched my face. "Belle, I thought ... " Then his arms pulled me in tighter than before. I felt his breath, as he whispered into my ear. "I thought I'd lost you."

I took his face in my hands. "You could never lose me." I closed my eyes and melted against him.

He gently moved a lock of my hair from behind my ear. "But Sister Bridget's your friend. And she's a nun. Why would she lie? Why would she do that to us?"

I took a deep breath. He'd said "us." Despite it all, I couldn't believe I was about to defend her. "She must have been under the illusion that she was ... protecting me."

"From me?" He laughed softly and nuzzled my ear. "Doesn't she know I would never hurt you, never in all my life?"

I felt my knees buckle, but luckily Baloyi held me tight. I was back home right where I belonged.

A knock on the door alerted us someone needed our room.

Baloyi and I quietly filed past handcuffed prisoners waiting to be interrogated. He opened the main door to the station, and we flew out into a vibrant and colorful world. When we reached my vehicle parked among the trees at the side of the building, a cool breeze washed over me. Thunder clapped only seconds before large lazy raindrops descended. I leaned against the car and watched Baloyi's playful expression return. His twinkle was back. I studied his dark eyes, the way the tiny lines crinkled when he smiled. He pressed me up against my car and leaned in.

"Someone will see," I lightly admonished him.

"But, you're my girl, remember?"

He kissed me, then pulled away, surrendering, his hands in the air. "Keeping it simple, in case Sister Bridget's watching." We both laughed. Before I turned to get into the car, I grabbed his shirt and pulled his mouth to mine.

I was breathless and Baloyi looked at me as if letting me leave was the last thing he ever wanted to do. But he eased me into the car, leaving the inner me screaming for more.

I drove back toward my friend who knew nothing of love between a man and woman. Had I said love? I smiled all the way back to the school.

Seventeen

The Memorial

By the time I arrived at the Mother of Angels School, I was ready for Bridget. I had released most of my anger. She was alone in her office, seated at her desk.

When I sat down in a chair facing her, she whipped off her glasses. "What happened? You're all wet."

I ignored the question. "Thank you, Bridget, for wanting to protect me."

"What?" She jerked her head back in surprise.

"I appreciate your wanting to make sure I didn't get hurt, but the thing is I am in love with Baloyi, and I can take it from here. You don't need to worry. I'm a grown woman. And he makes me happy." I couldn't translate the look on her face.

"But you'll leave."

"Maybe, but we will work it out. And you may be forced to leave Malamulele, despite your valiant effort. And, you will have to work that out too."

She sat tall in her chair, her dark eyes avoiding mine.

"So what I'm saying is, don't be a mamgoboza." I was controlling my anger quite well I thought. I waited for a defensive argument. Surprisingly, Bridget's face appeared embarrassed. Absolutely nothing could have surprised me more. I continued my attempt to allay her fears. "We've done nothing wrong, Bridget. Nothing for you to be worried about. So if by chance you're concerned about my soul, relax. God and I have that covered." Then I flashed a big smile that took little effort. "Just be happy for me."

She seemed exasperated, then melted and blew out a breath. "Fine."

"Is that all you have to say?" Then it hit me. "Bridget, are you worried about *our* friendship?"

She wore a decidedly guilty look.

"You know that you don't have to worry. No matter where I go or don't go, I will always Skype you, text you, phone you – always. Having someone in my life will not affect our friendship. You do know that, right?"

She sat back in her chair, sporting a small grin. It was so simple. I had said the exact words she needed to hear.

The next morning my eyes fluttered open to the sound of chirping birds. I glanced at the clock on the nightstand, then rolled over and inched my head under my pillow. The birds sounded so close, like I could have reached out and touched them. Then I remembered—those birds were my new ringtone. I grabbed my cell.

"Ahh, hello Mr. Baloyi." My voice surprised me. It sounded sexy. No need to tell Baloyi it was allergies.

"You up for Wimpy's? I've got a few ....."

I didn't allow him to finish. I replied in the affirmative, closed my cell, dressed, threw my hair up in a crazy twist, brushed on lip gloss and was out the door. I drove up to OK Furniture in record time. Baloyi opened the door before I'd had a chance to turn off the motor.

"You mind driving?" he asked as he jumped into the passenger seat. A mysterious musk filled the car. I took a deep breath. He wore jeans and a thin black wool sweater under his leather jacket. His handgun was well hidden.

"What's on your mind this morning?" I asked.

"Coffee." He laughed as I drove down Main Street to the highway. A light conversation made the day so normal. Then my cell rang.

Bridget's voice was clear. "When are you coming?"

I hesitated, uncertain how to answer. "I'll be there by two?"

"Are you with ... him?" Her voice sounded different. Was it stress?

"Yeah, is everything okay?"

"No." She hung up.

I hit speed dial. She didn't pick up. I sighed, wondering if she could be reacting about yesterday. Was this her way of getting attention? Then Baloyi's cell rang. He spoke in Tsonga. At least I could recognize the language now, even if I couldn't speak it.

He hung up. "Accident at the school."

I skidded the car around. Fifteen minutes later we walked into the Mother of Angels Elementary School to see the staff scrambling up and down the halls.

"Where's Bridget?" I cried to no one in particular.

A teacher flying down the hall said, "She was poisoned."

I heard a blood-wrenching scream and ran to the fourth door on the right, but I was shaking so badly I could hardly open it. The door swung open and I saw Sister Bridget sitting beside Junie, the secretary, who was lying on a cot.

Junie murmured something. The next second her dark eyes looked lifeless. The nurse put a hand to Junie's throat and shook her head. Bridget bent over her secretary and wept. I went to Bridget and wrapped my arms around her. "Thank God you're okay. I thought it was you." I burst into tears. Before I had a chance to say more, Baloyi rushed in. When I let go of Bridget, he faced her.

"I'm sorry about your friend."

She nodded and sniffed into a lone tissue. I reached for the tissue box and grabbed two handfuls—one for Bridget and one for me.

"What happened?" Baloyi asked.

Sister Bridget stood like a tethered animal, agony on her face. "First, she brought me tea. I was busy checking a report. Had to fax it to Pretoria. No time for tea. I told *her* to drink it." Bridget's voice cracked. "She drank the tea, but then she dropped the cup and grabbed her tummy, falling to the floor."

I softened my voice. "The tea was meant for you."

Tears filled Bridget's eyes as they locked onto mine. "But, Junie." She got on her knees and began the Hail Mary prayer. I knelt beside her and cried too, cried for the innocent woman who had died so senselessly.

A few minutes later, Bridget rose and faced Baloyi. "I'm sorry. I'm sorry." She waved her hands in the air for emphasis. "Sorry I told you Annabelle shouldn't be with you."

Baloyi reached out and tenderly patted her hands. "Don't you worry about that. We're okay. Right?" He waited.

Sniffing, she nodded.

"Can we go down to your office?" he asked. "Let's see if we can figure out how this happened."

In her office, he helped Bridget into her chair. "Have you seen anyone around who didn't belong here?" Baloyi asked.

"No." Bridget took a minute. "No, nothing, no one."

Baloyi put on latex gloves and headed for the kitchen. After giving Bridget a hug, I followed him. He picked up fragments of Junie's teacup and put them in a plastic bag, then strung blue DO NOT ENTER tape across the break room door.

Baloyi looked at me. "Forensics on its way."

Junie's service was on Saturday morning at St. Benedict's Catholic Church, a short walk from the school. Once a pile of rubble, the small church had been restored to its original structure after a fire gutted it three years before. A beautiful grotto built by the parents to honor the Blessed Mother stood near the driveway. Despite the cold winter, flowers peeked through the stacked rocks sealed with mortar. A peaceful, lovely place.

People arrived from surrounding villages to attend the memorial service of Junie, who had left behind three teenage children, her own mother, and an ex-husband no one could find. Sister Bridget and the Malamulele nuns dressed in navy blue skirts, white blouses and matching jackets and sat up front representing their religious community.

Baloyi sat beside me in the back of the church on a wooden pew with kneelers. I wept openly, but I felt like a fake. It wasn't for Junie. Her death angered me, but I hardly knew her. I could not stop thinking how it could have been Bridget lying there. We'd been lulled into a false sense of security by days of peace from the murderer. How could we have been so blind?

Hand-made flower wreaths and school drawings decorated the casket. Live African music, which began as a funeral dirge, quickly grew joyful as the memorial service continued. How on earth could evil be lurking about?

All day Sunday I rarely left Bridget's side. Baloyi and I were in constant contact, texting and updating one another, but for now we simply couldn't resume our real lives, our normal lives again. I worried ceaselessly about how Bridget had been a target yet again. The police undercover person, namely Aimee, had been ineffective at the school. Now she knew the danger was real, Baloyi was confident she would step up. Would she? We needed a break in the case.

Monday, Baloyi invited me to go to breakfast. He urged me to leave Bridget in Aimee's care, assuring me that the officer was quite capable. And Bridget was in cahoots with him—she practically begged me to leave her alone.

"If I'm late to pick you up this afternoon, will you get a ride with someone else you can trust?" I asked.

"You worry too much, Annabelle." But when I refused to leave without her assurance, she begrudgingly gave it to me.

Once I saw her safely to school, I drove away and joined Baloyi at Wimpy's, where he soothed my fears by reiterating that Aimee was an excellent officer.

The waitress had cleared the table and Baloyi and I were on our second cup of coffee and discussing the latest attempt on Bridget's life. "The method of attempt has changed. Poison, this time. No snake. No machete. Could it be a different killer? " I asked.

"Couldn't get the job done with snakes." He stared intently at his coffee mug.

"When do you think you'll hear about the tox screen about what killed Junie?"

"Potassium cyanide."

"Whoa, excellent turn around!"

Baloyi dropped his head, then confessed. "Well, not official, but the quick death thing—it's either cyanide or a derivative."

"You're charming." I flashed him a smile. I wished I could forget about murder and focus only on love. "There has to be a reason for these murder attempts. If we could figure out the why, we could find the who."

"Tell me about Bridget's family."

I summed up what little I knew. "Sister Bridget's father taught economics and her mother taught kindergarten. That's all I know. Anyway, how could dead relatives from Ghana be important?"

"Not sure." He twisted his napkin and his eyes found the edge of the table where he apparently had discovered a manufacturing flaw.

"How can I leave until I know she's safe?" I buried my head in my hands and rubbed my forehead. When I looked up, I couldn't help but notice that the smile lines at the corner of his mouth were about to be deployed. "What?"

"Nothing, nothing at all."

"I'll have to take a leave of absence from my job in Denver." I watched the edge of those chocolate eyes crinkle.

Then abruptly he changed the subject. "We need to put a warning sign at the borehole."

"That's random."

"Something I've been meaning to do. You ready?"

A half-hour later Baloyi pulled off the highway near the borehole where we searched the trees and scraggly shrubs thoroughly.

"Are you sure we're in the right spot?"

"Yes, I'm sure." He pointed to a fresh mound of dirt. "Someone's filled it in. But why would they do that?"

"Look at this Baloyi." I pointed to tire tracks. I returned to the bakkie and grabbed my SLR from my bag. I placed my pen next to the tracks to document size. My mentor in Denver had always said snap everything.

Suddenly, I wondered again about Zula.

"Baloyi, I'm still suspicious of Zula. It's obviously true she has a rough life, but falling into that borehole? The more I think about it, the more farfetched it seems."

"You're still on that?"

"Are you saying you still believe her?"

"Yeah, she was too scared, must have been an accident."

"But maybe the muti killers threatened to hurt her children if she didn't help them."

"You have a very scary mind."

"I still think they could be after you."

"If they were, then they would have rushed out of the grass as soon as we found Zula. Do I need to remind you, that didn't happen?" He grinned at me.

I couldn't help chuckling. "Okay, I see your point."

With that, we loaded ourselves into the bakkie and headed back.

"I have the afternoon off." Baloyi's voice was mesmerizing. I could listen to it all day.

Eighteen

Nun Danger

When I stepped into the convent I was greeted by the furrowed brow of Sister Mary. "Where have you been? I've been calling and calling you."

I looked at my phone and it was on silent. Before I could respond, Sister Mary continued her disgruntled questioning. "Have you seen Sister Bridget?"

All that came out of my mouth was, "She wasn't in chapel?"

"No. No one's seen Bridget since she left the school early afternoon."

Damn it! I'd thought Bridget would be getting a ride home to the convent from Officer Aimee. What had happened? Apparently, I couldn't trust anyone but myself to keep track of Bridget outside of school hours. I urged Sister Mary to call absolutely everyone she knew who could possibly have had contact with Bridget. I grabbed my cell, threw on my black pea coat, threw my crossover bag over my head and ran out the door fishing for my keys. My speed dial to Baloyi went to voice mail. I drove the few blocks to the Indian shop, the only place I knew to start looking.

The sky kissed twilight goodbye as I parked. My cell sounded like a bunch of birds and I quickly answered. I alerted

Baloyi to Sister Bridget's disappearance and told him where I was. In a hurried voice he said he was on his way and instructed me to wait for him. I said I would, but every second counted if Bridget was in trouble. He knew it and I knew it.

I entered the store as if I were a shopper. The owner and his friends were nowhere in sight. The place looked identical to the night Bridget and I had visited to buy her airtime. Electric blankets snug in plastic wrap, a variety of lamps and several washing machines were powdered with dust.

Something blue lying on the floor caught my eye. I bent down and picked up a cobalt blue scrunchie that held a few black strands of hair. A chill raced up my spine. Sister Bridget had been wearing it this morning. The style was unique because I'd sent it to her from Colorado. I stuck it in my hip pocket and moved forward. At least I knew she'd been here. I was on the right track. I looked around for security cameras. Nothing. Laughter broke out down the hall. Common sense told me to wait for Baloyi, but urgency pushed me forward. I crept to the back of the store and entered a hallway with several doors on either side. Luckily, a small crack in the wall gave me a quick peek into the back storeroom.

Stacked boxes stood like book ends on either end of the cot, and on it lay Sister Bridget stretched out, deathly still. My heart nearly stopped when I saw the two African men standing against the wall. One was short and balding, the other taller and brandishing a pistol.

As I opened the door, I tucked my hand into my coat pocket and pointed my finger, using fury to sustain me. "SAPS," I screamed. "Against the wall." That Citizens Police Academy back home had given me a badass voice. For a few moments, I wagered that I could fool them into thinking I was the police. I had to detain the two startled Africans until Baloyi arrived. They threw their hands in the air, the gun skimming across the floor. Both looked terrified, glancing at one another and back at me.

I picked up the gun on the floor, as the taller one blurted something in Tsonga. He threw a box at me, and when it struck my shoulder they both peeled out of the room and disappeared. I ran to Bridget. Her arms were bare and stone cold. How long had she been lying there? I spanked her cheeks. "Bridget, Bridget, are you all right?"

Her eyes flickered and closed. I shook her. She was alive, thank God.

Baloyi rushed through the door with his gun drawn. He surveyed the room before holstering up and kneeling beside Bridge. He opened her eyes one at a time, then let her lids close. He bent near her mouth and smelled her breath. "She hasn't been drugged the same, not like the others." He picked up her hand and let it drop. "But she was bloody well knocked out with something."

"What others?" He didn't answer, but he didn't need to. I knew what others. The victims of the muti killings.

I checked Bridget's breathing. Slow and steady. If anything happened to her, I'd never forgive myself. I watched Baloyi pull his cell out and call for an ambulance and police backup.

"Don't worry, they're minutes away." He removed a box out of the stack and slit it open with his pocketknife. Carefully, he pulled out stuffing that looked like pale hay. Then he lifted a large glass jar out of the box.

"What is it?"

He turned and showed me. I wish he'd kept it to himself. At least a dozen eyeballs floated in the liquid, looking back at us as if pleading for someone to end their misery.

"Where ... where was it being shipped?"

"Durban." He opened another box.

I monitored Bridget and watched Baloyi open one of the largest boxes. A gruesome head stared back at us. The woman's dreads wildly struggled to swim free. Almost a look-a-like to Medusa. Luckily, no one I'd met. Or, if I had, no one I recognized. Still, someone had known her, loved her. She had been someone's little girl once upon a time.

"This box was headed for India," Baloyi said. "A bigger can of snakes than we thought." He looked over at Bridget with downcast eyes. He didn't need to say that Sister Bridget would have been next.

The rest of the boxes were small bottles with what looked like spices and herbs headed to all points on the map. "So it's an International operation. Now we know for sure." I checked Bridget again. "When is the ambulance coming?" I realized we were standing right in the middle of one of the muti killers' centers of operation. Just blocks from the convent. Dear God. That put all the nuns in danger.

Baloyi took a breath. "Maybe the killer thought she'd bring greater muti. You know, a nun, all holy and everything. Believe me, Bridget's a lucky one."

Horror twisted in the pit of my stomach. Dear God, how could people be so cruel?

While Baloyi explored more boxes, I hurriedly broke the lock on Punjab's roller top wooden desk and found hypodermic needles. The second drawer held vials of a substance

I couldn't read, but I was pretty sure each one contained a knock-out drug.

"Confirmation that this is how they get their victims." Baloyi shook his head. "Just as I thought, they shoot 'em with narcotics, transport 'em to the bush. No one can fight or call out, nothing. Poor bastards. No wonder we couldn't catch a break."

I envisioned the ambulance sliding up as I heard the gravel crunch outside.

I rode with Bridget to emergency, where a doctor and two nurses began checking her vitals. I stayed close but pulled out my cell and pressed Sister Mary's number. She answered on the second ring.

"Sister Bridget's in emergency." No need to tell her the hospital. There was only one in Malamulele.

Pocketing my cell, I turned to Baloyi. "Sorry the bad guys got away."

"Don't be. You're okay, she's okay. Plus, what a find!"

Baloyi pulled out his iPhone. He walked into the hallway and paced while he spoke to someone probably on the Limpopo Task Force. When he signed off, he glanced at me. "They're stoked." Then he made another call. He smiled like the proverbial cat that had just caught a big plump canary.

I waited near the door for Sister Mary, who a few minutes later rushed in.

"She's okay," I said, gently grabbing her arms and making eye contact with a very frightened nun. Then I quickly explained how I had found Bridget in the back of Punjab's store and that she had been drugged.

Sister Mary's eyes grew wider and she wrapped her arms around me. "You're a guardian angel, you are." Her reaction startled me. Now the question was could I possibly protect *all* the nuns?

We had been so lucky with Bridget, who was now hooked up to a monitor. As I watched the clear solution drip ever so slowly into her tube, I felt relief so strong it overpowered me. "Sister Mary, I won't leave Bridget, but you'll alert the others? Right away?"

She laid a hand on my arm. "Of course. We'll all be praying for both of you."

Nineteen

Bloody Enough Already

Bridget's eyes opened on her blank face with deep pillow impressions. "Where am I?"

"You're in the hospital. You were drugged." I didn't want to go into the details too much until she was more lucid.

"I had crazy dream."

"Tell me."

"I went to buy time. Mr. Punjab, he gave me tea."

"That's your dream?"

"Stuff was swimmin', swimmin' in my head." She lifted her shoulders and scrunched up her face as she searched for more. "I think you and the detective were there."

"Dreams can be ... so funny."

By the next day Sister Bridget was alert and the doctors were scheduled to release her midday. Meanwhile, gossip was rampant. Even the nurses were giving us side-glances.

Apparently a wildfire of fear scorched Malamulele. No need for national or local news. Accuracy, however, could be dicey. The local rumor traveling at lightning speed was that the police had caught the muti gang. Comforting, but not true.

Also, muti killers had been working out of the local sectarian high school. Also, untrue.

So I figured it was time I told Sister Bridget as much as I knew. "Bridget, I need to catch you up on a few things."

Her dark eyes grew serious. "Mr. Punjab's dead."

"No, no, he's not dead." I thought as quickly as I could. "But, he was dealing in more than outdated appliances." Ready or not, all I could do now was forge ahead. "Mr. Punjab is involved in the ritual killings."

"No!" Bridget shook her head furiously. "No! I know him." She leaped out of bed, jerked her I.V. out of her arm, and pulled her clothes from the bag in the corner. I faced the wall as she dressed. This was not the time to change her mind.

"Bridget, I went there Monday night looking for you. When I went into the store, I heard a noise. That's when I found you— drugged and unconscious."

I thought a minute, then continued. "Oh, and boxes of body parts were stacked against the wall. We now have a few clues about the muti killers, thanks largely to you. And in a strange way to Punjab too."

The room was quiet. I turned around. She was fully dressed and hiding her face behind her hands. "Why does everybody want to kill me?"

The next day Bridget and I met Baloyi at the police station to check out images of potential suspects in hopes of identifying the men she'd seen that night. I was looking for the two men I saw up close and personal.

When we entered the Malamulele Station I was surprised to see a crowd. The police officer behind the wall-to-wall counter reminded me of an overworked air traffic controller.

"Next."

Baloyi bypassed the slow entry process. Walking under the counter bridge and through an open door leading to two interrogation rooms, we entered a cozy office with a beat up desk and two straight back chairs. Baloyi left and returned with an additional chair he managed to squeeze into the tiny room just as a task force member walked in. He was a white man about five foot ten, a few extra pounds with a head of coarse gray hair. Without any pleasantries, he sat down and opened a folder.

"What were you doing at the Indian store Monday night?" He looked directly at Bridget, but I took the lead in answering.

"I went looking for Sister Bridget that evening. She buys air time there."

The official turned his head to Bridget. "You know the owner?" he asked in an accusatory tone.

"Yes, he's my friend." She said it truthfully, but her eyes darted around the room, and even I would have thought she was lying if I didn't know better.

"Friend? You're a religious, a missionary. You're friends with criminals?"

"He's not a criminal." Sister Bridget sat up straighter in her wooden chair.

"Bridget, we found you drugged on a cot in the back of his store. Tell him the last thing you remember."

"I ask the questions," the official barked. I could just see his younger self in the apartheid era. He would have fit right in intimidating suspects and scaring everyone to death.

"Sorry." I glanced at Baloyi wondering why he wasn't

assisting us.

With serious eyes Bridget looked squarely at the official. "I bought time..."

"Phone time?"

"Yes." She thought for a moment. "He offered me tea. I remember I turned to go and my head was spinning. I was dizzy, dizzy. Mr. Punjab helped me to the back room to lie down. That's all."

Then, miraculously, the task force member softened. "You're principal of the local school?"

"Yes. And Mr. Punjab is a good friend."

"Not so. Do good friends kill you?" His eyes blazed at Sister Bridget.

"Am I dead?" Bridget spat back at him.

Then he looked at Baloyi, and shifted into Afrikaans that only Baloyi and Bridget understood. They all got up and walked out of the room. I followed.

When we reached the entrance, Baloyi said Bridget should return to the convent. The official had said Bridget was confused, and he would talk with her again. On the way to the car, Baloyi slowed and let Bridget walk ahead of us.

Under his breath Baloyi said, "I need to see you tonight."

I nodded, then waved as I drove Bridget back to the convent.

———————

That evening as the nuns gathered for the latest on the attempted muti killing, I am sure they were thinking "there but for the grace of God." *What you do to one nun, you do to all.*

Despite everything, I was astonished that the nuns handled it so well. A murder in their own convent. And now one of their sisters had been drugged in preparation for a ritual killing. What on earth would it take to push them over the proverbial edge? Hopefully we'd not find out.

My cell rang. Baloyi said he was waiting at the front door. The two officers standing guard at the door was the only distraction. Otherwise, Baloyi would have reminded me of the boy next door asking me to come out and play. Instead, he waited in the entrance hall as I ran to my room. I brushed my teeth, hit my lips with gloss and slipped on my warm coat, wrapping a red wool scarf around my neck.

Once we were inside his vehicle, he officially became Detective Baloyi.

"I needed to talk to you." Without hesitation he asked if I knew Punjab.

I blinked in surprise. "I met him only once. That's all."

"Punjab said he didn't know the guys who barged into his store, threatened his family, unloaded boxes and demanded that he ship several a day until they were finished."

"Think he's telling the truth?"

"I do. He had no knowledge of the contents. Other than shipping, I don't think he was involved." Baloyi pulled his bakkie out slowly and took a right turn. As we passed the Indian shop, he continued. "Apparently Sister Bridget walked in unexpectedly. To avert a confrontation, Punjab panicked and drugged the tea with his own sleeping pills. When the tea knocked her out, the bad guys relaxed. They had no interest in Bridget, proving that they were just in charge of transport."

"So the sleeping pills were not the drugs muti killers use on their victims."

"Nope."

"But, the syringes?"

"His son's allergies."

"Bridget thinks Punjab's her friend, so maybe it's true. What do you think, Baloyi?"

"I'm hoping he's innocent, especially since we let him go."

Baloyi drove a few minutes down R526, then eased the car off the main road not more than ten feet. He drove it beneath a large naked baobab tree, then stopped the motor. The full moon cast shadows over the countryside giving it a fanciful look as the coal fires puffed clouds over the village.

I took a series of small breaths and let my window down an inch or two. The cold air felt good in my lungs. I breathed in the faint aroma of winter fires and a touch of creeper blooms. It occurred to me that this was the most privacy we'd ever had. It was pitch black with only the full moon above, assuring us the bakkie was well hidden from passing traffic.

Baloyi pushed his seat all the way back, stretching his long legs. "Try it," he said. "You'll be more comfortable."

I eased my seat back. "More comfortable?"

He leaned toward me. "For this." He slowly slid his long fingers into my hair massaging me, sending chills in all directions. I barely whispered, "So I am your girl." I could feel the smile register on his lips.

"Oh, yeah." His voice was low, mixed with a heated breath that I could feel as he so very carefully unwrapped my red scarf once, then twice. He gently slipped my scarf away from me, I felt stripped bare in an alternate universe that heightened my senses. His warm lips touched mine, exploring seductively. His hands suddenly found places I thought I'd locked away permanently. I gasped, my body quivering.

He drew away. "Belle, we're too old for this car thing."

I fought to stop panting. "You're right." I tried to pull back from my state of delirium.

"The convent's out," he said.

"That's a given." The mention of the convent doused imaginary cold water on a bed of hot coals. We were parked under a stunning starlit sky in the southern hemisphere, yet after living with celibate nuns, there was a part of me feeling conflicted.

"Have you notified the school?" He snapped his seat upright, and reluctantly, I did as well.

"The school?" My mind was reeling. "Oh, you mean the university." I lowered the window slightly. "Not yet."

"Are you serious about stayin' longer – for six months, I mean?" His eyes studied me.

"Of course. I can't leave until I'm sure the nuns are safe."

"I can tell what's going on here." He paused.

"Can you now?" I turned in my seat to face him.

"Let's do the cards on the table thing. I'm trying to keep you innocent for the nuns and all, but I admit I'm having major trouble." He shook his head in exasperation and started the car.

"Look." My hand grabbed his arm before he put the bakkie into gear. "I am right there with you. But I live with nuns who can see straight through me, the minute I make out with you. It's crazy. I can't imagine what they'd say if I were ... you know."

"Sleeping with me? So what do we do?" I could see from the dashboard lights that Baloyi was staring straight ahead at nothing in particular.

"Baloyi, believe me, you're not the only one who's frustrated."

As he pulled off the gravel road, I could feel my heart screaming "bloody enough already."

Twenty

Rebellion

Sister Bridget was home and leaning against pillows on her bed, staring at her laptop. She looked up at me. "What happened?"

"Absolutely nothing." Baloyi had said goodnight leaving me breathless with a stunning kiss, frustrating me even more. "How are you feeling, Bridget?"

"Good, good." Her eyes jumped back to her computer.

"What are you up to, Bridge?"

"Up to? What do you mean 'up to'?"

I was testy. Who could blame me? My emotions had been jerked around all evening. On the brink of sexual fulfillment, Baloyi and I had clung to our silly consciences. I took a breath. "What are you doing?"

"I'm writing a letter to Ireland telling them we will remain in Malamulele."

"Good for you!" It was refreshing to see Bridget moving forward. At least one of us was. "I'm proud of you. I'll make tea, okay?" She nodded.

On the way to the kitchen I passed Sister Mary carrying a stack of laundry. "Hey, Sister Mary, doing laundry?"

"Packing For Johannesburg. How is Bridget?"

"But, Sister Mary, what about the letter?"

"I kept a copy."

"No, not that letter, the one Bridget is writing."

Her quizzical expression surprised me. She didn't have a clue. Rather than interfere, I changed the subject. "Bridget's fine."

As she stepped into her room, I said good night then headed for the kitchen. I plugged in the hot pot. From the pantry I selected the battered red tray, filled a plate with mini chocolate cakes. When the electrical pot boiled, I plopped two rooibos tea bags into the teapot, added scalding water and popped on the top.

When I walked into Bridget's room, she pulled a chair over for the tray of goodies,

She handed me her laptop, then poured tea into the cups as I sat down on her bed to read.

Mother of Angel Convent
House Number 7772
Section D
Malamulele
Limpopo Province

Dear Reverend Sister Mary Michael,

Thank you sincerely for your letter. After a lot of prayer, reflection and dialogue with the local laity, we have decided not to leave Malamulele at this time. As an enduring Mother of Angels congregation for over ten years, we believe we have yet to complete our job here. The decision to stay is through the guidance of the Holy Spirit and our God who has called us

in His service. We pray that we will all be united in prayer and allow the Holy Spirit to direct and guide all of us.

We have notified the nuns from Brazil that we will not be leaving.

Renewed thanks and God's blessings.

Sincerely yours,
Sister Bridget Lolker

"Wow, Bridget! I'm proud of you!" For the first time in days, I was grinning ear to ear.

Bridget beamed back at me. "I have prayed about this, and it seems best. I have work here to finish."

"Yes, yes you do. Like building an auditorium, right? You should add that to the letter."

"But, I have no more funding." She punched a few computer keys, then looked up. "I will find more. I'm working on it."

"You're going to ask all the nuns to sign it, right?"

Bridget put aside her laptop. She stood and paced in a circle. "No, but excellent idea, Annabelle. Excellent idea!" She was a woman on a mission. Literally. Her strides quickened and I could practically see thoughts shooting in her head like colored balls on a pool table.

She scooped up her laptop with pure determination and quickly headed for the office printer.

It would be a minimum of 24 hours before the Superior General or the Regional Director could possibly receive the letter by e-mail and perhaps seven to 10 days by snail mail. I was anxious to see the response.

I was in the kitchen the next morning to grab a quick coffee when voices surprised me from the dining room. One was Bridget's, the other Sister Mary's. I admit I tarried stirring my coffee, while I listened as best I could. A reporter's habit. Snooping.

Sister Mary's voice sounded reprimanding. "Bridget, you can't send it with all our names on it. It will look like an Irish rebellion. And you know where that got us."

"Fine, I'll send it myself." It sounded like Bridget was folding paper and sliding it into an envelope.

"Bridget, I've been a nun for over fifty years. I took a vow."

"I took a vow, too, but this is a new day."

I silently clapped in support. *Good for you, Bridget.*

"You have too many American ideas," said Sister Mary.

I threw my hand over my mouth to keep from protesting.

"You listen to Annabelle too much. And don't get me wrong, I love Annabelle and you know how much I loved her aunt, Sister Cecelia. Annabelle has done marvelous things for us. But she lives in a different world."

"Yes, she lives in a free world." Bridget said, and walked into the kitchen, surprising me. "You were listening?"

"No, getting coffee," I protested.

She touched my cup. "Your coffee's almost cold."

Sister Mary joined us. "Come sit down Annabelle. We need to hear from you." She motioned for me to join them.

I felt like a proverbial lamb being led to the slaughter, and even Bridget was carrying an ax. Before I could protest, I found myself sitting at the dining room table across from both of them.

"You must tell Bridget not to send this letter." Sister Mary's resistance rode on her shoulders.

The only response I could come up with startled me even as I said it. "Maybe we should hold off and come up with other ideas. All the nuns could sit down together tonight and discuss it, then proceed."

"No." Bridget said it emphatically.

"Why not?" I asked.

"Every time they say hold a meeting, the answer is no."

"You asked me for my ideas. I say, explore all the ideas before you send the letter."

Sister Mary looked pleased and quite surprised as she readjusted her glasses to take a better look at me.

Bridget twisted her mouth in protest but agreed. "Okay, I will listen, but then I will send the letter."

"Tonight after supper?"

They both agreed, and we retired the subject.

I returned to my room and showered. Looking into the cloudy mirror, I remembered the fiasco under the baobab tree. Baloyi and I seemed to be heading toward a mature, adult relationship, yet it never happened. The stress was stringing me out. It wasn't natural. We needed to work something out. In our situation, I knew what would make the nuns happy. Our marriage certificate. Even then, I wasn't sure it would make all the nuns happy.

But a marriage certificate was only a piece of paper. And in just conscience, I couldn't marry someone just to give us a license for sex. And no matter how much we worked on it, the situation with the nuns would remain constant. They wouldn't change. They couldn't change. And I couldn't leave Malamulele until the murder was solved. I saw no way out of the dilemma. How I hated loose ends. One thing for sure ... I had to notify the University of Denver that I'd be taking a leave of absence next semester.

As I combed my hair up into a ponytail, my cell rang as if by magic.

"Minjhani." His voice reminded me of warm syrup over pancakes. Suddenly I was hungry.

"Minjhani to you."

"How are you this morning, Miss Annabelle?"

"Wonderful." And suddenly, I was smiling with not a care in the world.

"I need to see you."

I paused. I wondered what he meant exactly. And before I could ask the question, he answered.

"To talk."

"I'm leaving in a little over a week and...." I had no idea why I said that when I was already planning on extending my leave. Maybe I wanted to see how much he wanted me to stay. Was I playing games?

"So you *are* leaving."

"I might stay ...." I couldn't control myself. I wanted to hear the words, his confession that he wanted me, some declaration. How very old school of me.

"And what exactly does it depend on?"

I pulled my stomach in and tried to feel a smidge taller while I held my phone to my ear. "I'm not sure." *Cop out, cop out. Annabelle, you have no guts.*

"We need to talk to clear ... to clear the environment."

I smiled. "Clear the air?"

"Same." He coughed.

A chill ran through me. Maybe he was going to break up with me. Maybe that's what he meant when he said he had to clear the air. Maybe he couldn't take this being physically apart any longer. That had to be it. After all, he was a grown man with needs. Holding back in that department couldn't be easy. But I had needs too. "Where should we meet?" He was a patient man, but I feared he'd lost patience with me.

"OK Bazaar at nine-thirty?" Baloyi asked.

"Nine-thirty it is."

Words rattled in my head. Baloyi couldn't break up with me. We weren't even going together. I breathed in. I didn't know how to handle myself anymore. It'd been too long since I'd dated. Was that what we were doing? Hardly. I had a crush on a hot African detective, even though I knew there could be no future.

As I pulled up in front of the OK Bazaar, music filled my head. It was like watching a sexy television commercial. Baloyi in tight jeans, leaning his lanky body against his bakkie, with legs crossed at the ankles exposing scuffed up cowboy boots. A faded Gap T-shirt under a black leather jacket. Dark sunglasses. I stopped. He opened the passenger side door and slid in like a movie star. I gulped and managed one word. "Minjhani."

"Better."

"You want to talk?" I admit I said it as formally as if I were a lawyer questioning the prosecution. Stiff. I'd decided I wouldn't drive far because afterwards, I'd have to drive him back to his car and suffer the humiliation of being dumped. Funny, now that I thought about it, I couldn't remember a time when I had been dumped. Well, there was Toby in the third grade. *Annabelle, pay attention.* I drove for five minutes down the highway

I pulled onto a nondescript, skinny two-lane dirt road and cut off the engine. This seemed to be the only place where we could talk and be away from prying eyes. The trees were mostly stick-like, it being winter, but somehow it felt private still with small bushes here and there. I might as well get this over. I turned and faced him. I could be courageous when I had to.

"About that air you wanted to clear?" I smashed the ball squarely into his court.

He turned sideways in his seat. What a seriously gorgeous face. Oh, how I would miss those deep, soulful eyes.

"You ... are ... extending your stay." He punctuated his comment by pulling me into his arms and bringing me close, catching my full attention. Then he pushed me back as if he wanted to take a look at me.

Confused, I struggled to make sense of what was happening. "But..."

His fingers roamed tenderly through my hair, as if there was nothing he'd rather do. I would have collapsed if I'd been standing. His hands sensuously moved elsewhere and after last night's prelude, I was on the brink of instant ecstasy. Then his fingers tenderly brushed my face. This was a crazy way to break ... up.

"Now say this with me, Annabelle." He waited for me to catch up. "I ... am ... extending ... my stay." His lips glided onto mine like butter on a warm southern afternoon. He pulled back as his fingers lifted my chin close to his. "I will ... extend ... my stay. Repeat, Annabelle. I will ... extend ... my stay."

It was apparent I was in the throes of having my very first heart attack. "I think...." I said, but his lips got in the way.

"No thinking, Annabelle." Gently he shoved me back into my seat, opened his car door, walked around to the other side and pulled me out. He walked backwards, playfully pulling me with both hands and enjoying my surprise and utter wonder, as I laughed with each surprise step. I couldn't control my composure any longer. I was lighthearted and felt giddy as my body relaxed and enjoyed the sheer pleasure of being in the moment. When we reached an open area beneath a large baobab tree, his arms encircled my waist and he pulled me up off the ground as if he wanted to ravish me like in a romance novel. As he kissed me, he twirled us around. Then his lips met mine and just as I thought they might stay there, he twirled me again. On the next twirl, I laughed and surrendered to the euphoric moment. He pulled me close and whispered in my ear. "Happy?"

"Oh, yes." I had floated into his magical world.

Baloyi looked at his watch. "Quarter of twelve." He picked me up again and whispered. "Good afternoon, Mrs. Baloyi."

I pulled away and grinned at him. "What?"

"Mrs. Baloyi. Our tradition. Kissing you three times under a baobab tree before noon. We're married now. No more worries about the nuns. Brilliant, isn't it?"

"Married!"

His face glowed with anticipation. "It's the answer, don't you see? Now the nuns will relax, it saves a lot of red tape, no license, no minister, easier, quicker and now we don't have to feel guilty no matter what we do. And I am so ready to ...." Then he burst into a raucous laugh the likes of which I'd never heard. "Of course I'm kidding, Annabelle."

Twenty One

Poppycock

After Baloyi went off to work and I headed back to the convent, my emotions crashed and burned as I recalled the make out session under the Baobab tree. While I took a moment to reflect, I waited for cows to cross the road. The word *marriage* reverberated in my head. After my disastrous marriage, I'd sworn I would never repeat that mistake. But what had I felt in that split second when I believed Baloyi and I were actually married? Elation? Frightening elation?

I slammed on the crazy brakes. I might love Baloyi – OMG – was I admitting it was possible? Marriage? No way. Commitment? Yes. Marriage? No. A definite no. But all I could think about was Baloyi lifting me up and twirling me. The euphoria I felt with him. My feelings of wonder and surprise.

I stepped on the accelerator as the last cow ambled to the other side of the road.

What would the nuns think if Baloyi and I allowed our relationship to go to the next level without a marriage certificate? Never mind. I did want Baloyi. I could commit to Baloyi. But no marriage. Then a feeling of sadness fell over me. It was as if I had struggled forever to find ... him. Could there be something to the soul-mate theory? Of course not. But silently I thanked

God for sending Baloyi to me, and although I didn't have a clue what I was going to do with him, I smiled at the possibilities.

My cell rang, jarred me back to reality. It was Bridget. "Aren't you coming to the school?"

"Yes, yes I am, I am coming just now."

I arrived at the school shortly after lunchtime. The playground was vacant and the early afternoon view of the countryside was breathtaking. Never had I seen a sky so brilliant. Crisp cumulus clouds floating above so perfectly. Despite it being winter, tall poinsettia trees reached the roof of the school and added crimson splashes of color. Treadless tires painted bright primary colors looked like giant lifesavers defining the playground. A light breeze fluttered my hair as I walked into the Mother of Angels office. The buzzing of activity had died down. Soon it would be teatime, a tradition from the British colonials. When I entered Bridget's office, she sat squarely behind her oversized desk, her half glasses perched on her head.

She sat back further in her chair with her arms folded. "What happened?"

"Nothing."

"Something's different about you."

If I hadn't known better, I'd have thought I was a bug under a microscope. "How do you mean?"

A knock on the door caused us both to glance up. Baloyi bent his head and walked through the door. "Afternoon, Sister." Then his eyes found me. "Annabelle, a word?"

"Of course." I may have floated out the door.

We walked down the hallway and past the secretary and the admin assistant, then found his bakkie parked a short distance from the front door of the admin building. He leaned his back against the driver's side door and faced me. Of course, with Sister Bridget, her staff and hundreds of children scrutinizing us through the open windows of the office and classrooms, it would be scandalous to touch him.

"Annabelle, I wanted to make sure you were okay."

"Quite. Why?"

"I just wanted to make sure. I think I freaked you out this morning and I wasn't ...."

I interrupted him. "My dear Mr. Baloyi, you rocked my world this morning." It was torture to not rush into his arms. I lowered my voice even though I didn't think anyone could hear us. "And that was just with a kiss." I glanced at the front windows dotted with faces of teachers and staff members. I motioned with my head. "I think you must be a rock star to others as well. Wanna tell me about that?" I laughed.

He ignored my comment. "I didn't want to scare you off, that's all."

I eased in a half inch and met his eyes. "If you wanted to scare me off, that was definitely not the way to do it, Detective Baloyi. Besides, I'm not easily scared."

"The Baobab tree nearly did you in, admit it." His eyes switched from laughing and flirty to serious and intense. "It's okay. Now I know not to mention the M word."

I put my hand on his sleeve. "No, I'd like to explain ...."

"Look, you don't have to say anything. How about tonight? Give us time to talk, and this time, I mean talk."

I considered Bridget's meeting at the convent after supper. "Is nine too late?"

"No, it's all good. I have paperwork to catch up on.

Nine it is."

I made my way back to the office without looking back. I heard the engine start and his car slowly drive away. I was enjoying watching the young female staff and off duty teachers scattering back to their posts. By the time I entered the building everyone appeared to be extremely busy.

I walked to Sister Bridget's office and closed the door. She was ready for me.

"Let's go, I need bricks."

"It's too late to go there and back, Bridget. We've got that meeting and all."

"Let's go."

Then I realized it wasn't bricks she was after.

We gathered our purses and laptops and said our goodbyes to the office staff. Comfortably seated in my rental, I turned the key and drove the car for no more than two minutes when Bridget popped the burning question.

"You want an African man?"

"Excuse me?" I wasn't sure what she meant at first.

"You heard me very well."

She was right. I had heard her very well.

"Everybody says you want him," she said flatly with no emotion.

"Everybody?" I cringed at the thought of people discussing my private life. "I don't know what you're talking about." Usually Bridget and I could discuss anything. Openly and honestly. But this subject swept me into uncharted waters.

"Did you kiss him today?"

"Yes." I was shocked at my pertinent honesty. "Really, he kissed me."

"Will you kiss him again?"

"Maybe." I rethought that. "No, no definitely." Even as I spoke to Bridget, my head was somewhere else. I thought about meeting Baloyi tonight. Where would that lead? Nothing could be as good as this morning. Perhaps because this morning was unexpected? Because it was fanciful? It seemed our relationship might be on the cusp of change. "Yes, definitely, I will kiss him again." Although I tried, I couldn't wipe the smile off my face. I kept talking. "Maybe we'll get married." *Where did that come from?*

Bridget ducked her head, her face shining like a lighthouse. "Maybe you'll stay in Africa!"

The next moment we were both laughing joyfully. Apparently she didn't need bricks anymore.

An hour later, Bridget and I were assembled with the other nuns in the lounge with Sister Mary presiding.

For ten minutes, Sister Mary explained the role of total obedience and dug in her heels on the side of the Irish congregation. Despite my knowing that she herself did not want to leave, you could have fooled me during those first few minutes. She explained why all of these hardworking nuns should do as they were told. She let it be known that she expected them to pull up and leave because the transfer notice had been sent ordering them to a convent in Johannesburg.

Sister Margaret stood up with a half scowl on her face. "I think this vow of obedience is a bunch of poppycock. It's not God's will, it's whoever wakes up on the wrong side of the bed's will."

I dare say Sister Margaret's comments shocked us all.

Sister Ann, the youngest nun, picked up the conversation. She acknowledged that she was new, but she was delighted to stand with Sister Margaret and Sister Bridget. Sister Ann, who also had taken the vow of obedience, felt that communicating with Ireland was extremely important, but certainly less important than communicating with God on a personal level.

"I was raised in a protestant church where I was taught that God would guide me. And despite my conversion to Catholicism, God convenes with me on a daily basis and directs my path," Sister Ann said. "Besides, many of the nuns running our order have never been to Africa. Why should they be in charge of deciding our fates? They know nothing about what we are going through. It's highly inappropriate for them to make judgment calls."

Sister Bridget's shoulders dropped with relief and a slow smile broke across her face. But she waited for the last nun to enter the debate.

Sister Benignus, staring at her kerchief, said that in all her days she had always gone by the rules. But, she had to agree with Sister Margaret. "We would just get up and going good on an assignment, like Uganda, and then because of who knows why, we'd be moved for no reason. Never mind our projects, never mind leaving people who desperately needed us. It wasn't right. It wasn't."

I admit I was absolutely stunned. Our meeting was giving the nuns a forum. Here I thought Bridget was the only one, but nothing could have been further from the truth. Everyone was in agreement except for one. We all grew quiet as our eyes focused on Sister Mary.

"Well, if that's the way you feel, good night." Sister Mary

picked up her empty cup and walked out the door. I followed her to the kitchen. She turned back and stared at me. "Your American ideas are corrupting our congregation." Her remark felt like a slap in the face. Sister Mary had been my aunt's best friend and up until now one of my biggest supporters.

"I think your congregation is wonderful. I wouldn't be here if I didn't. How many summers have I come to volunteer?" I didn't wait for an answer. "I believe what you are experiencing here in the simplest form is the beckoning of the future. Just think. Wouldn't it be great to select the country, the assignment, and perhaps how long you want to stay? Wouldn't that be great?" I hesitated as she stared at the floor. "Sister Mary, I know you would like to stay here in Malamulele near the hospital where you are making an extraordinary contribution."

"It's too late for me." She coughed and wiped her nose with a tissue.

"But not for Sister Ann and the ones to come. Why not give them this gift? Change the future. Maybe joining Sister Bridget would give the movement a voice. Maybe it's not too late. You're barely sixty. You have thirty years left at least."

She stared straight at me, then quietly walked out of the kitchen and headed down the walkway.

I had a strange feeling in my gut. How much longer would I be welcome at the convent? As I paused to take it all in, I heard cheerful laughter. "I like that, I like that, put that in, Bridget," said one. The nuns were negotiating like a group of policy changers. Fascinating. They had no idea how their decisions this night might affect lives. The simple act of standing up and taking that first step was about as exciting as anything I'd ever witnessed. The Malamulele Rebellion. Had a nice ring to it. I hoped this subversion among the ranks of the nuns wouldn't end up biting them later. I didn't want them to be punished for their freethinking actions. Subversion in the church was not welcomed, I knew. But at least whoever wanted Bridget dead couldn't have known about how she would become a leader among the nuns inciting them to a form of disobedience. *I* might think speaking up for themselves was long overdue, but the Reverend Sister was unlikely to share my views.

Listening to the vigorous voices and camaraderie of the nuns, I suddenly truly felt like the outsider I was. The clock in the lounge chimed nine. I grabbed my coat and hurried to the side door.

Twenty Two

Ritual Murders

The waitress at Wimpy's delivered our late night specials – club sandwiches with bacon, tomatoes and lettuce. Baloyi took a big bite and wiped his mouth with a serviette. "I don't get not ever having sex and then saying it's for God, you know, like the nuns."

I sipped my diet cola. "Look at it in a different light."

"How do you do that? I'm just sayin'." He took a sip of coffee. "Course, I can relate to giving up sex," he said sarcastically, then batted his eyes at me. "Maybe God turns off that switch, you know, for the nuns."

"No, I think if God turned off the switch, it'd be easy to be a nun." I took a sip. "You know what's difficult is when they're older. I think it must be difficult to wonder what might have been." I paused. "You know like not having their own children and all."

"Speaking of what might have been ... " Baloyi shook his head.

The drive back was quiet. The phrase "what might have been" lingered in the air.

Baloyi parked on the street a short distance from the convent. As we both got out, I could hear him exhale. Before he walked me to the door, he pulled me into the shadows of the overhanging tree and kissed me in the cold moonlight. I tensed. Baloyi must have felt it. He whispered in my ear. "This is way, way hard. That's what it is. We're grown-ups, for God's sake."

I didn't need to ask what he meant. He was right. And if I weren't staying at the convent, things could be different between us. As I drew out my key, it occurred to me that after Sister Mary's comments earlier this evening, I might be looking for other accommodations anyway. And very soon. I locked the side door behind me and moved quietly down the interior walkway toward the kitchen. A screaming teakettle suddenly went silent. I walked in.

Sister Mary was wearing her thick robe. "Oh, lo' and begorrah, you half scared me for sure – what are you doing up?"

"Just got in."

"You've been out? Where?"

"Wimpy's." I smiled. "I had a date."

She scrutinized me. "With whom, may I ask?"

"Guess."

"I haven't the foggiest."

"Malamulele's finest Detective ... Detective Baloyi."

"Is that safe?" Her eyes were wide.

"Safe? How could I be safer? He's a cop."

She picked up her mug of steaming tea and walked into the dining room motioning for me to follow her.

The vinyl seat was cold as ice. I needed my robe but I held out. "I'm just curious - why would you think I wouldn't be safe?"

"Well, not that *you* wouldn't be safe."

"Well, he was certainly safe." I laughed at my wit. Something made me just blurt out my latest worry. "Is it going to be a problem if I stay on for a couple of extra weeks? I need to be here for the murder investigation."

Sister Mary frowned. "Annabelle, you are always welcome here. And I am so ashamed for the remark I made. You know, the American influence." She looked at her lap. "I've been under a tremendous strain."

"Sister Mary." I reached across the table and patted her hand. "You know I didn't take it personally."

Her shoulders relaxed. Her lips were considering a smile. "You're right, of course. At times like these I miss your aunt so much. You know she was my best friend."

"I know. I know you two were close."

"I thought I might die when I heard the news." She sniffed, then wiped her nose.

Silence and stillness joined hands for a few moments.

"I wish she could have met Baloyi."

Sister Mary looked at me with tired and disbelieving eyes. "Surely it's not serious?"

"He's a wonderful man." I hesitated and prepared myself for telling a lie. "But no, it's not serious." Sister Mary didn't need another worry.

It seemed I had barely fallen asleep when my cell rang at 4:32 a.m. It was Baloyi.

"Got a fresh one. Investigation's at daybreak and it's a long drive."

I struggled to open my eyes. Standing at the lavatory in my room, I turned on the water. Nothing. I groaned. This very moment I admitted I was tired of the hard life. I wanted the comfort of hot and cold running water and I wanted Starbucks.

Throwing on my robe, I reprimanded myself all the way to the kitchen for being so privileged and spoiled. As I made my way through the pitch black night, the kitchen light shined like a beacon. I walked in and Bridget, dressed in navy sweats, stood at the stove pouring rice into boiling water.

"Oh, you're going to Mass." She beamed.

I hated to disappoint. "Not this morning. Why aren't you at prayers?"

"Finished."

I hoped she'd said some for me.

Bridget continued to stir. "Why aren't you going to Mass?" She was always concerned about my soul. Usually, that gave me comfort, but this morning it irritated me. I guessed it was the lack of sleep.

I looked under the cabinet and pulled out a black Dutch oven. "There's been another murder. I'll catch up with you later."

"Why do you like murder?" Bridget asked.

I stared at her for a moment in surprise. "Bridget, I don't like murder – I like figuring out who did it. Like solving a puzzle." That seemed to satisfy her.

I walked out of the kitchen with my oversized pot and headed for the four-foot plastic container of water in the garden. From the wall light I could see a large bug spreading its legs in the rainwater. I slid him over and dipped the heavy pot into the water and let it fill up. When I pulled it out, a palm leaf came with. Lucky for me, the other debris had settled. Hated to think what was in the bottom of the barrel. Most days I would have heated this wash water, but no time today.

Bridget breezed through as I used rainwater to brush my teeth. I scrubbed my tongue and remembered not to swallow. It was best to drink only boiled rainwater.

I jumped in my car and backed out carefully. The streets were dead quiet and void of people except for the queues at the bus stop. As I drove up to the furniture store, Baloyi stood with his hands in his pockets, breathing out clouds. When he saw me, he quickly opened the passenger door of his bakkie.

"Minjhani."

Instead of good morning in any language, I responded with "Am I late?" I looked at my watch.

"We've a bit of driving. We're going to Northern Limpopo, one hundred ninety kilometers or so."

We both got in the car.

"Isn't that out of your jurisdiction?" I asked.

"Not now. I've been officially assigned to the Task Force."

"For the Ritual Murders?"

"Yep." He glanced at me, then pulled onto the highway. "It'll take some sacrifice, like working on Sunday."

"What a coup for you."

He yawned, then smiled. "And you are my official photographer," he said as he handed me a point and shoot.

"I can do that." Then I hijacked the conversation. "Any more thoughts about Sister Valaria?"

Although I'd asked the question, I suddenly realized murder was the last thing I wanted to talk about. I looked forward to a beautiful sunrise. But it was too late. Sister Valaria was on the table.

"When we find the muti killers .... "

I ventured a guess. "You think Valaria's murder is connected, don't you?"

He nodded and said, "Hmmm."

"I wish I could believe that. But something doesn't fit."

"Like what?"

"Have you forgotten the Boomslang in your bed and the cobra in my car?"

He furrowed his brow. "Girl, you think I could forget somethin' like that?"

I laughed, then yawned and did my best to hide it.

"You're a woman after my heart."

———————

At 6:32 a.m. Baloyi pulled off the road and into a dirt parking lot where a small grocery store was lit up like a Christmas tree. "We need coffee." The whitewashed frame building looked like it'd been hit by hard winds. A truck so beat up it could have been lifted from a demolition derby stood out front. Sitting next to it was a sleek new red convertible.

"Is this an okay place?"

"Oh, yeah, my cousin works here. Be right back."

In less than two minutes, he returned with two very large black coffees, sweetener and cream packets. We were on the same page. I mixed my coffee and was swigging it down. Then he handed me a brown paper bag. Four large fat cakes. How I loved them, but there was a reason they were called fat cakes.

As we drove north, the South African sun streamed across fields of pineapple and avocado farms. It could have been a lovely road trip had I not remembered the reason for it.

So I decided to lighten the mood momentarily. "What do you think about when you're driving to a scene?"

His eyes flitted over to me and then back to the road. "I try not to think."

"I try to think of beautiful things like the way I felt the other morning when we were in the middle of nowhere." I waited for a reaction.

Baloyi shot me a look. "Girl, you're extremely distracting, you know that?"

"You have to see the beauty in the world, as well as what you must see every time there's a murder. Otherwise, you'll be drawn into a dark and depraved place."

Baloyi smiled, then began to slow down. "That's the turn."

"What street are we looking for?"

"No street names out here."

"What do you do?"

"Figure it out."

"There's a sure sign." I saw cop cars and a koombie parked on the side of the narrow gravel road. Baloyi eased up behind them and turned off the engine, then opened his door. I followed.

Yellow crime scene tape wrapped around trees cordoned off the area. A few feet into the field I spotted a black tarp covering what I was sure was the victim. On the other side of the tape, an African woman stood alone, head bent, hands clasped. Dear Lord, was she the mother of this victim?

I stayed where I was, unsure of what to do as Baloyi took a preliminary look. After talking to the officers on scene, he motioned me over, and I slipped under the tape. He introduced me to the cops and then he eased back the tarp.

It was like watching a movie in slow motion. I saw the dew balls roll off the tarp and beneath it lay a beautiful African girl, sixteen or seventeen, short stylish hair, perfect skin—she could have been a model or a beauty queen—except that she had no lips, eyes or breasts. I saw the girl's muddy blue taffeta dress discarded in the grass. How had this lovely young woman gone from being a prom queen to a muti victim?

I forced myself to operate the camera, but tears filled my eyes and I had to wipe them away before I could focus. While Baloyi and members of the task force scrutinized evidence, I took pictures, including one on my phone in case Baloyi would need to send it in quickly for any reports.

My grisly task finished, I slowly made my way over to the woman still standing behind the crime scene tape. Her sorrowful eyes stared at me like people do when they are trying to remember where they might have met you. Then she looked straight ahead at nothing in particular.

"Do you speak English?" I asked hesitantly.

She nodded sadly. "Little."

"She is your daughter?" I should have used the verb "'was," but it was too soon.

She nodded again, her heart surely breaking into a million pieces.

"And how old was she?"

"Eighteen."

"When did you last see her?"

"Last night. She go to dance."

"Who with?"

There was no hesitation. "Vince."

"Do you know Vince's last name?"

A shake of the head.

"Where was the dance?"

"Thohoyandou." That was halfway between where we were and Malamulele. "Big dance" was all she could manage.

"What is your daughter's name?" I kept my voice soft.

"Cici, Cici Malana."

I nodded, then saw Baloyi motioning for me.

"We will find Vince. I promise you. We will find him."
I touched her shoulder as I turned to leave. I met Baloyi at
the bakkie.

He opened my door, climbed into the driver's seat and
started the engine.

"The mother wouldn't talk to us."

I stared straight ahead.

"Did she say anything to you?"

"The mother is heartbroken..."

He interrupted. "Believe me, I understand that, but ...."

I interrupted him. "Her daughter's name is Cici Malana,
eighteen. She left for a dance in Thohoyandou last night with a
guy named Vince."

"She what?" He shook his head. "Unbelievable."

"Just lucky." I wiped my eyes with a tissue.

"No ... no, you're good." He gave me a look of validation as
he pulled out onto the highway.

"I'll run the name Vince by Sister Bridget. She knows a lot
of people."

"Long shot," he said.

"They're my favorites." I cut my eyes over at Baloyi. A half
smile told me the long shot he was thinking about wasn't the
one connected to the case.

Twenty Three

"You're Killing Me"

Baloyi turned left at a bright green highway sign indicating Malamulele was twenty-one kilometers to the right.

"Malamulele is that way." I pointed in the opposite direction.

"Surprise!"

"I don't do surprises!"

"Close your eyes and breathe, Annabelle. Breathe."

"Tell me, tell me where we're going." I pretended to pout.

"Uh-uh."

"At least, give me a hint."

"Okay then." Baloyi thought for a moment. "It's something my father gave me."

"Like that's a clue." I was so exhausted that I was in no mood for games.

Baloyi slowed and turned into an undefined parking area near a small building overshadowed by a heavy growth of vines. A solitary gas pump stood out front. No signage. A Toyota was parked at the side of the building next to three aging vehicles needing visible repairs.

"Your dad left you an auto repair shop." I waited for his reaction.

"No, but behold our equivalent of your 7-11. You are hungry, right?"

"Not so much."

"You need to eat. Let's go." He got out and so did I. Baloyi took my hand and led me up three stairs to the tiny store. We walked through picking up chicken and mayo sandwiches, bags of chips, pieces of fruit and two drinks. Scrambling back to the car, I jumped in and opened one of the sacks. Miraculously, my appetite was intact after all.

Baloyi reached over and with one hand grabbed my sacks. "Not so fast, girl. Just wait." He proceeded to drive a short distance, then pulled onto a dirt road. Off road competitive types would have had a field day. He carefully drove up and down the next few hills that reminded me of a miniature roller coaster, then turned right down yet another unmarked road and stopped the car.

"Where are we?"

"My father's house."

"Your father left you a house?"

"He did."

Through the thicket of acacia trees, I spotted a small cabin with a fading coat of white paint accentuated by dense woods decorated with an abundance of red flame creeper. The rectangular windows were draped with bougainvillea, which fell lazily down the sides.

"When's the last time you were here?"

He looked at his watch. "Bout seven hours ago."

"But I thought you lived where the snake came calling."

"Nope, just crashed there that night."

"Then someone *was* following you."

Baloyi shot me a glance. "Can you ever just turn off, Annabelle?"

"You want me to turn off? But then who would be there to turn me on again?"

"You're killin' me." His shook his head.

We gathered our things, and went up the wooden steps to the front door. He turned the doorknob and went in.

"Detective Baloyi, you don't keep your doors locked?"

"Not way out here."

The first thing that impressed me was how neat the house was, the only exception a shirt hung over a blue wooden chair.

"I'll get plates. You can take a tour, if you like—but let me warn you, it won't take long."

The kitchen ran across the back wall of the cabin, and in front of it was a small separate living room, complete with a flat screen television and dark brown couch. A hall to the left led to one bedroom and bath. The bedroom had a small antique dresser and a double bed, covers so tight they would have passed any inspection.

I walked back into the kitchen. "Beautiful."

"No," he said, pulling me close. "You're beautiful."

I looked into his eyes. All my emotions rose to the surface. Images of the mutilated dead girl collided with the thought of living in the moment.

Live now. Right here. Right now. Away from prying eyes. I pulled the band from my ponytail and let my hair fall around my shoulders, then massaged my temples.

"Here, let me do that." He pulled out a kitchen chair. Standing behind me, he slowly ran his long fingers through my hair, rotating my scalp, working magic. I moaned.

Baloyi swept me up into his arms and carried me to his bed laying me down with a pillow beneath my head. His hands traveled the length of my leg and slipped off my tennis shoes, first one, then the other, He kicked his own boots off and then lay facing me, studying me, stroking my arm oh so softly. Lifting my hand to his lips, he found the tender spot on the inside of my wrist, delivering sweet and gentle kisses, as if they were a prelude to a symphony. My breath came quick as he reached the pulsating vein in my throat and all I could think of was this was the moment I'd been longing for. I looked into his eyes and he asked the question.

"Are you okay with this – cause if you aren't, just say."

"It's okay Baloyi, it's okay," I whispered with the little breath I had left. I felt perched high on a hill as if the wind sailing in had blown all the air across an ocean and I had little left.

His arm gently dug beneath my waist and lifted my torso up high next to him as his hands pulled at my T-shirt, caressing me ... just as I heard the piano riff from my cell. I pulled it out of my jean pocket and threw it on the table, but Baloyi retrieved it.

"Baloyi, please no."

"It could be important." He handed me the phone and brushed his hot cheek against mine before he moved away and eased out of bed.

I struggled to say hello.

"What are you doing?" Bridget said in a perky voice.

I immediately felt guilty like I was doing something wrong. What the hell? I couldn't believe she had called at this precise moment. And I couldn't believe I had left my cell on. I answered her with a high-pitched irritation. "Bridget, I told you already that I was going to a murder scene. I'll fill you in when I get back."

"When?"

"Later."

"Where are you?"

"Good bye, Bridget." I hung up. I was numb. Numb from the interruption, numb from the victim I had seen today. And okay, I admitted it. Numb from anger toward Bridget. It wasn't her fault. She had no idea what was happening. Or, maybe she did. I stood and straightened my clothes, then walked into the kitchen to find Baloyi staring out a small window over the sink.

"Lunch break?" He turned and embraced me.

His hug calmed me. The hot romantic spell, like a bubble, had burst. We sat down at the kitchen table. Baloyi made light conversation, ate his sandwich while I picked at mine. I moved our dishes to the sink and began washing the plates.

Baloyi put his arms around me from behind. "We've got nothing but time." He turned me around and kissed me on the forehead and pulled me close again.

"I need a shower," I said.

Baloyi smiled. "Okay, but I've got to warn you."

"Oh, yeah?"

"The shower." He hesitated. "It's got an American head and it's awesome."

"And the water?"

"What water?" He threw his head back and laughed at my reaction.

I knew I'd never be able to recreate that exact beautiful moment again.

Baloyi turned the shower to a perfect temperature, then kissed me on the cheek and left me alone. I had envisioned his hard body against me in the shower, but that apparently wasn't going to happen. I stepped under the spray and was well into recreating a romantic mindset when the warm water ran out.

Wrapping myself in his robe, I opened the door and found Baloyi stretched out on his bed sound asleep. I scooted next to him.

Darkness was well on its way when we finally awoke. And without thinking, I said what was on my mind. "I wish I could stay here forever."

He whispered seductively, "You can, but the question is ... will you?"

But we both knew we had to head back—back to reality, and danger, and murder.

Twenty Four

Glimmer of Guilt

"Where were you yesterday?" I jumped at Bridget's voice and looked up to see her leaning against my doorway.

I didn't want to answer that question so I asked my own. "Want to go to Tzaneen and shop?" I needed to reconnect with Bridget one on one.

Her face beamed as she yanked her braids into a makeshift ponytail. "First, take me by the school and come back for me in a few hours?" She turned and dashed to the shower.

"Perfect." My cell rang.

Baloyi's voice was raspy and seductive. "Want some Wimpy's?"

It wasn't easy to turn him down, but I explained that I'd pledged my day to Bridget.

"Girl, does it take a crime scene to get your attention?" Then he laughed softly.

"I believe you quite appropriately caught my attention last night."

"Ahh, so I did." He sounded pleased with himself while I marveled at how a mere conversation could raise my blood pressure.

"Talk to you tonight."

After dropping Bridget off at school, I decided to kill some time in Malamulele and fill up my rental in preparation for our trip to Tzaneen. The main street was swollen with throngs of people milling around from shop to shop selecting fruit and vegetables from small vendors on the side of the rural road. In less than two kilometers, I pulled into the petrol station at the corner of the Giyani highway and the unnamed road that defined Malamulele. I patiently waited for the attendant to fill up the tank. This was Africa, where people didn't pump their own gas. If I'd insisted on doing it myself, it would have amounted to stealing from someone's pocket.

Three uniformed men hustled over asking to fill the car with petrol, check the oil and wash the windshield. It reminded me of bees buzzing around a hive. One attendant in particular caught my attention. Early 20's, dark chiseled features. He had come to collect the R145. I gave him two R100 bills. When he returned with change, his face mesmerized me. With his muscular arms, he reminded me of a young Taye Diggs. Why wasn't he on the cover of *GQ* or *Rolling Stone*?

I noticed a patch of material hanging by a thread. I took a guess. "You're losing your name tag." He looked at me like I was an ice cream cone on a sweltering day. His pearly white teeth sparkled and I felt a catch in my chest as he glanced down at his shirt, straightening the embroidered name. Now I could read it. *Vince.*

As I drove toward the exit, the lipless face of the teenage victim who'd gone to the dance with "Vince" flashed into my head. I punched number two on speed dial. Baloyi didn't pick up. I hit speed dial again. This time he answered on the second ring.

"Admit it, girl. Can't do without me."

I was barely breathing and it wasn't because of Baloyi. "Remember Cici, the last victim, the girl on her way to the dance?"

"And good morning to you as well."

I ignored him. "The mother told me her daughter's date to the dance was a guy named Vince. Remember?"

Baloyi's voice grew serious. "Yes, yes I do."

"At the Malamulele petrol station ... " I stopped to catch my breath.

"Go on, Annabelle."

"A guy named Vince filled my car with petrol five minutes ago."

"Description?"

"Handsome, twenty something, engaging smile, a charmer. Don't you see? He's the kind of guy who could get a girl to go anywhere, do anything ... "

"Where are you?" Baloyi's voice was elevated to high alert.

"I'll be picking up Bridget in a couple hours."

"Good. Now listen carefully. Stay away from the petrol station. I'm halfway to Joburg. When I get back, I'll check it out. Just you stay away from there, do you hear me?"

"I will. I will."

But as I continued to drive back to the school, I had several second thoughts. Vince was privileged. Anyone that good-looking must have gotten everything he'd ever wanted, one way or the other. It was "the other" that sent chills down my spine. What if unknown circumstances caused him to suddenly disappear? What if I lost track of him? I couldn't take the chance. I turned around and headed back.

I had plenty of time before I needed to pick up Bridget. I couldn't lose Vince. As I eased past the pumps, I parked at the back of the station. I opened my door and stepped out, locking my car behind me. I scanned the area. Several attendants feverishly worked offering services to a variety of customers. An Afrikaner with attitude and a weathered face waited while a young man filled his bakkie at the first pump. A tall African in dungarees and a baseball cap cleaned the windshield of a brand new Volvo. This was a happening place. Then a raucous laugh drew my attention.

Two attendants lounged against the side of the petrol station. I walked toward them. One looked up at me and concluded break time was over. Vince, however, leaned against the building with one foot hooked up behind him as he sipped from a bottle in a brown paper bag.

I forced a big smile. "Vince!"

He cocked his head and pursed his lips, looking me up and down. Flipping his cigarette to the ground, he flashed that million-dollar smile. "Need somethin' princess?"

Suddenly, he looked like a punk. A vibe screamed for me to steer clear. But the stubborn reporter in me declined.

"What can I do for such a finnneee woman as yourself?" His eyes settled on my chest, as if he were able to see cleavage with X-ray eyes.

I pulled out my cell. I had sent the photo of Cici to Baloyi earlier but luckily had not deleted it. "Did you know her?" I showed him the gory picture. It was the kind of picture that usually sent someone over the edge. I waited for his reaction.

"Shhhhhit! What a bloooody mess." I would swear I saw a

glint of pleasure in his eyes. "No fuckin' way." Then he smiled, staring right at me. No shock registered.

"Would you look again? You picked her up for a dance Friday night." A slight liberty with the truth.

His black eyes met mine. "Wasn't me, lady."

I felt a shiver up my spine. I had seen that same look in the eyes of everything from corporate CEOs denying their crimes to college students caught cheating on exams. I called it the glimmer of guilt. Guilt from the lie or maybe the murder. Fury filled me.

"Would you come to the police station and answer a few questions?"

"You a cop?" His head snapped back in surprise.

"No. Crime reporter."

"Oh." He laughed, flashing that masterful smile that would have convinced almost anyone that he was completely innocent. "Television or web?"

"Both," I lied.

"Will my picture be on YouTube?" he chortled.

"If you had anything to do with her death, it'll go viral!" I laughed aloud as if we were playing a game. I had him in my grasp. Like a bloodhound, my journalism professor always said.

"Ahhhh, well then, if that's the case, I'd better change." He turned and walked into the retired garage that was still standing behind the newer service station. It was dark and empty with a strong smell of petrol, but I wasn't letting him out of my sight. I stopped a few feet in and waited for my eyes to adjust to the darkness. "Tell them what you know. Make it easy on yourself."

"I'll make it easy, bitch." He came from the shadows, catching my throat in the bend of his arm. I couldn't breathe. Then I felt a sting under my right ear and floated into blackness.

Twenty Five

Kidnapped

My head ... hurts. Oooooh, my eyes ... heavy, can't open. Did I sleep in my contacts? Too much to drink? Focus Annabelle ... focus. Dear God, what happened to me? My legs won't move. Oh, God, don't let me be paralyzed! My brain is burning. What is wrong with me? Oh, wait! I'm tied up. I'm okay, just tied up ... with rope. I must remember ... Vince. I followed him ... inside ... inside the darkness ... then a bee sting. Vince and the dance girl. Poor beautiful dance ... girl.

Garbled voices floated through the air. Two, maybe three. The voices grew louder, then explosive. Complete silence. The door clicked. I closed my eyes.

"Vince, what were you thinking?"

"I was thinkin' she'd be worth a fuckin' fortune. Who knows what corn silk hair would go for? And as for the rest, I'll check that out later."

"Tonight she scream real good." A childlike voice. Quick laughter. Then someone else.

"Stay with her. Don't touch." It sounded like Vince, but I couldn't be sure.

My heart fluttered as fast as hummingbird wings—like when I had my first tap dancing recital. *Where in the world did that come from?* I had to get control. If I pretended to sleep, maybe they wouldn't drug me again. Whoopee do! I was on my own. And in no state of mind to think—about anything. High as a kite. *What did they give me? Dude, I could fly.*

Annabelle, wait. Someone's opening the door. Holy crap. I couldn't see who it was in this fetal position facing a concrete wall.

Someone grunted over me, smelling like beer. What felt like fingers stroked my cheek. It was all I could do to keep my eyes closed. Then a hand slid between my legs and with a sudden jerk, grabbed my crotch. I groaned from the unexpected pain.

"Oh, you like."

Bingo! Like lightning, an idea hit. I moaned softly. Cheap trick, but it was all I had.

What felt like giant hands rolled me over. "Me Moto. Me like."

Despite everything, I let my eyes open slightly. I saw a large twenties guy, and forced myself to smile as if I were about to be handed a chocolate candy bar. "You're cute." I slurred my words so he'd feel he had total control.

He took a pocketknife out of his breast pocket and opened it. I held my breath. This couldn't be the end. Not like this. Please God! Then he reached over and cut the rope that bound my feet together. I moaned again.

"You horny." A childish laugh filled the room.

I thrust my hips provocatively. "Hands. Need hands. Make you feel gooood."

"Moto like." As he untied my hands, I let him pull me up to him.

I was wobbly but at least able to stand. My hands caressed the boyish face of a man who towered over me leaning his head close to mine. I took a breath and gave him a hot wet kiss.

"Sit." I pleaded like a small child begging for a bedtime story. I eased him onto the edge of the cot and quickly straddled his lap, my bent knees against the mattress, enabling me to have height. I moved seductively, rising high and arching my back, then bending over him as my hair fell into his face. I brushed up against him, pretending I was still half-drugged, which wasn't too far from the truth. With my life on the line, I scanned the room, desperately trying to concoct an escape.

Moto reached for the zipper on my jeans, but I touched his hand. "Slow, real sloooow." As his hands moved to my butt, I scanned the room for weapons. Nothing. Only the cot we were on. As I moved, I lifted myself up high and leaned over his shoulder. This time I felt something. Another knife, this one in a leather sheath at the back of his belt.

I'd never killed anyone, but I was far too weak to kick and punch my way out. I had to escape, even though all I wanted to do was roll over and take a nap. *Come on, Annabelle.* "Sloooow," I whispered into his ear, and I led him further and further into his fantasy world, his hands now roaming freely. I raised up high on my knees, eased the knife out of its scabbard and with one quick downward thrust, I shoved it between his shoulder blades.

Moto's disbelieving eyes looked at me as I jumped off him. He rolled onto the floor then twitched, reaching for my foot. I jerked away. His mouth bled, and his eyes closed like in the movies when someone is dying.

Shaking, I turned and looked back. "I'm sorry. I'm so, so sorry." A pang of regret hit me, but I couldn't deal with my bloody conscience right now.

Survival was a bitch.

Twenty Six

Zombie

A loud clap of thunder unnerved me as I held my breath. Opening the door inch by inch, I listened. Nothing. The smell of oil and petrol permeating the wooden structure grew stronger as I carefully slipped into the next room. Uncanny. No one was there. Shivering from fear or drugs, I struggled to put my arms into the sleeves of a heavy jacket I found lying on a chair. The comfort wrapped around me, giving me the courage to search the room for anything I might be able to use.

When I saw the dustbin, I hit pay dirt. My handbag lay on top of dried up miele. I grabbed my purse to my chest like a child with a baby blanket on a scary night. But my iPhone and wallet were gone. No surprise there, but at least my captors had overlooked my Mag light zippered into a pocket. Also, I found the credit card and a few hundred Rands I'd sewed into the lining of my bag for emergencies. For a split second, I felt like a frickin' rock star.

My whole body shuddered as I staggered into the late afternoon. Falling temperatures hit me. I was in a wooded area of poplar and acacia trees. The building I'd left appeared to be a deserted garage, and I saw no other buildings nearby. The road leading up to the place was paved with dirt, and overgrown.

Fearing the return of more of my kidnappers, I decided to stay well off the road.

As I entered the trees, the first few drops of rain fell. At first, it felt like a gift from heaven, but the farther I walked, the more Heaven decided to show off. Rain poured down, which told me one thing: It was not freezing out here, it only felt like it was.

I spotted an abandoned three-sided lean-to and managed to take shelter beneath it. I had no idea how to get home, how to find a phone, how to let Baloyi and Bridget know where I was. Even I didn't know where I was. It was cozy under the lean to. I curled into a ball in the corner. I would rest my eyes for only a moment.

When I awoke, it was pitch black. I had no amnesia. Unless of course I didn't remember it. I smiled at my sense of humor even at a time like this. Truth be told, I had no way of knowing what I remembered and what I didn't. Oh what drugs do! My head hurt and I couldn't see a thing. I fished around in my bag for my black Mag light, flipped it on and could have lived forever without what I saw next.

A snake coiled in the corner of the lean to raised its head and turned from side to side looking at me. I held my breath and pretended I was a stone statue. The head of the snake was irregular. I had only studied the poisonous snakes and I didn't remember this one. It seemed to be observing me and obviously knew I was no threat. A red tongue popped out and then the snake lowered itself quietly and slithered out of the shed.

What a terrible odor. I didn't realize snakes smelled so awful. I crinkled my nose. Whew! Then I sniffed at something dark smeared all over my jeans. I shined my Mag light and sniffed again. Yuck! Blood. But I wasn't bleeding. Dear God, was this Moto's blood all over me? Maybe he didn't even die. That idea was even scarier.

Please get me home! My prayer was hysterical and demanding. *Stay focused, stay focused. God helps those who help themselves.*

I would walk to the highway, but in which direction? It had been a mistake to leave that dirt road, which would eventually have led me to the highway.

I was filthy and looked like the wrath of God. *Sorry God, just an expression.* Suddenly nauseated, I puked and instantly felt better. Of course, it could have been worse. I could have been served up this very night to the muti killers and Baloyi would have had to carry me away in a body bag. I licked my dry lips, grateful I still had them.

My mind flitted from subject to subject. The impact of having stabbed someone weighed on me. How had I gone from the little girl, who picked up spiders in the house and released them outside, to a person who could murder someone? But I was sane enough to realize the alternative was too grim to consider. I had done what I had to do. And now I had to concentrate on staying alive and getting back home to Baloyi and Sister Bridget. Then I could have a meltdown.

By now both Baloyi and Bridget would surely realize I was missing. They must be frantically searching for me.

I hated being so hopelessly lost. Why hadn't I listened to Baloyi and stayed away? Confronting Vince on my own had been unbelievably stupid. What had gotten into me?

Fury. Fury over Cici had made me take leave of my senses, and I had almost paid the same price as that poor young woman.

My breathing was becoming erratic. I staggered out of the lean-to, feeling dizzy, then steadied myself against a small tree. Oh, how I needed a phone. I moved forward having no clue where I was going. My heart pounded. I took a deep breath and coughed. Smoke! I smelled smoke. I must be dreaming because then I heard music. And laughter?

Paranoia hit me like a sledgehammer.

I retreated a few feet and leaned against a poplar tree. *Think, Annabelle, think.* I had no idea how far I'd traveled, but on foot I couldn't have gone too far from where the muti killers had held me prisoner. And, let's face it, anyone could be linked to the muti gang. Moments later, I took my next step and immediately found myself face down on the ground. I squelched my scream and lay still and listened. No footsteps in my direction. I was safe. I pulled myself up and sat cross-legged. I shined my flashlight on my bloody hands. I wiped them on my jeans and looked back at the root of the tree where I'd tripped. I hugged my legs and buried my head silently weeping until my body felt drained.

Pity party, be gone! I stood up. *One step. That's all you have to take Annabelle. Just one step.*

That music was still playing. I lifted a branch back and looked ahead toward the sound. I saw a small campfire about ten meters away. In front of the fire, a couple was making out on a red blanket, and beyond them was a small pitched tent. I watched the man sweep the young woman up into his arms and laughing, carry her into their love nest. Chances were good this wasn't a muti killer hideout.

I considered my options. With my zombie look, I could

walk up and frighten them to death. Or I could quietly steal their Jeep, which was parked about twenty-five meters to the left. I could take it to a phone and then send it back safely with the police—along with a warning to the couple to change their campsite.

The second option appealed to me. Not only was I probably a murderer, but now I was about to become a thief as well.

Groggily, I scurried forward as fast as I dared. When I reached the white Jeep, I hoped this guy had a similar habit to my friend back home who always left his car keys in the ignition when camping. Luckily, the door on the driver's side was unlocked. As I eased it open and lifted myself onto the seat, I threw my bag on the passenger side. Shivering, I closed the door quietly and locked it. Searching the glove compartment, I checked the floorboards and seats. I had only seen someone hotwire a car in a movie, but how hard could it be? I flung my head back in desperation only to see the keys dangling in the visor above me. *Now that's what I'm talkin' about!*

As if the rain had waited for me to get inside the vehicle, it now pounded the windshield. I flipped a switch and the wipers came alive.

Twenty Seven

The Accident

My eyes opened and all I could see was white. *Where was I?* Tubes streamed from my arms. I looked up and an African man was stroking my hair. "No!" I heard myself screaming and then an angel patted my arm.

"You're okay, Annabelle. You had an accident."

"Help me! Help me!" No, no not again. I pulled my arms and jerked a tube out. The woman stuck me with something and suddenly I was flying ... flying ... away.

Two strange women stood beside my bed. I closed my eyes pretending to sleep. They whispered to one other and the larger woman caught me peeking at her.

"Annabelle! Look, her eyes are open. Thank God."

A tall dark man loomed over me. Who was he? And who were these women? And who in the hell was Annabelle?

A woman in white asked how I was feeling. I wondered how she thought I was feeling all hooked up to tubes. I wanted to see...I wanted to see...I couldn't remember who I wanted to see. I brushed the tears away.

"You must rest now. You are disoriented. You had an

accident," the angel said. Then I went...sailing away.

A soft voice reverberated from far, far away and I realized as my eyes fluttered open that it was Baloyi bent over my bed.

"Annabelle, please wake up. You're everything to me. I never told you ... please wake up so I can tell you how much I love you, how much I want you, how much I neeeed you." He took a deep breath. "Come back to me. I'll even go to church. I will. You should have seen me prayin' with Sister Bridget. We were so scared we'd never see you ...."

I swallowed, then struggled to form the words I intended to say.

"Fat chance."

Baloyi jerked his head up. "Annabelle?"

A tear trickled down my face.

"Who am I, Annabelle?" He wiped the tear away. "Who am I?"

"A rock star."

"No, my name, my name. Say my name." He waited, begging me for an answer with those chocolate eyes.

"You forgot your name?"

He leaned over me, planting a gentle kiss. I could have flown out of the room and taken the tubes with me. And it had nothing to do with drugs.

His cell rang.

"She's awake. Annabelle is awake and she remembers, she remembers!" Then he clicked off.

"Sister Bridget." He slipped into the bed beside me and pulled me into the crook of his arm and I could feel him all around me. I could only think of one thing. I didn't remember how, but somehow I was home.

Twenty Eight

Lynch Pin

I realized the killers depended upon one sure thing to protect their grizzly crimes. Fear. Village people were terrified. No one knew exactly who was connected to the operations, leaving the wide-open possibility that it could be a neighbor, even a family member. Consequently, villagers kept vigilant and silent, frightened at what might happen to them or their children if they talked to police. After my ordeal, I couldn't be more sympathetic.

Also, ritual killings were bad for tourism. If news leaked that an American woman was caught up in the middle of a salacious muti murder, it could create an international incident. A scent of scandal would have been a detriment to the muti operation as well. So far, in everyone's interest, that had been averted.

Miraculously, Baloyi kept my name out of police reports, which kept television and newspaper reporters away. I was grateful. And the jeep I'd smashed had been repaired and returned to its rightful owners—who were given a false tale of ordinary theft to explain its disappearance.

After a few days of convent bed rest, I was almost myself again. The biggest problem was psychological. I mourned the fact that I had killed someone, though Baloyi said they hadn't found any bodies in the place I had described. They had found blood, though, so at least he knew I hadn't made the whole thing up, even though apparently I sounded like I was raving when I gave him the story. I figured Vince wouldn't have left Moto's body for anyone to find.

My mind played scenarios in which I might have escaped another way, but I always reached the same conclusion. Stabbing Moto was the only thing that had saved me from a gruesome death. I might take that guilt to my grave, but I was still glad to be alive.

The good news was that there had been no more attacks on Sister Bridget in my absence. Also, the muti killings in Limpopo Province had come to a halt. At least for the moment. Unfortunately, the women and children in the outlying villages of Gauteng Province all the way south to Durban in KwaZulu-Natal were disappearing, a testimony to the kidnapping strategy developed in Limpopo. When confronted, the muti killers had shifted their operation to another area. It haunted me to know that Vince was still enticing women to their deaths. I vowed to find Vince and stop him. Baloyi and I were a team now, part of it being that he didn't want me out of his sight.

He said he had something to show me, but I wouldn't go with him until Sister Bridget was safely inside the locked convent doors for the afternoon. Then I allowed him to stow me into the bakkie and drive away.

Twenty minutes down the highway he pulled into a wooded area that after following the road for a mile or so disappeared. A bit further and we were looking out onto an escarpment. It was second only to God's Window, a tourist attraction in Mpumalanga Province. The clouds and mist stretched out below us. Baloyi stopped the car, reached in the back seat and pulled out a padded manila envelope.

"What's this?"

"Open it."

My eyes popped when I saw the glint of the metal. I recognized the 9 mm pistol. "No, I'm sorry, no."

"Annabelle, you *need* to carry this. And you're going to learn to shoot."

"Why?"

Baloyi hesitated. "Because ... Vince or someone who fits his description is back."

He waited for my reaction. As I searched his eyes, I could feel the blood drain from my face.

"You are going to learn to shoot this gun."

"I can shoot." I opened my car door.

Baloyi pulled out empty glass pop bottles from his boot and placed them at a respectable distance. I allowed him to show me the proper stance. Then he stepped back with his arms crossed waiting for his student to perform.

I had handled a 9 mm at the Citizens Police Academy. I didn't need to tell him that all the actual shooting I'd done there had been simulated, like a video game.

Minutes later Baloyi surveyed the chards of green glass. "You have a knack for this." He patted me on the shoulder. "Now keep that gun with you at all times."

He must have seen the lack of commitment in my eyes because he paused. "For me, do it for me."

"Do you really think he'll come looking for me?"

Baloyi pinched his lips and spoke softly. "He, or someone

he hires. The grapevine says he's pissed, Belle. Oh, and Moto Messini, he's back as well."

"That's not funny, Baloyi!"

As I watched his serious face, he didn't blink. "You're serious?"

He stared me down.

"Moto's alive?" Strangely, my heart soared. "He's alive!"

A huge block of guilt riding on my shoulders suddenly sprouted wings and flew away. I hugged Baloyi. "I didn't kill anyone!" I joyfully pounded my fists on his chest.

"What?" He caught my arms. "You're happy you have two guys now after you?" Baloyi kissed me and made it all better for both of us.

As the early morning sun graced the wet grass, the school grounds looked like a field of sparkling diamonds. Bridget and I sipped rooibos tea in her office waiting for the rest of the world to wake up. She organized her stack of mail as I scanned headlines on my laptop.

Bridget answered her cell on the first ring. I could only hear one side of the conversation, but it was apparent she was talking to Reverend Sister Mary Michael who was inquiring if the nuns from Rio had arrived. I watched with silent amusement as Sister Bridget dealt with her.

"No, the nuns from Rio de Janeiro are not coming." She said her words calmly. "As we told you in our letter, the Malamulele nuns have decided to finish their projects here. You mustn't worry. We contacted the Rio nuns and told them they weren't needed at the moment." She smiled and glanced at me for support.

I put my hand over my mouth to smother my laughter. I could hear Sister Mary Michael's voice from where I was standing three feet away. I watched as Sister Bridget held the phone away from her ear. Then she pulled it close again. "We sent you a letter last week. Did you not receive it?"

Sister Mary Michael bordered on screaming. I distinctly heard her say, "You nuns are conducting a mutiny? You don't know who you're dealing with!"

Bridget took a deep breath, then silently let out her frustration. "We explained we will remain in Malamulele. We have work to complete here. Thank you, Sister Mary Michael. The peace of Christ be with you."

When Bridget hung up, our eyes met. "She's going to be a problem." Then she made the sign of the cross and opened her next envelope.

The morning was full of surprises.

Bridget received a call from a Durban businessman who informed her that he was on his way to Malamulele to see her, and that he had good financial news for her. I was impressed. No one ever came to Malamulele on purpose. It wasn't even on a map. Bridget's fundraising efforts for the school auditorium must be bearing unexpected fruit.

Twenty minutes later Officer Aimee performed her secretarial duties to perfection, announcing the businessman from Durban who then strode into Bridget's office. Aimee lingered in the hall and mouthed H-O-T to me. I hid my smile as I viewed the silver-haired fox from my chair against the wall. He bent to shake hands with Sister Bridget.

"Lovely to meet you," Bridget said. "And this is Annabelle

Chase, my friend from America." She gestured to me with a flourish.

"Ian van Riebeeck." He gave me a cool nod as if he expected me to leave.

My read when he shook my hand was that this attractive man was feigning his pleasure to meet both of us. He sat in a straight back wooden chair in front of Bridget's desk. Very curious now, I stayed where I was.

"This is ... private business," he said to me with a smile and actually tilted his head toward the door.

"She can stay," Bridget answered. "We are excellent friends, and Annabelle is closely concerned with all matters that concern the school."

He hesitated as if puzzled, then ignored me as he continued. "Sister Bridget, you are a busy woman, so I will facilitate this matter quickly. It's rather complicated, but I'll make it simple for you."

And he talks down to women.

Bridget sat at her desk and gave him her full attention, her hands tightly clasped in front of her.

"Johannes Locher, your grandfather, came to the aid of my grandfather while he was traveling in Ghana years and years ago. The story is that my grandfather was lost and your grandfather assisted him. At any rate, my grandfather offered Mr. Locher five percent of a company he was forming. He wrote the agreement down on a scratch piece of paper. At the time, only dreamers would have done so. My grandfather had merely a small plot of land, nothing else. Nevertheless, your grandfather, when offered the chance, bought in. Neither of them ever spoke again. I believe your grandfather died leaving only one child, your father, now also deceased." He took a deep breath. "School teacher, am I correct?"

"Yes." Sister Bridget's eyes grew serious.

"We lost track of you for a while, but the deal was legal and binding." A few drops of perspiration dripped down his face.

Bridget looked puzzled.

"As it happens, I am selling the Piet Retief Diamond Mine, my father's company and my grandfather's company. I want to retire, and the buyer needs full disclosure. I have an offer for you. I think it's....no, I know ... it's quite generous." He handed Sister Bridget a small piece of paper. "It's a check for R500,000."

Sister Bridget's eyes nearly bulged out of their sockets. Her face lit up. I knew she was considering how this money would end all of the school's financial woes. I, on the other hand, knew it didn't seem like much for part ownership in a successful diamond mine.

The CEO whipped papers out of his briefcase, stood up gallantly, and laid them in front of Sister Bridget. He handed her a gold pen and put his finger on the blank spot. "By signing here, you acknowledge that you accept this amount as payment and forfeit any further interest in the business."

Sister Bridget picked up the pen. Thankfully, her eyes found mine. I shook my head furiously, my eyes pleading with her to say no.

She paused, then handed the check back.

Our visitor's mouth fell open.

"I will review the papers," Bridget said.

"But I've flown all the way from Durban. I assure you these papers are legal and binding."

"Nice of you to come." I admit I was sarcastic, but I

didn't trust him.

He stepped back and looked me up and down. "I was conferring ... with Sister Bridget." A haughty look rode his face.

Sister Bridget stood. "Yes, and I will confer with you later, as I said." Nothing made her madder than someone being rude to me. I wanted to laugh, but I kept my composure until he gathered his briefcase, turned and calmly addressed us. "I look forward to hearing from you."

We stared out the window watching his African driver open the door of the black Mercedes. Then the Silver Fox crawled like a weasel into the back seat.

"Why?" Bridget whined. Her eyes were filled with regret.

"Something is wrong. If you own five percent of a diamond mine, believe me, it's worth millions, not what he offered."

"I don't need millions. I'm a nun. I've taken a vow of poverty."

"That's why he knew you'd sign the papers. He knows where you live, that you work with the poor. He was sure you'd take it." I patted her shoulder. "Don't worry. I'll find you an excellent pro bono lawyer in Joburg. You need to look into this, vow of poverty or not. Think of all the good you could do with that money."

The owner of a huge diamond mine had come all the way to Malamulele. Didn't send his lawyer, came on his own. He needed Bridget, obviously, and he was so arrogant he thought she'd sign immediately. For sure she was the lynch pin of the deal. What I intended to do was find out just how wealthy Sister Bridget actually was.

Twenty Nine

Betrayal

Bridget agonized well into the night about what she could do with R500,000 and whether she should have given the check back. She also pledged me to secrecy, afraid of what would happen if the news got out.

"Of course, Bridget," I reassured her. "I won't tell anyone."

I dragged myself out of bed at 4:30 the next morning and headed for the kitchen. I walked in on Sister Ann slumped against the counter waiting for the water to boil. When she heard me, she quickly straightened up. "Good morning."

"How are you this morning?" I couldn't have appeared perky if I'd wanted to.

"Wonderful!"

Question asked, question answered. But I discerned a huge disparity in her answer relying solely on my observation of her red swollen eyes. Nuns are people too, and they have troubles like any of us. However, they rarely show it to the outside world. Thanks to Sister Mary, I knew that Ann suffered from the HIV virus. Or it could be something else entirely weighing on her shoulders.

"Couldn't sleep?" I asked casually.

"Going to the clinic a wee bit early today."

"Everything okay?"

"Never better." It was then I realized she always said "never better."

"Sister Ann, how are you *really* feeling?"

Anxious eyes stared back at me as she pushed her short dark hair behind her ears. She studied the floor considering my question.

"Can I help you?" I asked.

"Oh, sure and begorrah, I'm fine, don't you worry about me." Then with a fabricated smile, she left the kitchen with her hot cup of tea. I suspected she was headed to the lounge, so I followed.

I walked into the dark room and flipped on the overhead light then sat down in a rattan chair across from her. "Sister Ann, I don't want to pry, I really don't. But I'd like to help. I'm not a nun, so whatever you say goes no further. You can tell me anything. Use me!" I laughed, attempting to lighten the mood.

Her blue eyes darted from the door to me to her teacup on the small rectangular table between us. She pulled her wool sweater close, then shivered as she laced her slim fingers around the cup of tea and studied the floating lemon bits. Sister Ann appeared anxious. "It's Sister Valaria."

Something told me I didn't want to hear it.

"First, I have to explain something else." Her eyes met mine. "I have HIV and no I didn't have sex – it was an accident at the clinic."

Since I wasn't supposed to know this, I feigned surprise.

"But I know you were an AIDS activist and so, I hope you will keep my confidence and you're right – I do need your help."

I reached over and touched her hand. "Anything."

"I don't know how, but Sister Valaria found out I had HIV. She threatened to tell my family. She insisted they needed to know."

"And?"

Sister Ann's face transformed. Filled with anguish trumped only by anger, she spat out the words. "She didn't know my family. It was a dreadful, dreadful idea. It would have alienated us forever."

I moved to the couch beside her. "You didn't kill Valaria, did you?"

Her head popped up like a deer on the first day of hunting season. She wiped the tears streaming down her pale face. "Oh, sure and begorrah, you can't think I did that."

I kept quiet and waited as she wrestled with what to say.

"But, I might as well have." She stood and ran her fingers through her hair as she paced around the room. "A patient at the clinic I'd grown very fond of—Ella was her name—had come in for testing. She was HIV positive. I thought if I confided in her that I had the disease maybe it would help her to accept her own situation. Later I told her of my frustration with Sister Valaria and how worried I was that she would tell my family."

"What a terrible strain on you."

She continued. "It was the next night Sister Valaria was killed." Sister Ann buried her face in her hands and sobbed outright. I handed her a fresh tissue and waited helplessly, wishing I could say something, anything helpful. "Oh Annabelle," she said, mopping her face, "I've been afraid to tell anyone about Ella's possible involvement but the guilt is eating me up. What if she had something to do with Valaria's death?"

I patted her shoulder. "Did you ask Ella if she had anything to do with the murder?"

"No. No, I never mentioned it. I was too scared. I may have caused her to sin. That would be unforgivable."

I paused. The fact someone might have hired a killer had occurred to me, though I never expected it to be someone this close to home. "But, Sister Ann, she may not have had a thing to do with it. You might be carrying this burden for absolutely no reason at all!"

"Would that were true." She hesitated. "But, I'm sure she had something to do with it. She smiles at me, as if we share a secret. I believe Ella found someone to kill Valaria."

"But that person would have to have known the layout of the convent." I shook my head. "Very unlikely unless you gave her all the details about the sleeping arrangements of all the nuns?"

Sister Ann looked up at me with innocent eyes. "No, I didn't and I never thought about that."

"I don't see how she could have known where Valaria was sleeping."

We both went quiet. Could this possibly be true? If Ella had befriended Sister Ann and arranged for someone to kill Valaria, then the muti killings had absolutely nothing to do with our in-house murder. Plus, that killer had not been after Sister Bridget. The whole landscape of the murder investigation and the attempts on Sister Bridget's life would change if that were the case. I could see my theories wrapped up in black ribbons flying out the window.

"Please say something," she pleaded with tearful eyes.

"I need to talk to Ella." I hesitated. "I'll be discreet."

The problem was, murder was not discreet. Sister Valaria's threat to reveal Sister Ann's secret to her family was not a crime. Perhaps it should be, but it wasn't. If I were completely objective, Sister Ann had a powerful motive for killing Sister Valaria. However, this petite nun could not have dealt the blow that nearly took Valaria's head.

And, the fact that Sister Ann had told Ella about Valaria threatening her was not a problem, unless Sister Ann had indicated she needed Ella to fix her problem.

Maybe Ella had wanted to repay Sister Ann for her kindnesses at the clinic and had taken matters into her own hands, believing death was the only way to keep Sister Valaria from talking. However, murdering a nun to repay a kindness was pretty farfetched. I was more inclined to believe that all the fears in Sister Ann's mind had run away with her. How to find out the truth? Someone impartial needed to talk to Ella and sound her out on the subject. That was why I was the right person to follow up with this lead.

I flipped open my computer to search for the diamond mine's annual report, which I suspected would be pure fiction if the Silver Fox had had anything to do with it. My gut said Bridget was worth millions, but proving it would require finding an honest pro bono lawyer.

As I Googled the Piet Retief Diamond Mine, a magnificent website in splendid color brought up a professional picture of the very man we had met earlier. Ian van Riebeeck. CEO and Chairman of the Board of the Piet Retief Diamond Mine. It was smaller than the famous De Beers Consolidated Mines. No surprise there. But the fact it took me so long to find details like net worth was significant.

Wading deeper into the website I found full financial records. The conglomerate, of which Sister Bridget owned approximately five percent, was worth over R20 billion. Suffice it to say, Bridget was mega wealthy. We needed a lawyer all right, and he would need a kick ass accountant. But it was essential to keep all this info under wraps. If it became public, who knew what the repercussions could be? What would someone do to get a piece of Bridget's fortune? A chill ran through me. Suddenly, the attempts on Bridget's life lined up front and center.

Had van Riebeeck hired a contract killer? With failed attempts on her life and his arrogant nature maybe van Riebeeck had decided to take matters into his own hands. He assumed correctly that Sister Bridget would have accepted the R500,000. That may have been his last ditch effort to handle the matter. Had I endangered Bridget by advising her to not take the check? Unless there was another attempt on her life, how could we ever prove van Riebeeck had been behind any of this?

Thirty minutes later I was staring at a hot guy who was half awake. I had decided to tell Baloyi about Sister Ann. I wanted to tell him about Bridget's wealth because it would explain so much. But Bridget had made me promise not to tell. How I hated secrets.

I elaborated the story of how a woman at the clinic might possibly have put Sister Valaria's murder into play. My info was thin, and after the attacks on Sister Bridget in the intervening weeks, I doubted that someone had killed Sister Valaria independently. However, shouldn't we track every possible clue?

Baloyi looked around as if he needed coffee. "You need to let the police handle it."

"But, I'm the one Sister Ann talked to. And she'll never talk to police," I said adamantly, and saw his eyes shift to the floorboard. I wasn't getting through and I couldn't understand why. "What's wrong, Baloyi?"

"Nothing. But you're not a cop. Let us handle it."

I handed him my coffee. "Here, you need this more than I do. To get the cobwebs out."

He took a couple of sips. "Annabelle, I know you want to help. And believe me, you're great with theories. Plus, you've been up close and personal with the muti killers. I get it that you want to solve Valaria's murder. But this sounds like a wild goose chase to me, and in your case chasing geese seems to have a way of turning deadly. I thought you would have learned that from this last episode. You need to quit taking foolish chances!"

I bit my lip. "Okay, you're right, it was stupid to confront Vince by myself. But this is a completely different situation."

"You can't possibly know that in advance." Baloyi's eyes simmered. "You need to back off now. Let us take it from here!"

I leaned back, feeling the heat of his anger.

He took a breath and seemed to will himself into a better frame of mind. "Listen," he said as he moved closer and took both my hands. "The Task Force thinks you're too involved. First, you're American, plus you're a woman. Now, before you say anything, I know it's old fashioned and all, but it's how the guys feel. Just sayin'."

"I didn't realize you men were living in the dark ages." A snippet of the tough women cops who'd interviewed me right after the murder played in my head.

"Belle ..."

"But, you have women on the Task Force ... surely."

"Uh, not on the Task Force. Our Deputy Minister of Police is a woman and we have women through the ranks—and in important positions—but on the Task Force, no."

Quickly I considered losing my source, my only source to the police department. I softened my pitch. "Look, I know you're in the middle here. So let me give you a heads up and you forward my ideas to the team." I hesitated. "Teamwork. Like we've been doing. Except, I have to handle the AIDS clinic. I realize it's probably nothing, so you shouldn't be bothered anyway. And she confided in me, so please don't mention that to anyone, okay?"

He sighed deeply and threw up his hands. "Understood, but please, don't take unnecessary risks."

"Agreed. So are we okay?" I waited for a response.

His eyes crinkled at the edges. "I know what could make us better."

"Baloyi. Be serious."

"Oh, I am." He put the bakkie in reverse, backed out and drove us away.

Thirty

Boom

After the quick stop breakfast, Baloyi dropped me at my car on his way to a rescheduled Limpopo Task Force meeting. I headed for the AIDS clinic. Baloyi's comments had infuriated me, but I willed myself to appear flexible.

Sifting through my theories consumed me so much that I was shocked when I glanced up and saw Tzaneen. Time had flown. Within minutes I pulled off the highway onto a narrow road leading to the AIDS clinic a few blocks down. In front of the clinic stood an old 1995 Ford, a dilapidated bakkie and an out-of-commission ambulance that might be 70s vintage with two missing tires. I parked behind the bakkie, walked to the door and entered.

Surprising bright yellow walls welcomed me to a spotless clinic. Toddlers and their older brother and sisters entertained themselves with toys on a yellow and orange rug, while grandmothers in gray folding chairs sat around a coffee table waiting for appointments. All eyes were glued on me as I entered.

AIDS was a dreaded disease and rampant all over the African continent. The nuns attended a minimum of one or two funerals every Saturday. Relatives of the deceased pretended that their loved one had died only of pneumonia, flu or some other illness. No one ever died of AIDS. People believed if they didn't talk about it, it couldn't be true. Meanwhile, the disease had wiped out a whole generation of young parents, with grandparents assuming parental duties. Over the past ten years, educational campaigns finally had crept out to the smaller villages. This trip I had been relieved to find giant billboards on Malamulele's main street urging people to seek testing and encouraging them to "be safe." Education had finally arrived.

Now in the clinic I searched the faces of these worn out women sitting before me, mostly grandmothers. I wondered if one of them might be Ella, Sister Ann's friend. The women talked back and forth in their native languages. The oldest straightened her bandana, walked over to the magenta and khaki straw basket on the window ledge, grabbed a handful of plain, foil-wrapped squares and stuck them in her pocket.

When Sister Ann walked into the waiting room, she looked at the next patient, then her eyes fell to me. "Annabelle, I'll be with you in a few moments."

I nodded and sat down.

Two women came in dragging a reluctant husband or lover. I leaned back against the wall pretending to ignore them. My eyes wandered and then my legs followed suit. The office had one computer and no secretary. It looked like the college computer I'd trained on years ago. The clinic needed a serious upgrade.

Sister Ann came back with her patient in tow. She exchanged goodbyes as the woman picked up a toddler and a handful of condoms. She called to her grandchildren, who dropped their toys and followed. From the window I watched the children scamper down the steps and out to the dirt road for what would most likely be a long walk home.

Sister Ann motioned to me. I followed her into a consultation room. She closed the door. "What are you doing here? Do you need an AIDS test?"

"No, no. I'm good." I drew closer to Ann and put my hand on her arm. "Sorry to disturb you, but I forgot to ask you how to contact Ella and I need to."

Sister Ann looked as if she wished she had never told me her fears.

I lowered my voice. "All of us need closure. The only way to do that is to find the person who killed Valaria." I raised my voice with the last sentence and mentally squirmed when I realized it.

Her voice was a whisper. "She works at Milady's in the Tzaneen mall."

The streets of Tzaneen were filled with a stream of flatbed trucks, bakkies, Mercedes and rentals. I tried Baloyi, but his number went straight to voicemail. My short message was "At Milady's. Lunch at Wimpy's?"

I pulled into the refurbished underground mall entrance toward a man waving his arms like I was an airplane heading toward a hangar. Double glass doors gave entrance to the lower level. I rode up one floor to Milady's

A customer was checking out racks of colorful garments. She thanked the store clerk who then turned to me. The striking woman, tall and stately in a long sheer skirt and wool sweater walked over, her head of curls bobbing with each step. "Gooood morning. You must try that on." I had picked up a sheer gray blouse with a silver sequined collar. She whisked it away from me and carried it into a small dressing room, allowed me to enter, then swept the curtain closed. I thanked her, jerked off my black T-shirt and slipped it over my head. I walked out of the dressing room searching for a mirror.

"Stunning." She flashed a smile. "Absolutely stunning."

"It looks okay?"

"You look lovely, dear."

"Are you Ella?" I refrained from saying "the Ella who knows Sister Ann."

Her brown eyes grew wide, her red mouth appearing not to know what to say next. "Why, yes, I'm, I'm ... Ella. How do you...?"

Her cell jingled a song. "Excuse me." She smiled. "My grandson." She walked a distance away.

I quickly changed, yanked on my coat and grabbed my faithful crossover bag just as everything went dark. I blinked. Yes, I was awake. But nothing. No background music, muffled conversations or ambient noise. My heart quickened thinking how deep I was inside the belly of the building. Below me was the basement. Above me was the second floor. I was caught in between. My heart accelerated. What happened? A power failure? Claustrophobia sat on my shoulder like a crow waiting to attack. I felt my way forward.

"Ella, where are you?" I yelled.

A torch blinded me. I reached for my cell. I squinted and instinct made me back up – from what I wasn't sure. A hand grabbed me, but I jerked away as a loud rumbling noise rocked the building.

Fighting through soft and silky materials, I panicked. Pitch black. Couldn't see a thing, could barely breathe. Who would be able to find me down here? Miraculously, my new iPhone rang.

I spotted the light shining through a pile of sheer debris. I struggled to move, but my legs were pinned down. I stretched out my hand and managed to grab it on the fourth ring. "Baloyi!"

"Annabelle, where are you?" A panic rose in his voice.

"Something's happened, I can't see anything." And then my brand new phone went dead.

I coughed and punched the air with my fists. Someone was choking me, damn! Then I discovered my crossover strap was tangled around my neck. But little mattered. With the amount of coughing I was doing, I wouldn't be able to breathe much longer. Panic filled me. I unzipped my bag and fished around until I felt my Mag light. I flipped it on and screamed as loud as I could. "Help me!" It felt strange saying those words. What was happening?

A bouncing beam of light blinded me. I pulled back and winced from the pain then looked up at a face distorted by a clear respirator mask.

The man jerked off his mask. "Annabelle. It's me." I'd never heard a more glorious sound than Baloyi's voice. He replaced his mask, then fitted another over my face. "Can you move?" he asked, voice muffled now.

I honestly didn't know. I tried to help as Baloyi and a medic shoved mounds of fabric and lifted a few heavy pieces of debris off me. I winced as my detective reached down and picked me up. The medic's flashlight beam focused on a victim lying in our path. The dead eyes looked vaguely familiar.

I yanked my mask off. "That's Moto. Omigod Moto!"

Baloyi pressed the mask back onto my face. "We have to get out of here," he said, his words distorted. "There might be another bomb."

"A what?" I felt disoriented. Here I was on the other side of a news story.

"Bomb."

The medic raced ahead shining his torch and leading us out. Baloyi's grip grew tighter on me as he struggled to climb over the rubble. We reached a shaft of bright light that looked like it was from a hovering spacecraft. As my eyes refocused, I realized daylight was shining from a hole in the second floor above us. Then glass windows decorating the roof suddenly shattered. Baloyi ducked under an overhang to avoid shards raining down.

The medic, who reminded me of someone I'd known in a previous life in Denver, crouched a short distance in front of us. Baloyi moved forward, maneuvering us around a hole in the floor, exposing the basement where a fire was raging, and thick clouds of smoke billowed toward us.

"Hurry." The words had just left Baloyi's mouth when another tremor shook the building. Baloyi and the medic steadied themselves, hurriedly hooking me into an evacuation swing. Before I could protest, hands grabbed me, yanking me out and throwing the swing back down. Baloyi came up quickly and immediately hoisted me up into his arms, running with me and dodging falling debris to the front door of the mall.

Baloyi laid me on the sidewalk and headed back toward the mall. Thankfully, firemen and policemen grabbed him and held him back just as a series of explosions rocked the mall, collapsing the entire roof.

"The medic ... " Baloyi sat next to me on the ground and bowed his head on his knees.

I put my arm around him, wishing the mask would let me talk.

Baloyi pulled his mask up. "He was the only who volunteered ... to help me find you." He gasped. "Then he made me go first in the swing...." Tears filled his eyes.

I slipped off the uncomfortable respirator mask, but the fresh air was filled with dust, soot and ash. I struggled to talk. "So sorry." I felt like I was having a vicious allergy attack. "But what happened here?" I asked.

"Underground parking ... car bomb ... then one by one each car fueled it." Baloyi turned his head and strained to clear his lungs.

"Moto was in there," I said before putting the mask back over my face. Oxygen streamed in.

Baloyi looked grim. "One less worry for me," he said.

What a strange turn of events. The bomb that had devastated the mall had somehow preserved my life. Moto must have followed me—and I didn't doubt he'd been moments away from kidnapping me again, this time with revenge on his mind.

I must not have hurt him nearly as badly as I thought. And now he was dead, with no help from me.

Baloyi asked if I felt strong enough to ride with him back since the Tzaneen Hospital was way past capacity. To appease him, I agreed to a check up at the Malamulele Hospital. The ringing in my ears would subside, they told me, and I had no broken bones, which was an absolute miracle. My left shoulder was painful, but a sling and 'round-the-clock Panadol should make it manageable. Whenever I felt a pity party coming, I remembered how many had died in the mall that day.

On a positive note, the nuns were spoiling me. I could barely turn my head without one of them offering me tea or toast or good company—especially Sister Bridget, who hovered over me the same way I'd hovered over her for the past few weeks. When I objected, she just smiled and made jokes about payback.

Stellar news was that I had splurged and agreed to the full insurance package with Beavis car rental. I would not have to pay one cent. Plus, they would deliver a shiny new car the next day.

The bad news was my investigation was on hold. On the first list of mall victims, Ella's name did not appear. Since they had not found her body, she must have slipped away before the explosion. Best guess was the phone call she'd received was a tip off.

The next afternoon I was in a lawn chair tucked inside a navy blue blanket. I pretended to relax while I waited for Baloyi. A rapping on the front door of the convent jarred the silence. Flora put down her broom and answered the door. With her hands on her hips, she stared up at Baloyi as he ducked his head and walked inside.

"Is Annabelle here?"

Flora pointed to where I was sitting.

His first words to me were, "She doesn't like me."

"No, she doesn't like me being with you."

We laughed softly as he gently held my good arm and escorted me slowly to the bakkie. After I was comfortably seated, he slid in on the driver's side and leaned over and kissed me softly for the first time in days. He beat Panadol hands down.

Baloyi slipped me the updated list of mall victims I had

asked for. My eyes ran down the page as he started the car. "Have they gone through all the rubble?"

He shook his head. "Not yet."

I wondered about Ella. Could she be buried under the rubble?

"There is one thing." Baloyi rubbed the back of his head like he did when he was considering something he wasn't sure he wanted to share. "Jimi from bomb squad said the initial explosion was triggered accidentally while being attached to a specific vehicle."

"Whose?"

Baloyi paused.

"Your rental."

I heard myself gasp. "Someone was attaching a bomb to my car?" My mind raced. "It wasn't Moto. He was upstairs with me. So who was it?"

"Somebody who may never be identified."

Twenty minutes later Baloyi and I arrived at his one bedroom house in the woods. Winter sun had forced beautiful buds on a variety of surrounding trees. Living in the moment was my new mantra, including my time with Baloyi.

My heart hit double time when he opened the front door, and I could hear the Hallelujah Chorus as visions of my last visit played in my head.

Movement ahead of Baloyi caused my eyes to refocus. Someone was there.

I stared in shock.

It was Ella.

Thirty One

Dirty Laundry

My legs collapsed and I fell onto Baloyi, who caught me, carried me into his bedroom and gently laid me down. My head was spinning. I pulled a pillow to my chest and rolled over to face the wall. Nothing made sense. Why was Ella here?

Baloyi sat on the edge of the bed. "It was too soon to get you out. It's obvious you need more rest. "

Ella tapped on the open door, hesitated, then walked in with a steaming cup of tea. "You had a terrible shock, my dear. A terrible shock."

I nixed the tea, asking Baloyi to fetch me a blanket. When he left the room, I faced Ella and spit out my words.

"What are you doing here?" I hissed.

She stared blankly at me, and then Baloyi returned.

Ella said, "Let the poor girl sleep ... she's had a terrible ordeal."

Baloyi covered me with a throw, then followed Ella, leaving the bedroom door open.

I could hear them whispering to one another, but I couldn't make out what they were saying. Closing my eyes, I kneaded my forehead with my fingertips. When I told Baloyi about Sister Ann's suspicions that someone was possibly involved in the murder of Sister Valaria, I hadn't mentioned Ella by name. Was she an accomplice? Could Baloyi be involved in the muti killings? Being a detective would be a nice cover. But no. He'd been alone with me repeatedly, and had plenty of opportunity before now to drug me. However, at the moment I didn't trust either of them.

Baloyi returned with the same cup Ella had offered me earlier. "You gotta drink this. It'll make you feel better—it's herbal. Now drink, Belle." He said it playfully, certainly not menacingly. Was I willing to die to prove he was not involved?

I took a sip, then drank it down. He took the empty cup from me as Ella walked in.

"Better now?" If this woman had anything to do with murder, she was a terrific actor. "Yes." I hid my clenched fists beneath the covers.

"Oh, I'm sorry, I forgot to introduce you. Belle, this is my Nana, Esmeralda."

"Ella, for my friends," she said, with the sweetest smile. Her face was pure, innocent, so convincing.

"Does that include your nun friends?"

Her eyes blinked as fast as hummingbird wings.

"Uh, I'm Presbyterian. I don't believe I know any nuns." Her eyes desperately pleaded with me. Then I got it. Of course she hadn't told anyone about the nuns or the clinic or that she had tested positive for HIV.

"My mistake." I felt better having leverage. But wouldn't that give her an even more compelling reason to get rid of me? If she'd arranged for someone to take care of Sister Valaria, she could do it again. I turned to Baloyi. "Would you leave us? Women talk." I concentrated on giving him an innocent look.

He winked at me and left the room.

When the door shut, I sat straight up. Sometimes, circumstances demanded a violation of confidences. "Ella, I know about your talk with Sister Ann. Were you involved in setting up Sister Valaria's murder?"

Her hand flew to her chest. She sank down on the edge of the mattress. "No, no, of course not." Tears welled up in her eyes. "Please don't tell my grandson about, you know, the other." She thought for a moment. "And don't tell him I was working at the store. I promised I wouldn't work anymore. He thinks I need to take it easy." She attempted a smile as she wiped a tear away. Bingo! That's why Baloyi wasn't worried about his grandmother when the bomb blew.

"Ella, did you tell anyone that Valaria was causing Sister Ann problems?"

She began to shake her head. Then she stopped.

"I might have mentioned ..."

"Who," I said. "Tell me, who did you tell?"

"I told my ex-husband, but he's the Police Commander. You can't think he had anything to do with it." Her eyes were those of a trapped animal. "And I never mentioned the nun having, you know, the disease."

She couldn't even say HIV. And from her body language, I believed her. I had interviewed a lot of guilty suspects over the years. Ella was absolutely innocent.

Relief flooded through me. I reached for her hand. "I will never tell a soul about your HIV. Never. You can relax." I put my arm around her shoulder. "I had to know you weren't involved in the murder. I'm sorry for upsetting you."

Baloyi knocked. "You women done? Breakfast is ready."

He gave us a sideward glance, but seemed content to believe we were simply chatting.

In the kitchen, the table was decorated with bowls of miele pap, scrambled eggs, bacon, and toast. I helped Ella to her blue chair and eased her under the table. Baloyi did the same for me.

As I dug into the scrambled eggs, Baloyi introduced a new topic. "Nana, what do you hear from Marcus?"

Ella looked up and smiled at Baloyi, who gave me a serious glance. "That's my brother. He's studying in Europe, or so he says."

"Now, Baloyi don't be that way." Ella said it with a melodic voice. She had recovered from my unexpected questioning. I was impressed.

"Where is he exactly?" Baloyi passed me the platter of scrambled eggs as I handed Ella the bacon.

"Traveling around Venice. But how can he travel with school?" She looked at me, then placed her napkin in her lap. "Sorry, didn't mean to—what is it you Americans say? Shake the dirty laundry?"

"Air the dirty laundry," I said softly.

"I just wish he could be more like Baloyi. So stable. Such a good boy." She reached over and squeezed Baloyi's hand. "But Marcus did say he's coming home next week. Spring Break." She paused. "Annabelle, you should come to dinner."

"Sure." Baloyi stared at his plate.

"Tell me about your family, Ella."

"Please, call me Nana." She smiled my way then continued. "Well, my one daughter Lacinta married Ru Baloyi. Marcus is her younger son, and you know about this one, N.F. I'm sure he told you how he got his name."

"Now Nana, don't start." Baloyi threw his head back and laughed.

"I haven't heard that story yet," I said, remembering my first meeting with Baloyi when he'd brushed me off about his initials. "N.F.?"

"I'll tell it, Nana." Baloyi clasped his hands behind his neck and rocked his chair back. "Okay, then. My Mom, well, remember she was incredibly young, didn't have nothin', very poor. So she named me, all legal and all, No Furniture Baloyi."

It was a funny story, but in that moment I felt such sympathy for him, for his poor mother, for his having that name, for his parents having died too early. I only said, "N.F., finally I have a first name."

"And he told you their story, how they died ...."

"No." I swallowed. I could hardly speak, looking at Baloyi.

He gave me a look of understanding. "A long time ago now," he said. "Car accident took both of them when I was fourteen."

"I'm so sorry."

"Long time ago," he repeated.

Ella seemed eager to change the subject now. "I married a boy who didn't know nothing," she said. "He had R5 in his pocket." Her mouth made a movement from side to side. "And he sure weren't the police chief back then!" She tossed her head back and forth with an attitude. "His name was Chugue Langa. He got a job sweeping floors at the police station." She took a sip of her tea and continued. "Then one night he was asked to watch the office cause everybody else was out chasin' a chicken thief. And that's how he began his forty years with the department. Only now it's payin' off. He's got some type of special retirement. I'm really happy for him. I'm also really happy we're divorced." She laughed at her own comment.

I smiled and understood completely.

"So how about dinner, my house, Saturday night? You can meet Marcus and have you ever met Chief Langa?"

"No, I haven't." I could finally meet the Police Commander Chugue Langa, Baloyi's grandfather.

Something was pushing my subconscious like a cattle prod. I couldn't quite put my finger on it.

"I have to warn you. Chief's quite the charmer!" When Ella said it, I could hear the affection in her voice peppered with a smidge of sarcasm.

I threw my robe around me the next morning and tapped on Bridget's door but she'd left already for prayers in the chapel. I wondered if I should have joined her. I had a feeling I would need all the prayers I could muster. But instead I dressed slowly and waited until chapel was over. Then I headed into the lounge. Sister Ann and Sister Bridget were sipping tea and looking terribly serious. I turned to leave, but they motioned me back in.

"You guys planning the next big take down?" They looked at me as if I was speaking another language.

"Never mind." I laughed. What's up?"

Bridget grinned. "The nuns from Rio will not be coming."

"That's awesome!"

Sister Ann lowered her cup. "Perhaps." She seemed pensive. "They'll just send more nuns."

"But, not today," I said exuberantly. "One small victory at a time. Look, you've taken a stand. You've canceled the new nuns from taking over the school. It very well *could* be permanent."

Together both of them relaxed their shoulders as if they'd practiced synchronicity for hours. I wished I had a video camera.

"You're right," Bridget said.

Sister Ann agreed, then excused herself.

Bridget's eyes studied the rug.

"What else is wrong?" I waited patiently.

"I got a letter from the CEO. He said that I will lose my five percent of the mine if I don't settle right away. He offered me R600,000."

"Aha!" I said with a grin, as if I were a master detective.

"What?"

"Don't you see? We have him on the run. You are a very wealthy woman." I leaned toward her. "Please tell me you turned him down?"

"Yes, I did. But it was hard."

"I can't wait to hear what the lawyer I found for you has to say."

Thirty Two

Who's Come to Dinner?

Saturday night arrived faster than expected.

I was apprehensive about meeting Baloyi's family, which may be why I spent so much time honing a positive attitude and finding the perfect outfit. Black slacks, a black Merino sweater and my black leather jacket. This would be one of those defining moments where I would absolutely be charming and adorable.

Baloyi arrived and whisked me out the convent door. In the shadows outside he pulled me close and nuzzled my neck, his warm breath igniting my pilot light. "You look fine, girl." I grinned when I realized he was wearing black jeans, a black sweater and a black leather jacket.

Jacaranda 94.2 played the "African Footprints" album as we headed for the highway. My eyes dampened listening to the words. I'd loved this continent from the first moment I'd arrived and stepped off the plane taking my first breath in the Southern Hemisphere. Even the air itself was different.

Baloyi pulled into the first Giyani petrol station. I had calculated that it would take an hour to an hour and a half to meet and eat, leaving us with some alone time. "How close are we?"

"You nervous?" He gave me a sideways glance. He seemed to be enjoying every moment of my mild anxiety as the gas station attendants danced around the vehicle squirting fluids on the windshield and filling us up with petrol.

Baloyi pulled onto the highway, then surprisingly turned at the next corner and drove two blocks. He slowed near a black iron fence on the left. Although the night was moonless, I could see from the front porch light that the house was brick and had a detached garage to the right of the driveway. He guided me up the brick walkway leading to Ella's front door. A contrasting picture of the round mud huts down the road flashed before me. Chief certainly must pay his alimony, because working at Milady's would never buy Ella this sort of comfort. Plus, he was sending Marcus to college in Europe? *Follow the money, follow the money.* What was wrong with me? Baloyi was right. Could I not ever turn off my suspicious mind?

A quick knock and the front door opened. Smiling, Ella looked radiant in a white European jeweled sweater over a long black skirt. "Welcome," she said, graciously inviting us in. "Chief called, he'll be late. Why am I never surprised?" She laughed, as she hung our coats in a hall closet. We were in a small entrance with several adjoining hallways.

"Like old times," Baloyi bantered.

"Seems like, doesn't it?" She ushered us toward a blue velvet couch into a comfortable room with a blazing fireplace. I wondered where the four archways led. From the aroma, one definitely went straight to the kitchen. And from where I sat, I could see a small beautifully decorated dining room. The table was set for six with pastel linens and probably imported dishes, complete with sparkling wine glasses.

When Ella returned, she handed us each a glass of dark merlot.

"Aunt Jenna's coming," Ella said matter-of-factly.

"Haven't seen her in a while."

"You can't have a table for five, now can you?"

"Guess not." Baloyi squeezed my hand.

"Would you two excuse me? I need to check on Flora."

When Ella left, Baloyi took my wine and set it down on the small glass coffee table. He pulled me close. "I need to tell you about Aunt Jenna." He had a pensive look.

"What?"

The doorbell rang and Baloyi whispered, "Later."

I could hear Ella greeting someone.

"That's Aunt Jenna," Baloyi said. "And Chief's probably right behind her."

A tall woman with bright auburn dreadlocks created quite an entrance in her shocking pink caftan complemented by strings of red and orange aurora beads. It was unavoidable. I liked her instantly.

Ella handed Jenna a glass of wine. After introductions, Aunt Jenna tilted her glass toward Baloyi and me. "To the future of this lovely couple."

Yes, I definitely liked that woman.

The doorbell rang again.

A ruggedly handsome man just over six foot walked in. Baloyi's grandfather had a look that demanded attention. Immediately I felt drawn to him and stood with Baloyi waiting for introductions.

"You haven't met Annabelle, have you Chief?"

A smile broke across Chief's face and smoothed out the jagged scar on his left cheek. As he took my hand, his ring scratched my skin and I jumped in surprise.

He didn't seem to notice. "You are quite the detective, I hear."

"Sometimes." I gave him my best all-American smile. I was surprised by the color of his eyes, blue as the Indian Ocean. Absolutely mesmerizing. For an older guy, he was quite a handsome dude. "Now I know where Baloyi gets his good looks."

"Did you hear that, Esmeralda?" The Chief's face lit up.

"Oh, my yes, I heard every word." She controlled her laughter. "I may be your ex-wife, but I admit you've still got the charm." There was an underlying hint of seething heat between them that lay like a familiar dog on a kitchen floor.

Ella moved toward me and under her breath said, "Which is why we're not married anymore."

Her comment told me everything I needed to know. Another ex who couldn't remain faithful. We had more in common than I'd realized. I smiled as Jenna greeted the latest guest.

"Chief," she said, as she walked over and gave him a smoldering look. He cradled her in his arms for a quick moment, then whispered in her ear. They fell onto the couch laughing hysterically.

The doorbell rang.

When I heard Ella scream, I knew her other grandson had arrived.

"I wasn't sure you'd make it." Then she came in and said, "Look everyone, here's Marcus."

Baloyi drew me to him and whispered. "We'll eat quickly and leave." I laughed, then looked up to see a chiseled face that would have made Adonis blush with envy.

There stood Vince, my kidnapper.

Thirty Three

Dysfunction at its Finest

I was stunned.

Chief and Baloyi stood an arm's length away, but it might as well have been miles. It was like watching an accident happen in slow motion. You see it and you cannot stop it. Vince sauntered over, lifted my hand to his lips in a playful romantic gesture, bowed and kissed my fingertips.

"Rumors of your allure and how you have transfixed my brother precede you, Annabelle Chase."

The fact that he was this near sucked the breath right out of me. Scenarios played over and over in my head. Was the Chief aware of Vince's involvement in the muti killings? Vince wasn't attending university in Europe. Maybe trafficking muti to the superstitious and wealthy. Could his grandfather have sanctioned his lifestyle? Ella had said earlier that the Chief had a great retirement gig. Maybe he was in on it. Maybe they were all guilty. But what about Aunt Jenna? And Ella? I shook my head clear of obvious absurdities. The culprit as far as I knew for sure stood directly in front of me.

"Brother." Vince reached to shake Baloyi's hand, upsetting Baloyi's wine glass and spilling it all over the walnut parquet floor. "How clumsy of me. I'll get you another." Vince walked out of the room and in two minutes, he returned with a fresh glass of wine. Baloyi lifted his glass and took several sips, which I was quite sure he needed.

Assembled in front of the blazing fire, the family sat in a circle with me frozen beside Baloyi on the velvet couch, Chief and Jenna across from us on the love seat. Ella sat in a high back imported chair and Vince stood at the fireplace, as if he were heir to the throne. After a few minutes of polite conversation, Baloyi's head drooped onto my shoulder. I gently rotated my shoulder and whispered, "Baloyi, Baloyi." But he was sound asleep and didn't budge. My mind returned to our initial conversation about his University of Texas experience and the partying on Sixth Street in Austin. No way one glass of wine would render Baloyi drunk.

Vince laughed. "He never could handle his booze. Chief, an assist?"

Ella ran to Baloyi. "He must be ill. I've never seen him like this. Baloyi doesn't get drunk!"

Chief turned to her and gently held her back. "He's fine. We got this Ella."

I watched protectively as Vince and his grandfather each picked up an arm and dragged Baloyi down the hall into Nana's room. They laid him on her bed. The Chief put his arm around Vince, and they walked back down the hall like fraternity buddies.

I sat on the side of the bed and checked Baloyi's breathing. It was normal. But I couldn't wake him—which wasn't normal at all. Then it hit me. Baloyi had been given a pinch of something. Vince. Like a game of cat and mouse, he was toying with me. Since I had kept my mouth shut, Vince thought he was in control.

I pulled the thick satin comforter from the chair and covered Baloyi, then returned quickly to the other room. *As soon as Baloyi awakes, we're gone.* Until then, I wanted to hear every word of Vince's conversation.

Chief sidled up to Ella, and I overheard him say something about *Baloyi is fine and we have a guest for God's sake.* She looked back at me, then at Chief.

With a bright smile like an ad from the dentistry tech mag, she said, "Six is now five. The poor boy must be so exhausted from his work. I suppose we should eat?"

We took our places around the table, Ella at the head. I sat to the right of Ella with Marcus across from me. The chair to my right was empty. I prayed Baloyi would miraculously wake up and claim it. Aunt Jenna sat to the right of Chief who was at the other end of the table. This must have been what their marriage was like. Chief on one end, Ella on the other, with a beautiful woman in between.

Flora, who had apparently signed on for an evening gig, served the first course. I watched as she ladled shrimp soup into each of the bowls. Why had she been hiding her talents at the convent? I didn't know she could cook anything but Irish stew. And why did she hate me dating Baloyi? Had she been trying to warn me away from the family? Was it possible she might well be my only ally in the room?

"Excuse me." I stood up and pushed my chair under the table. "I'll check Baloyi." I wandered down the hall to Ella's bedroom. Baloyi looked like a sleeping prince. I sat beside him and ran my hand down his arm.

His eyes flew open. He sat up and swung his legs off the bed, holding his forehead for only a moment. "What happened?"

"You fell asleep."

"What?" He sat up and stretched his arms, then rotated his head in all directions.

He didn't realize he'd been drugged—and how could I tell him what had really happened with his family in the next room? "They're waiting," I said, my heart hammering so hard I thought it might break apart.

Baloyi rubbed his forehead. "Man, I feel so out of it."

"You need heavy-duty caffeine."

We walked into the dining room, and I requested two large cups of coffee.

"You look better, Baloyi." Ella, so innocent, was maybe the only one at the table who actually was. She and Aunt Jenna. I was getting a few quirky vibes about the Chief so I couldn't be sure about him.

The meal continued with Vince staring at me from across the table. I could never call him Marcus. Due to his amazing face and GQ body, this putrid piece of humanity had enticed women to their deaths. I hoped he could read minds. *Vince, you may think you've got the upper hand, but I'm coming for you. I will get you no matter who your grandfather is.*

Then I looked at Baloyi. He had no idea it was his own brother he was chasing.

"Are you okay?" he asked me.

"I need to talk to you," I whispered.

"On the way home?"

I nodded. *How was I going to tell him? Would he even believe me?* I needed proof or else it was Vince's word against mine. And Vince was his brother. His blood brother. The man they called Marcus was a vicious killer. I was convinced he'd kill any of us in a flash. What a terrible ordeal this would be for Chief and Ella. At least Ella. I wasn't sure about Chief. And, if I helped bring Vince down, would Baloyi ever forgive me?

As we feasted on Peking Duck, the Chief's cell rang. He looked disappointed as he glanced around the table. He shoved his chair back, told Baloyi not to worry, that he wasn't needed, and apologized as he hurried out. Nine minutes later by the antique gold clock hanging on the dining room wall, Aunt Jenna developed a migraine and apologized as she left. Then there were four.

"We never finish meals here – never in all these years." Ella sighed.

Ella, Vince, Baloyi and I ate what would have been an exquisite meal, except it was apparent that none of our minds were in the moment. If I'd had to guess, Ella was envisioning Aunt Jenna and her ex at some undisclosed hideaway. Baloyi looked trashed. I kept a watch on Vince.

A few minutes later Baloyi pushed his polished wooden chair back and began clearing the table. Ella had given Flora the rest of the night off. Rare anyone would give their help the night off with company adding to the pile of dirty dishes in the kitchen sink. With Flora gone, that meant Ella or her guests would need to step up or leave kitchen work until the next morning. And that was something I could not see Ella doing.

"Ella, I'll help you." I stood with my plate in my hand and reached for an empty side dish.

"You and Marcus get acquainted. We'll do the dishes." Ella smiled and followed Baloyi to the kitchen.

"I believe we are acquainted." I muttered, but how could

I tell Ella that Vince had kidnapped me? Her own grandson? Blood is thicker. She would never believe me. And he banked on that.

Vince watched Ella disappear, then scooted his chair out and walked around the table. Leaning over me from behind, his hot breath hit me as he whispered. "So pleased to make your acquaintance." He jerked my chair back from the table. As I stood and turned to confront him, his right arm cinched me around the waist so tight I could barely breathe. I struggled, pushing myself away from him, but before I could scream he clamped his left hand over my mouth.

"You scream and I'll kill everyone in this fuckin' house, Baloyi and Nana included. And don't think I won't. That crazy bitch knows nothing and it's stayin' that way!" He yanked my left arm behind my back, pulling me so close I could smell his coffee-laden breath. "You and your buds will never escape. Not in a million years." He forced me down the hall to Ella's bedroom where he slung me forward and locked the door behind us.

"You're lucky, you know. Had I not hired a screw-up, you'd be dust, my sweetness. But what a waste that would've been." He threw me against the wall. "I'm going to enjoy every square inch of you. Starting now."

"Go to hell." I jumped up and pushed him back scrambling toward the master bath. But Vince's foot wedged in the door. I gasped as he clutched my arm with his iron fist and dragged me back to the bed. "I have something I want to show you, my love." He forced me down. "You make one noise and I'll kill Baloyi the minute he walks through the door. I swear to God I will. You got that?" His eyes burned with rage.

Baloyi was strong, but with the element of surprise I couldn't take the chance. The son of a bitch would do it. He would kill his very own brother. Fear gripped me. I had to protect Ella and Baloyi. I nodded and before I could blink, Vince was sitting on top of me, my hands trapped in Ella's scarf as he tied it to the wooden slatted headboard. He glared down at me. "You have fucked with my family for the last time." His hands in an instant had rolled up my sweater and jerked down my bra. "A thing of beauty. They'll be worth gold."

I gulped air and closed my eyes, desperate for this to be over.

"Open your eyes," he demanded. "I want you to remember this moment." Then he laid his hard body down on top of me as he unzipped his jeans and moved closer to my face. He displayed himself with a wild grin just as a knock on the door interrupted. "It won't be long," he whispered, then straightened up and unsnapped my hands from the headboard so quickly I was left wondering if any of this had occurred. I was standing straight up and ready to walk out the door like I'd been his windup toy.

"Tell Baloyi and I'll kill him. All I need is one more good reason." Then he shoved me into Ella's bathroom.

"Back off Marcus, she's mine," Baloyi said playfully on the other side of the door just as Vince opened it.

I could hear Vince through the bathroom door where I'd locked myself in. I was scared out of my mind to tell Baloyi anything. At least for now. I had to wait. I had to think. I had to plan.

"She's been puking. Brought her in to the big bathroom."

Of all the liars I'd ever encountered, Vince was indeed the best. Fighting real nausea, I washed my face with cold water to clear my head. I collected my thoughts so that when I walked in to speak to Baloyi, I'd be able to pull off the farce. Taking a deep breath, I looked at myself in the mirror, straightening my clothes. I certainly looked like I'd been throwing up. *Validation for Vince.*

When I emerged, Baloyi patted my hand. "You okay?" I nodded yes and we returned to the dining room and sat down for coffee.

"Annabelle," Baloyi said jovially, "did I ever tell you Marcus tried plenty to steal my girlfriends? Member Martha in Standard I?"

Vince laughed that infectious laugh that enchanted all the girls to death.

"You never even had girlfriends, Baloyi." Vince laughed so loud I cringed.

"I hid them!"

They joked with one other like real brothers with sibling rivalry. But only one was the good brother. Would Baloyi ever believe what I had to tell him? When I did tell him, would that put him in danger? Would his own brother actually kill him? I looked into Vince's menacing eyes when Baloyi turned to go back into the kitchen. Vince was able to turn it off and turn it on. Oh, yeah. He could kill anyone, absolutely anyone. Maybe especially Baloyi.

Thirty Four

Jackpot

You pay a price when you hold it together.

Dealing with a cold-blooded killer across a dinner table had left me with stomach cramps and a throbbing headache. On the way back to the convent, I didn't have to pretend I was sick. I felt like a canary staring at the wide-open cage door with a ravenous cat waiting to attack at any moment.

"Baloyi, have you and ... Marcus ... always been close?"

The dashboard lit up as his eyes darted from the road to me and back to the road. "Never. He's never liked me. He's tantalized me, tried to take everything from me. No one else seemed to notice but me. Sorry to say I was happy when he left for Europe or wherever the hell he's been. Suited me fine." He hesitated. "But in the end, he's blood. That's gotta mean something. So what can I say? He's my bro. Good with the bad."

Good with the bad. Oh, Baloyi, if you only knew. He really believed his brother was what he pretended to be. A mere rascal. This might require more thought on my part. As I got out of the bakkie, I turned to him. "Baloyi, be careful. Don't take any chances, even with those you know."

"Annabelle, you worried about something? Talk to me, girl."

I hesitated. "It's just that ... let's talk tomorrow. I'm exhausted." And suddenly I realized how much. It could wait for morning. Bad news was always better in the daylight. I offered my lips for a quick goodbye kiss, wondering how many more of those there would be.

Unable to sleep, I stepped out onto the walkway where the flickering candle flame pulled me toward the chapel. I needed to pray and I needed to feel safe. Though my faith waned from time to time, there was someone there who listened. I'd been talking to him—or her—since I was four or five.

I knelt and prayed intently for what felt like hours. When I stepped out of the chapel, I had clarity. I realized I had to come clean with Baloyi and tell him about his brother's involvement in the muti operations. If he didn't believe me, or if he did and it affected our relationship, I'd have to deal. I could not carry this burden anymore.

I saw Sister Bridget on the walkway heading to the kitchen. I walked in behind her and said good morning.

She turned and looked at me. "You look awful, Annabelle."

"That helps ... ever so much."

"You didn't sleep?"

"No."

"How was the dinner?"

I thought for a minute and decided to keep her out of the loop.

"Well?" She gave me a skeptical look as she flipped the switch on the hot pot and searched through the lower cabinet, finally dragging out the black dutch oven and setting it on top of the stove.

I yawned. "I'm tired, that's all."

Bridget shook her head and filled the pot with water, then flipped on the eye of the gas stove. Silently, I chose myself a coffee cup.

"You wouldn't believe me if I told you." I exhaled, wanting her to ask me again.

Instead of insisting, she seemed to go into a trance.

I'd been so consumed with my own particular problems! Bridget must be having her own difficulties. "What's up with you?" I stared at her until she looked up and spoke.

"That Johannesburg lawyer you found called yesterday. He says he's got all the information he needs and he wants to meet today."

"When do we leave?"

Her eyes came alive. "I was hoping you would go."

It would feel good to get away. "I'll go if we come straight back after the meeting."

She agreed. By 5:30 a.m. we were headed south toward the N1 and on our way to Johannesburg.

I'd pulled the lawyer's address up on Google maps and listened to the British accent on my iPhone directing us straight to the building on High Street. After parking underground, we trekked up to an unassuming lobby and spoke to the receptionist. She looked up through pastel framed glasses that accentuated the deep circles beneath her eyes.

"May I help you?" She looked at me, and seemed surprised when Bridget took over the conversation.

"We're here to see Mr. Fricker."

"Ahh, yes Miss Bridget ...."

Before she could get out the rest, Bridget corrected her. "Sister Bridget."

"Of course, Sister Bridget. Sorry." She pressed a button on the intercom, announced us, then told us to go in.

The disheveled lawyer reminded me of Albert Einstein. He stood and shook our hands, then pointed to seats on the other side of his desk. He grabbed a thick manila file folder. Smiling, he looked at Bridget, then me, then to Bridget again.

"You have a most interesting case. My accountant has spent hours analyzing it. I'm happy to say we have an accurate figure of what is due you from the Piet Retief Diamond Mine Corporation." He hesitated. If he were waiting for a reaction, I feared he'd be here quite a while. He must have assumed as much, so he continued. "May I congratulate you, Sister Bridget, for being clever enough to refuse the R500,000 check." He paused. "And it's a good thing you're sitting down."

Mr. Fricker straightened his file folder and picked up the first sheet. "Let's get right to it, shall we? With interest you should have been receiving over the years, plus inflation, taxes, etc. the amount owed to you is R1,855,995,213.08 plus change." He smiled, then sat back in his chair with his laced fingers firmly resting on his desk. He and I both stared at Bridget in anticipation of a jubilant reaction.

Bridget looked worried and disbelieving.

I nudged her arm. "Bridget, you're rich! I told you! A billionaire!" I laughed and clapped my hands like a child who'd been handed a Popsicle on a sweltering afternoon. "Will she have to go to court?" I asked the lawyer.

His elbows relaxed on the top of his desk. "I seriously doubt it. I sent a copy of our findings to the South African Treasury

Department and it will be forwarded to the courts. The managing director will acquiesce. That scoundrel hasn't a chance. Quite honestly, Riebeeck will be dodging a prison sentence for fraud, plus, it looks like he embezzled funds as well. The police will bring him up on a list of criminal charges. In fact, I spoke to the treasurer of the diamond mine already. He has sent me a check in your name to cover over half the funds." He took a deep breath. "Where do you want the money deposited?"

Sister Bridget looked comatose. In her wildest fantasy, she could never have dreamt this up. Oh, the things she could do now—the schools she could build!

"Sister Bridget," the lawyer prodded, "where do you bank?"

"I ... I don't bank." She looked like she'd seen a ghost.

I explained. "Nuns take a vow of poverty and are not allowed to have bank accounts or charge accounts."

I turned to Bridget. "May I suggest ABSA bank?"

She nodded and swallowed hard, still clutching the arms of her chair.

"The Amalgamated Banks of South Africa will be extremely happy to open you an account." Mr. Fricker smiled so big I thought he was going to burst out laughing. "And I will help you in any way I can. As questions come to either of you, please don't hesitate to call." He handed me a couple of his business cards.

I gave him a warm double handshake. "Don't worry. You will be the one we contact. You've been more than generous with your time. You will not regret it." I was positive I saw a twinkle in the eyes of Mr. Fricker as we turned to leave.

Outside his office, I pushed the down button for the small-antiquated elevator. "Bridget, you're rich. Rich beyond anyone's wildest dreams! It's like you won the lottery! It's like God is taking notice of all your good work."

"God?"

"Yes, yes, yes! No one could deserve this more than you!"

We stepped out into the bright sunshine.

She dropped to her knees right there on the sidewalk and made a sign of the cross and then folded her hands and looked toward the heavens. "Thank you, dear God. I promise to spend my money very well." Then she made a second sign of the cross. I ignored the passersby as they turned to stare at her.

"What is the first thing you want to do?" I asked, as I extended an arm to help her stand.

She brushed the dust off the knees of her pantsuit. "Build a new school?"

"Marvelous!"

We walked down the street and waited at the corner for the robot to turn green.

"Please, don't tell anyone, Annabelle. For now, no one must know about the money."

I entertained how that might work if Bridget wanted to build schools. Just as the green light prevailed, we stepped off the curb, and midway to the other side of the street I saw a dark Mercedes barreling toward us. With no time to think, I shoved Bridget forward sending her sprawling on the concrete between two parallel-parked cars, with me landing on top of her

"Dear God, that was close." Bridget had taken the full brunt of the fall. I rolled off her. "Bridget, Bridget, are you okay?"

A stranger's arm eased me up, then helped me carefully pull Bridget to a standing position. I scanned her quickly. A cut on her cheek, serious scrapes on her palms and knees bleeding through torn fabric. I pulled tissues out of my purse and bent to blot her knees. Her torn pantsuit would not survive another mending.

"He tried to run you down. I'm a witness, I saw it." The stranger, who was dressed in a three-piece suit, handed me a card. "Here's my contact information." I thanked him and the other bystanders who paused to inquire about us.

Screaming sirens whizzed past and stopped at the end of the next block.

"There's been an accident," someone shouted.

We limped half a block and in the distance could see the dark Mercedes wrapped like a crushed soda can around the frame of a heavy-duty lorrie. We joined the bystanders until the police unhinged the car door off the mangled vehicle. Paramedics lifted a bloody body out of the wreckage. I could see them desperately applying their skills to revive someone. A policeman on scene sifted through a briefcase. Minutes later a second medic pulled out a black body bag and with the help of two other paramedics sealed up the dead man.

When the ambulance drove away, a policeman motioned to us. "A witness said the Mercedes tried to run you over."

"Yes." It was all I could manage.

"Are you okay?" He glanced from me to Bridget.

She looked at him. "Scratches."

"Did either of you know the driver?"

I was pretty sure I could guess. "What was his name?"

"A Mr. Riebeeck from Durban."

"Yeah, we'd met," I answered. "He'd made several attempts on Sister Bridget's life. Only we never had proof until now."

"You need to come with me."

After answering questions at police headquarters for over two hours, the officer seemed satisfied and appointed a rookie to drive us back to underground parking to pick up our vehicle. He thanked us and gave us his contact card in case we had any additional questions. It was finally over.

As I drove up from underground parking, I inhaled as deep as I could, then relaxed. No one would be after Sister Bridget anymore. This lifted a great weight of anxiety off my shoulders, anxiety that had been nearly crushing me for weeks.

"How sad that Sister Valaria paid the price for that man's greed," Bridget said, and she bowed her head and began to say the Our Father.

She was right, of course, and I felt guilty because I'd barely thought of Valaria, focusing instead on Bridget's wealth and Baloyi's love. Well, I wasn't a nun, but I knew how to say the Our Father, and so I whispered it along with Bridget.

The street labored with afternoon traffic. When Bridget finished her prayers, she catnapped against the passenger window on the left, something I was now used to—both the fact that she was on the left side and the fact that she could fall asleep so easily. Poor thing was exhausted from the fall and also from the discovery that she was a billionaire. I smiled at the irony while Bridget slept. Truthfully, the sound of her snores was refreshing, certainly an insurance policy against my falling asleep at the wheel. I was exhausted too, but I could make use of this time. My mind flitted from the death of the CEO to the next immediate problem.

If—no when—I told Baloyi that his brother Marcus was Vince, the man who'd kidnapped me and led countless women to their deaths, would he believe me? Maybe Baloyi could persuade Vince to cooperate in identifying other muti murderers. My inner voice had one thing to say about that idea: *Fat chance.*

As I glanced into my side mirror, my eyes caught the downtown skyline behind us against a swirl of pastels painting the late afternoon horizon. Whoa. The beauty of Africa was all around us. But like at home, sometimes we got so busy with what we thought was important that we took breathtaking beauty for granted. Wished I had a lawn chair and a glass of wine.

We had four to five hours before we reached Malamulele. It wasn't very comforting to know that it would be pitch dark within the hour.

Thirty Five

Standoff

Although exhausted from our Johannesburg trip, I still awoke at 4:30 a.m. In the early mornings at home I'd lounge on my overstuffed couch, answering emails and sipping coffee until I was ready to greet the day. Here, dashing down the walkway through the brisk morning air, I shivered until the coffee was ready. Returning to my room, I slid my legs under the warm covers and counted the minutes until I could call Baloyi.

This African life had become ordinary.

Ordinary except that Sister Bridget, my dear friend, had become a billionaire and I was sworn to secrecy. Ordinary except that my boyfriend's brother was a killer and I was his target. I took a breath. I rubbed my head with my fingertips applying pressure to the painful areas. My head hurt. My shoulder hurt.

Think positive, Annabelle. I did not have to worry about someone stalking Bridget. The Silver Fox had met his deserved demise. Who would ever have suspected that a greedy CEO would stoop to killing a nun? As I reflected on the various ways he'd attempted to kill Bridget, Junie's death stood out. She was poisoned by Sister Bridget's tea. Something still niggled at me about that. Who had actually slipped the poison into the tea? It had to be someone inside the school. The hairs on the back of my neck stood up. We'd never discovered who Riebeeck's accomplice—or accomplices were. Now that he was dead, surely that would cancel the contract if there was one. But suddenly, my head felt like it would explode.

I opened the Panadol bottle on my bedside table, took two, then pulled out my iPhone and stared at Baloyi's name on speed dial. It occurred to me that I might not have many calls left from Detective Baloyi. Perhaps none at all. It was a bit like counting down to doomsday. I touched his number, waited a second, then heard his voice.

"Girl, what's up?" His voice was sleepy and warm as if he had just pulled me into his arms.

I closed my eyes. "Baloyi, I need to see you." My heart was sadly thumping as if it was closing a door.

"And I neeeed to see you." He chuckled. "Chief likes you. Invited us for Sunday lunch."

"Just us?"

"Only us."

"But before that I need to talk to you."

"Can't it wait 'til tonight? Task Force meetings all day." I could hear him moving around as if putting on his clothes.

"I'm not sure I can wait." I wanted to tell him about his brother while I still felt brave enough.

"I'll make it worth your while ... half past five?" His voice was soft and enticing and I longed to see him but dreaded it even more.

"Until tonight."

Baloyi whisked me away from the convent to his couch at home where we could be alone. With what I had to say, I knew this evening would not match his great expectations. I was practically tongue-tied attempting small talk and trying to ignore my feelings while knowing these precious moments could be our last. He poured two glasses of semi dry Riesling and handed me one. His familiar scent overwhelmed my senses as he sat down close to me.

"Tough day?"

I didn't realize how thirsty I was until I'd gulped down all the wine in my glass.

Baloyi gently took the empty glass and reached over to set it on the table in front of us. He turned to face me. "Annabelle, look at me. Seriously, what's wrong? You're worrying me."

"I don't know how ... to tell you."

"You can tell me anything." The crinkle of fine happy lines around his eyes had vanished. "Uh-oh, now I get it – this is the big break up? I must admit. I did not see this coming." He shook his head slowly and stared blankly. "I thought we were all good."

I moved closer and wrapped my arms around him. I kissed him and then again.

"Surely that's not the kiss of a woman breakin' my heart."

"No, no. I'm not breaking up with you," I said, thinking that he'd probably break up with me once I said what I had to.

"Then I can face anything." His face came alive.

I marveled at the way a person had the ability to light up someone's life and then snuff out the flame.

"Marcus, " I began.

"Yeah, I know."

"You do? You already know?"

"Yeah, he's a bit much, but hey, he's my bro. What can you do?" He scrunched his shoulders to his ears and then relaxed. "Let's not worry about Marcus," he said, pulling me close.

I pushed him back. "But, you can't let him run around killing people." I hadn't meant to say it like that, but relief filled me even as I saw the strange look on his face.

"What?" His head jerked back. "I never said Marcus was killing people!"

"So, you don't know ... and you've never suspected?"

"Suspected what?"

"Your brother Marcus ... he is Vince." I hesitated only for a second. "The Vince who kidnapped me, the Vince who's involved with the muti gang."

Baloyi stood and stepped away from me, staring as if I were clearly delusional. "Why would you say something like that?" His frown twisted the muscles in his face to one of pure disgust. "That's horrible, Annabelle, even as a joke."

I considered how this was affecting him but found a breath and continued anyway.

"You would be right, *if* I were joking. He is the very one who drugged and kidnapped me. You have been searching for your own brother." I paused. "Please, Baloyi, how could I joke about such a thing?"

He stared at the floor and began pacing from one side of the house to the other. His stride was wide and he used his hands as if they could somehow assist him in understanding. "Look, I know he's a handful and he could charm the stripes off a snake. And I hate him for it, but a killer? No, I don't believe it. You've got to be wrong, absolutely wrong."

I no longer had control over my trembling voice. "He nearly *killed* me. He is ... a muti killer. You must believe me." My words ended in a high pitch.

Baloyi's brows fell over his stone cold eyes as he stood in front of me with clenched fists. Unexpectedly, he dashed toward the kitchen table for his keys and headed out the door. I was right behind him, grabbing my jacket on the way out.

We traveled in silence.

"Baloyi, the man nearly killed me. Does that not matter to you?"

Baloyi stared at the road and sped up.

"Baloyi, are you listening to me?"

When he pulled in front of the convent, he stopped the bakkie and made no attempt to turn off the motor. His eyes stared straight ahead, his hands on the steering wheel as if he were holding the bakkie together, or maybe himself.

I climbed out, but before I closed the door, I leaned in. "Baloyi, think, why would I make up something like this? Vince nearly killed me for God's sake." Tears blinded me. "He threatened me the other night at Ella's." I left out the sexual assault. Baloyi stared straight ahead. Then my anger overcame me and I slammed the door.

As he sped away, gravel spun up behind him.

Tears flooded my eyes from relief and heartbreak, or perhaps the building anger that he didn't believe me. It was done. And tomorrow I would find a higher authority to report my findings to, someone not kin to the Malamulele Commander or the extremely stubborn and inept Detective Baloyi!

Thirty Six

Ritual

Instead of marching off to the authorities, I waited twenty-four hours hoping Baloyi would come to his senses. While I searched the web for the names of appropriate authorities, I checked my cell a zillion times. I spent time with Sister Bridget and counseled her on how best to spend her vast fortune. It was unusual for Bridget to be so absorbed with her own life that she had lost sight of mine. She had always been perceptive and played the role of a Mamgoboza. I missed her butting in. I needed her to butt in. But, if she did, she could be in danger.

Basically, it was the longest day of my life. Even if I convinced Baloyi that Vince was with the muti killers, could he ever forgive me for being the one to ruin his family? I didn't see how. And Vince was the Chief's grandson, nor did I know enough about the Chief to be able to trust he wasn't involved.

In a strange way, I understood why Baloyi would blame me and avoid me, but dammit, shouldn't the cop gene kick in and demand that Chief and Baloyi bring a criminal to justice, even if it was a family member?

Holding this inside left me numb. I had information to solve the muti murders. I had to tell someone who would believe me. Maybe someone on the Limpopo Task Force or

271

someone at the Johannesburg Head Office.

During my online search of the police task force roster, I found that Sgt. Youri Mara, a seasoned Johannesburg detective, headed it up. When I called, I was told that he'd be at a regional tactical meeting in Thohoyandou tomorrow at nine. A lot closer than Joburg. I would drive there, wait until his meeting concluded, then drop the bomb on him about the Chief's grandson, and hope that Sergeant Mara would believe me.

The next morning as I drove to Thohoyandou, guilt rode my shoulder like the ghost of Judas. How could I turn in Baloyi's brother? Then something snapped. *What was wrong with me? Vince bloody well nearly killed me!* It was true that my heart was heavy, but I was doing the right thing.

When I arrived in Thohoyandou, I eased the car into a crowded lot behind the police station, hit my key fob and found my way into the one story building, which sported a maze of plastic sheets cordoning off renovation. At the first station I asked the officer on duty if I could speak with Sgt. Youri Mara.

"He's busy." I sensed from his posture that the cop was preoccupied with computer issues.

"Can I be of help?"

He looked up at me, the tribal scars accenting his dark face. "No."

I hesitated, then continued. "Listen, when Sgt. Mara comes out, please make sure I see him? It's very, very urgent!"

He glowered in my direction, my presence clearly messing with his day. I headed for a folding chair next to a small table about two meters from him. I glanced at my watch. Nine-thirty. Baloyi's task force meetings lasted three to four hours. I opened my laptop, slipped in the 3G flash drive and began searching muti killings in South Africa.

Two stories written by reporters from the *Star* immediately flashed on the screen. I slipped over to the SAPS website and entered "tactical task force." A member list came up. Baloyi wasn't listed. At least I knew I wouldn't be running into him. For two hours, I surfed, then walked back and forth in the waiting area glancing at a multitude of unfortunate souls clearly as frustrated as I. It was nearly noon. I walked over to the cop on duty. "When will the tactical task force meeting be over?"

Anxiety clouded the officer's face, as he looked up with a blank stare.

"Over, when will the meeting be done, finished?" I repeated.

"Meeting finished half hour ago."

"But I've been sitting here all morning." My voice elevated to a high pitch. "I haven't seen anyone leave. How did I miss a group of people walking out?"

"Out back," he motioned as carelessly, as if he'd thrown an apple core into an ally.

"You've been so extremely helpful!" He didn't even acknowledge me. I stalked away promising myself it would not ruin my day. And neither would the knot in my stomach. I jumped into my car, slammed the door and let out a string of expletives. I pulled out of the lot with three cars lined up waiting for my space. Frustrated, my car screamed onto the street.

In my anger, I turned at the very first sign pointing to Malamulele. Probably a short cut, one of those back roads. I had plenty of time. I needed to think. And unwind. As I drove I was amazed at the lack of traffic, the rustic brush trees lining the road depicting a truly rural Africa.

A half-mile later I slowed down due to the gradual deterioration of the road. Yep, I was the new girl and hadn't gotten the memo. I hit speed dial for Baloyi. I would give him one more chance. Maybe he'd rethought what I'd said. It went straight to voice mail. Nope. He wasn't answering my calls. I didn't leave a message. I was afraid of what I'd say.

I dropped my iPhone into my purse with attitude. That would be the last time I called. Anger swelled inside me. Hell, it was his murdering brother that he should punish, not me. When would he come to his senses?

Two minutes later my rental coughed and sputtered, then stopped. I scanned the dashboard. Plenty of petrol. Three quarters full. I turned the key. Again and again. Totally dead. For the first time since college I regretted dropping that automotive elective. I tried Baloyi again. My phone said no coverage. It made no sense. I'd driven to the corners of South Africa and always had coverage. Why now?

In Thohoyandou the Internet worked fine. That couldn't be more than a twenty-minute walk. I pulled my keys out of the ignition, grabbed my crossover bag and stepped out of the car closing the door behind me.

I enjoyed the solitude of the empty road, but I admit I was relieved about fifteen minutes later to hear the rattle of a vehicle. I turned to see an aging Jeep wrangler, dust billowing up behind it. I waved the dust away enough to see a sunburned Billy Ray Cyrus look-a-like at the wheel, as he eased up beside me and stopped. He tilted his hat back from his eyes and adjusted his sunglasses.

"Problem?" he asked, with a thick Afrikaner accent.

"Could you take a look at my car?"

"Get in." His chin length hair hung over his face on one side and he squinted at me.

He didn't ask where my car was. My gut reacted. I wasn't doing this. "Never mind, it's okay. Just a short walk." I smiled. "I need the exercise." I turned to leave.

"Suit yourself, but watch out for snakes." He raced his motor.

"Snakes?"

"Found a nest of Rinkhals ten feet from where you stand."

"Shit," I whispered.

"Hey, look at me. I'm no serial killer." He laughed. "Have a little faith!"

"Could I just use your phone?"

"Sure, but it don't work out here."

I pictured the Rinkhals in the backseat of my car. Ever fresh in my memory. Anywhere would be better than here.

"Okay." I climbed up into his Wrangler. "Love your red Jeep."

Billy Ray made a U-turn. He stopped at the crossroads and paused for a car to pass. "Where you from?"

"Denver." Something about the way he smiled made my panic button blare. "You know, I do need the exercise. I'll walk, if it's all the same to you." But as I reached for the door handle, he hit the accelerator.

"Stop!" I kept my hand on the door.

He slammed the car to a stop. "Look, lady, I got to make a delivery. Can you hang on? Then I'll take you anywhere you need to go." Paranoia must be making me crazy. I sat and blinked at him. He flashed a smile of uneven teeth and changed the subject. "Pass me a cold one," he said, and nodded toward the cooler in back. Cooler. *What was in the cooler? Body parts?* Fear pounded my mind and I almost jumped out of the Jeep.

I had to know. As I turned in my seat and reached back, he jerked the Jeep forward again. I lifted the lid of a grimy red and white cooler. *No body parts.* I smiled and pulled out a Fransen Street and handed it to him. My mouth reacted as he twisted the top off and took a swig. Suddenly I realized how dehydrated I was.

"Tastes stellar. Help yourself."

"No, I'm good." I wasn't taking chances.

"Water in the thermos."

An unopened beer seemed safer. I grabbed one from underneath and twisted the top off. I took several gulps. It hit the spot. I leaned my head against the window. The afternoon sun lulled me as I listened to the plastic window covers flapping back and forth and back and forth, sending rhythmic and soothing music to my head.

My eyes popped open as I gasped for air. Panic filled my lungs and seemed to travel through my bloodstream at a frightening speed. I rolled my head to the side puking and luckily managed not to swallow. I lay my head back against something soft. Where was I? Not in the Jeep any more. Black plastic restraints decorated my arms and legs, holding me firmly down.

I struggled to hear the voices outside the door.

"Klutcher you old dog, how'd you find her?"

"Lucky break ... walking down old Thohoyandou road."

"What was she doing out there?"

"No idea."

Then there was the sound of high-fives and laughter. The last voice I recognized. So Klutcher was the name of my Billy Ray Cyrus. Good to have a name to the face. My brain felt like it was on fire and my eyes were heavy. I knew all I needed to know. Klutcher was with the enemy. My eyes closed as I tried to keep the room from spinning round and round.

When I awoke again, the smell of beer was still on my breath. My sinuses raged, my spine ached from my neck to my tailbone; my legs were pinched together at the ankles and right beneath my knees. Double binding. They weren't taking chances. How could I have been so completely stupid!

Then I heard a woman's voice. Low and breathy. Almost familiar. My head was too sore to worry about it. I stretched my bound wrists in front of me to see the time. No watch. *What did you expect, Annabelle?* Who knew where my purse was? By now my cell had been disabled or sold—again. Resources? Nil. Like last time. *Think, Annabelle. Think.* What were my assets? My eyesight. A definite plus.

Although bright sunlight blinded my eyes from the open door, I could make out a silhouette in a long skirt. Unexpectedly, the door slammed. Did I know the person on the other side of the door? Gauging the sunlight, it had to be mid-afternoon. The door rattled open and I closed my eyes from instinct until a familiar scent hovered over me. My eyes flew open to see Vince's face three inches from mine.

"You white fuckin' bitch. You won't bother nobody after tonight."

I gasped as his syringe delivered its familiar sting.

I smelled miele meal from the cotton sack over my head. I coughed and breathed in the dust residue of the grain, then coughed more and finally resorted to shallow breathing. Someone was carrying me like a sack of potatoes over his shoulder, then I heard the familiar sound of an engine. I winced as I was lifted up and thrown hard into the back of the vehicle, probably a koombie. I heard a door slide shut and listened as we drove. My ears screamed from whatever Vince had put into that syringe. Other than bouncing over a few rough spots, there was nothing to memorize. No horns, no turns, nothing. And the vehicle abruptly stopped.

Male voices speaking a Bantu language flitted back and forth. The door slid open and hands yanked me out. Someone grabbed me under my arms and another carried my feet. The journey was short. Every part of me cried for sweet relief until I was dropped onto a hard ice-cold surface. I was too frightened to speak and I barely could think when unexpectedly someone jerked the sack from my head.

"Thank you," I gasped, as I bent over and coughed freely. I looked up at a dark open sky above tree branches. Pinpricks of light shone down from stars. *How could this be happening on such a beautiful night?*

"It's the least I can do." That Klutcher had a knight in shining armor inside him just dying to come out.

I didn't recognize the man next to him who checked my restraints made of black, heavy-duty plastic securely fastening my wrists and ankles. He laid his hands on me and I kicked him with both feet. The man swung his rifle around to retaliate, but Klutcher grabbed it right before it slammed into my face. "Don't touch her!" Surprisingly, the other man backed off.

"Sorry, Annabelle." Klutcher said it with a soft, sincere voice. "Relax, it'll be easier." As he turned to leave, he muttered something about what a waste.

I squirmed to free myself, but the restraints weren't budging.

Near a thicket of trees surrounding us was a small group of African observers. Everything felt surreal, as if I'd stepped into my own nightmare. Had I? I didn't recognize anyone here but Klutcher, a man I'd only met this afternoon. Was he a new recruit? Then of course, there was Vince. I stared over at him from the large boulder where I now lay feeling totally helpless.

Vince moved toward me with another syringe.

"No, no more. Pleash, no more." I couldn't believe I was begging him for anything and I was slurring my words so much that I hardly recognized my own voice.

Without a comment, he stuck the needle in my arm. I hardly felt it. Whoa. I'd have to find out what that stuff was. But then the new drug coursed through my veins and I was instantly wide awake. Better than six lattes. I felt like I could run a marathon.

"Couldn't you warm the damn rock? I'm freezing." The old Annabelle was back.

Vince laughed, and if I hadn't known better, I would have sworn there was a trace of affection in his voice. "Won't hurt if you relax, sweetness."

Why did they keep saying that? Wouldn't hurt? They were fixing to bloody well kill me! What did they mean it wouldn't hurt? There was little left to do now except panic, as I waited what looked to be preparations for some sort of ceremony probably involving hours of agonizing pain. I wet my lips and hoped whoever used them for good luck would go straight to hell.

I hated being untidy. Bleeding all over the rock. And what would the Environmental Defense Fund group say? What would I look like when Vince was through with me? And what would they do with the rest of me? And when would Baloyi ever find me? And where was my Mamgoboza? Amazing how many thoughts can race through the human mind in a split second.

I wondered if they sterilized the rock I was lying on after each kill and envisioned my story to The New York Times. "African ritual killers spread diseases, selling muti to all points of the globe."

My head snapped toward the loud drumbeats. A tall masked man in a flowing robe writhed and danced around a glowing fire. He reached toward the heavens with a snake dangling in his fingers. As he threw handfuls of powder over the hot flames, the smoke became hues of blue, then mauve.

Scary stuff. And this ... was ... happening! Fuck! I hated that word. *I'm sorry God, but it just slipped out.* My heart pounded so I could barely breathe.

Baloyi, where are you? You should have believed me! And like a video I saw my birth, grade school, junior high, high school, my first wedding, and divorce ... my adventure had cost me everything. Then the image of Baloyi and I in the woods holding one another danced through my head. If I could just see him once more. Know he loved me. Please, I prayed. *One more time.*

Vince, holding the biggest machete I'd ever seen, strutted over to the fire. From my front row seat, I could see his eyes glistening pure evil as the drums beat faster ... faster ... faster. The masked dancer poured oil onto his machete, then Vince turned and slashed it through the air over the fire. The oil seared and slowly dripped down the scorched blade. *Oh, goodie, they do sterilize. I'm so relieved!*

Vince walked over and bent down as if to say something, but instead he laughed his hot breath onto me, then stood and aimed the machete at me. His dark wild eyes reminded me of an animal waiting for attack. Whatever drug he was on, it had lifted him to a whole new reality.

My head pounded and soon I couldn't tell if it was the loud drums or my heartbeats that I heard in my aching ears.

"Can you scream?" Vince asked, as if he were addressing a child trying to walk across the room for the first time. "Let's hear you scream."

"Go to bloody hell!" Tears filled my eyes and on the other side of the fire I saw the young woman who'd gone to the prom with Vince. Her image was as clear as could be. I blinked my tears away. Then I realized she was waiting for me. But where were my Mom and Dad and my aunt? I had always thought as I transitioned to the afterlife they would be there.

I jumped when Vince let out a wild laugh. He leaned close, sweat dripping off his maniacal face. "Baloyi believed his little bro right to the end." Then he screeched another laugh.

The pain ripped through me. Vince could slice me into a thousand pieces and it wouldn't hurt as much as those words ringing in my head.

"Wait, wait," I said, gasping for breath. "Question."

Vince shot me that million-dollar smile and roamed his hands across me. "Sure sweetness, make it quick."

"Did you kill Sister Valaria?"

He stepped back and glared at me, his eyes like hot coals as if he was staggered at my stupidity. "Hell, yes, but it shoulda been that principal."

"But how'd you get inside the convent?"

"Simple. Climbed on the roof, dropped into the garden. Door was bloody well unlocked. Escaped out the side, key dangling in the fuckin' door. Too easy."

My pain was fierce, but I hated loose ends so I continued. "But why?"

"Freelance for the white Durban boy."

Bingo. The Silver Fox. A brief satisfaction surged through me. Suspicions confirmed.

Vince hovered inches from my face and I could see his dark eyes ratcheting up to frenzy level with every drumbeat. Rationality was officially off the table.

"Who's the dancer?"

Vince motioned to the person in the headdress, who now held a black spitting cobra in his hands. He shook his head.

"Sorry."

The key dancer chanted feverishly, moving in wide circles, sweeping arms high to the sky as if offering up a gift. Guess that would be me. After all, that's why it was called a ritual killing.

It felt as if I were watching an old Tarzan movie until Vince held up his machete and slammed it full force. I didn't recognize the noise I made. It was as if a stranger had climbed inside me. And yet the blow was only a practice stroke, clanging against the boulder where I lay. Then from his pocket Vince pulled out the largest switchblade I'd ever seen. Starting at my ankles he slowly ripped the legs of my jeans feeling his way up to my waist. Then he grabbed my T-shirt in his fist, stuck his knife through it and tore the shirt apart. Luckily my sports bra remained intact.

Unexpectedly Vince slammed the switchblade into the fleshy part of my left thigh. My body shook from excruciating pain, as I let out a long, wailing scream.

"Way to go, girl! You got it. Let's try again. But this time with somethin' bigger." As he raised the machete up, I begged: "Wait, wait, one favor."

He laughed like a jackal. "No time."

"Just tell Baloyi I loved him." Then I realized I was talking about myself in past tense. *To hell with this.* My aunt's voice mimicking an American expression spoke as clear as a bell. *"It ain't over til it's over."*

"You loved him?" His devilish laugh filled the cold night air.

"Yeah." I fought back my tears, but they had nowhere else to go and streamed down my cheeks.

"Oh well, let me untie you. That makes all the difference. You lovvve him. But you're forgetting something. He's dead!" Taunting me, he shook his head back and forth. "How about I bury your bloody heart right next to his. How 'bout that?"

I hadn't believed he'd killed Baloyi. Wouldn't I have felt something if Baloyi had left this earth?

Vince's machete took aim over me. I gritted my teeth desperately searching for bravery or anything, absolutely anything but this. Panic filled my lungs and throat, but just then the frenzied dancer holding a Rinkhals in his hands waved Vince over.

The drugs were hitting Vince hard. He dropped his knife to the ground as he wobbled over to the man in charge.

Instantly, I rolled off the stone, grabbed the switchblade with my hands still bound and hacked through my leg restraints. Both hands worked as one. Vince's drug was turning me into a fighting machine. I felt like I had superhuman strength.

Dropping my knife, I somersaulted forward, thrust my whole body onto Klutcher, snatched his gun and pulled the trigger. Klutcher fell back onto the ground, crying out in pain.

I looked up to see the wild eyes of Vince as he raced toward me. I pointed the pistol at him, just as I pulled the trigger, a shot rang out from beyond the bushes. The dancer fell in unison with Vince as Limpopo officers rushed in like fire ants from every direction.

Suddenly there was Baloyi attacking his wounded brother punching him repeatedly in the face.

"He's alive." It was all I could say, as my body finally gave way to the shattering pain in my leg. A medic scooped me up, cut my hand restraints and tended my leg wound after giving me an injection that instantly eased the excruciating pain.

Suddenly Baloyi was kneeling beside me. "Annabelle, Annabelle, forgive me. I couldn't tell you about the sting." Baloyi cradled me in his arms.

Tears streamed down my face. "Thank God you came."

"I had no idea where you were until this afternoon."

"How?"

"Surveillance on Klutcher."

"Lucky me." I said sarcastically.

"I had a tracker on your rental, but they disabled it and the bug gave us nothing. I was crazy, absolutely crazy, Belle." His arms bound me to him. "I was nearly too late."

I cut him a break. "I'd say perfect timing." I never wanted to leave his arms, ever.

Two EMTs laid the headdress victim into a body bag, lifted it onto a gurney and as they rolled past, they stopped. Baloyi unzipped it for me to take a look as he shook his head.

"Aimee," I gasped in surprise. The undercover policewoman we'd left to watch over Bridget after Junie died from poison – poison meant for Sister Bridget. "She had to be working for the Silver Fox too!"

"The silver who?"

"The CEO." Then I realized Baloyi didn't have a clue what I was talking about. Sister Bridget had sworn me to secrecy. Since the Silver Fox and Aimee were now both dead, we'd probably never know how they'd connected.

A cop car with distinctive rotating lights slid to a stop sending gravel a car length. Chief rushed out, stopping only for a second to stare down at his grandson on the ground. As Chief stepped over him, Vince begged. "You can't think I was part of this." He grimaced from pain. "They shot me," he whined. His shrill voice was lost amid the chaos he'd created and the police sweeping the area for evidence.

Without another word to him, Chief walked over. "Too close." He took my hand in his, and then gave me a tender half hug.

"Not that close, Chief." I could not imagine how he was going to deal with his grandson up on multiple murder charges.

He nodded his head at me. "Sunday?"

"I'll be there." I looked over, but Baloyi had missed the comment because he was staring at his little brother on the ground receiving medical assistance.

Thirty Seven

Exploration

After a trip to the Malamulele Hospital where I received twenty-seven stitches for my leg wound, which now was completely numb, I deferred the powerful painkillers until later. I'd had plenty of drugs for the night, thank you very much. I insisted I was fine and Dr. Chake, the attending physician with a queue of patients, didn't argue. Baloyi called Sister Bridget to tell her he'd found me. I was beginning to feel fuzzy from something, drugs or relief I wasn't sure. Baloyi called a squad car to pick up Bridget and take her to his cabin in the woods, where we were headed.

When we arrived, Baloyi carefully carried me to his bed, placing pillows behind me as if I were a China doll. When he brought me a glass of water and two prescribed painkillers issued by the hospital, I took them now that I was under his care.

Hours later I awoke in an empty bed enjoying the comforting aroma of breakfast. Bacon for sure.

"Hey, Belle." Baloyi stood at the door staring at me with a relaxed grin as if he liked what he saw. Then he bundled me up and carried me to the couch in the living area. Sister Bridget was in the kitchen and she ran over to me. "Thank

God, thank God you're okay." Tears of happiness rolled down her face. She whispered, "I didn't want you two to be here, you know, alone."

I laughed and hugged her. "It's okay, Bridge. We've been here several times ... alone." I smiled. "You're being a Mamgoboza again," I sang. "And I love you for it."

Baloyi dished up fried bacon, eggs and toast. He poured steaming Ethiopian coffee into a mug, then delivered a plate of food to the coffee table in front of me. "I'll let you two catch up," he said. "I know you must have a lot to say." And he went outside to give me and Bridget privacy to talk.

"So what's happening in the world of Billionaire Bridget?" I asked, taking a delicious bite of eggs.

Bridget grinned. "I'm going to need you to stay a while longer," She paused. "Listen here, you won't believe it, but Ireland granted us another year in Malamulele." Before I could react, she continued. "God is good. But you must help me with the non-profit. In fact, I plan for you to take it over."

I knew I was a bit foggy and I wasn't sure I understood her. "You want me to be CEO of your non-profit?"

"Yes, yes, that's right. We've got a lot of schools to build." She beamed. "And I spoke with the lawyer. He verified that I can gift the money to you, make it legally yours. It'll be your money, and then I can remain a nun."

I stared at her, flabbergasted. Gift me millions? She must be losing her mind.

"We can build hundreds of schools across Africa, Annabelle!" Bridget spoke with great verve.

"Bridget." I put down my fork. "I can't take your money."

"You have to," she answered airily, as if she'd just offered to exchange rooms with me instead of giving me a crazy fortune. "You can't stop me, you know." She took my hand and squeezed it warmly before letting go. "I trust you. I know you, and you know me. And these last few weeks you've been there for me in a way that no one else could be."

"But Bridget, I—"

"This is the best way," she interrupted. "Otherwise I can't be a nun any longer. I know you understand that I can't abandon my calling. I took a vow of poverty."

"I know, but Bridget, don't you see? That money is a gift from God—to you. God didn't send it to me, He sent it to you."

"The gift from God is *you*." Bridget's eyes gleamed. Were those tears? "Without you, Annabelle, I would either be dead or I would have taken that first small check." She leaned in and hugged me. "I know it's hard for you to accept, but there's nothing you can do to stop me!" Her lilting voice held laughter as she listened to me sputtering, unable to speak a single coherent word.

She rose and headed toward the door. "I'm leaving for a funeral," she said. "Thank God I'm not going to yours." She made the sign of the cross and ran out.

I sat utterly stunned. Could I do this? Could I really be a CEO and help Sister Bridget build schools all over Africa? I worried a little about the corrupting effects of wealth. But then, I'd have Sister Bridget and the others to help keep my feet on the ground and my soul clean. Those nuns were a formidable bunch.

Maybe this money would also be helpful in supporting the nuns in choosing their own path of service and resisting the bullies in their hierarchy. I smiled to myself. Sister

Bridget wouldn't be able to stop me from helping her in my own way!

When Baloyi came in, I barely noticed he was there until he picked up my coffee mug and curled my fingers around the handle. What in the world would he think when he heard this news? I smiled at the prospects of surprising him, then decided to wait a while for that. I had to make sure he wasn't after my billion. I chuckled to myself, then laughed out loud at Baloyi's confused expression.

"Don't worry," I giggled. "I'm fine."

He walked over and turned on Jacaranda 94.2. As I stretched out on the couch, he tenderly placed an additional pillow beneath my head. He covered me with a navy throw and then knelt down beside me. Before he could say anything, I did.

"I am truly sorry about ... Marcus."

Baloyi paused. "I have a confession." Worry began to ease from his face. "He was my baby brother. That's why I naturally resisted hearing what you had to say. But Annabelle, I knew you wouldn't lie to me." He stared at my fingertips as he drew them near his lips. "It just took a while for me to come to my senses."

I nodded.

"Anyway, I took our suspicions to Chief." He paused. "At first, he didn't want to hear it either. But then, he realized we had to face the truth."

"What will happen to Marcus?"

"Should be turned loose with the kin of those he killed. But, we're a civilized society now." He sniffed the air. "Marcus will get life maybe, because his grandfather and brother are law enforcement. Maybe that'll help. Then again, maybe not. But if it's death, we'll have to deal." His shoulders fell. "I know how it must have been for you, Annabelle, your telling me, thinking I didn't believe you."

"What about Ella?"

"I'll tell her. She's dealt with a lot in her life. She'll be okay."

I struggled not to think of Ella's HIV. I would keep her secret. I only said something very true. "Sometimes life is more than unfair."

I pulled Baloyi near. He laid his head near my heart, letting it rest there for a few minutes. Then he looked up and squeezed in close. "I've been meaning to ask you ... " He traced my chin with his finger. "We haven't discovered the ringleader. Hopefully Vince will deal and give up info. But there's a lot more to do."

"Yeah."

He stroked my arm and despite the ordeal I had just been through, my heartbeat began to accelerate.

"Chief thinks you're good, a good investigator."

"Does he now?"

I watched Baloyi. I waited for that reassuring crinkle around his chocolate eyes that made the world seem perfect. There it was. Yes, indeed.

"You need to stick around, Belle—we need time to explore possibilities."

"You mean finding those responsible for the killings?" I hid my delight, waiting to see what else he had in mind.

"That too." I could see the pulse in his neck pumping faster and faster as he inched his body in closer to mine, allowing his hands to gently roam, accelerating my heartbeat and sending palpitations to all manner of hidden places.

I wasn't sure where this would eventually take us, but how could I deny this well-intentioned detective an exploration so absolutely essential to all attending parties?

About the Author

Darla Bartos has lived in Malamulele, Bryanston and Nelspruit, South Africa, as well as Zevenhuizen, the Netherlands, and the U.S. She now resides in Denver, CO, where she writes her stories and articles.

Her work has been published in *Fair Lady* and the *Star* in South Africa; *You and Yours,* Sydney, Australia; *Asbury Park Press*, Neptune, NJ; *The New York Times,* New York, NY; *The Plain Dealer,* Cleveland, Ohio; *The Oregonian*, Portland, OR; *Arkansas Democrat-Gazette,* Little Rock, AR; *D & B News*, New York, NY.

After receiving a Master's Degree in Journalism from Columbia University, Darla pursued work as a writer and crime reporter, teaching communications at the Metropolitan State University of Denver and at Northeastern Junior College in Sterling, Colorado. Darla attributes her first book to all the help she received from various members of the Rocky Mountain Mystery Writers of America, Rocky Mountain Fiction Writers, International Thriller Writers, Sisters in Crime and Romance Writers of America.

Darla writes full time and enjoys the fruits of her labor—five children she raised on three continents—and eleven grandchildren.